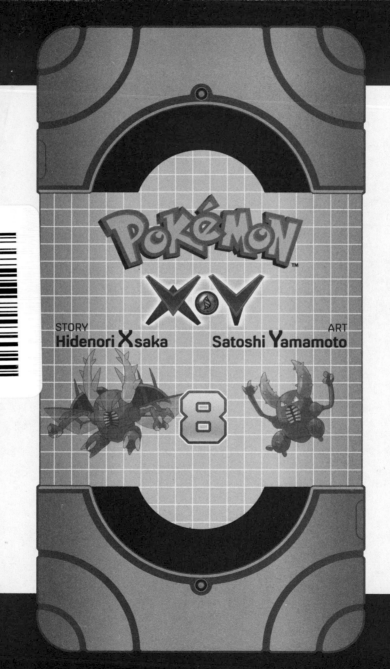

POKÉMON
X•Y

STORY
Hidenori Xsaka

ART
Satoshi Yamamoto

8

CHARACTERS

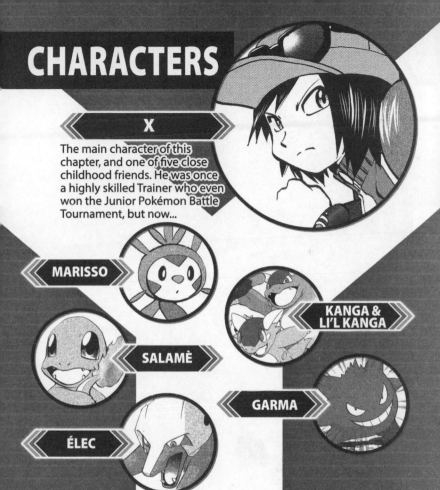

X

The main character of this chapter, and one of five close childhood friends. He was once a highly skilled Trainer who even won the Junior Pokémon Battle Tournament, but now...

MARISSO

KANGA & LI'L KANGA

SALAMÈ

GARMA

ÉLEC

OUR STORY THUS FAR...

In Vaniville Town in the Kalos region, X is a Pokémon Trainer child prodigy. But then he falls into a depression and hides in his room avoiding everyone. A sudden attack by the Legendary Pokémon Xerneas and Yveltal, controlled by Team Flare, forces X outside. Now he and his closest childhood friends—Y, Trevor, Tierno and Shauna—are on the run. X has a ring that Mega Evolves Pokémon and Team Flare wants to steal it. Turns out Team Flare has a nefarious plan to fire an ancient artifact called the Ultimate Weapon on the Kalos region and destroy it. Our friends launch an all-out attack to stop them, but Team Flare both escapes and steals Korrina's Key Stone!

MEET THE

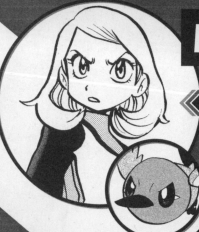

Y

X's best friend, a Sky Trainer trainee. Her full name is Yvonne Gabena.

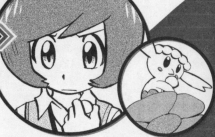

TREVOR

One of the five friends. A quiet boy who hopes to become a fine Pokémon Researcher one day.

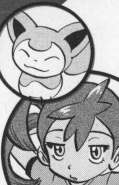

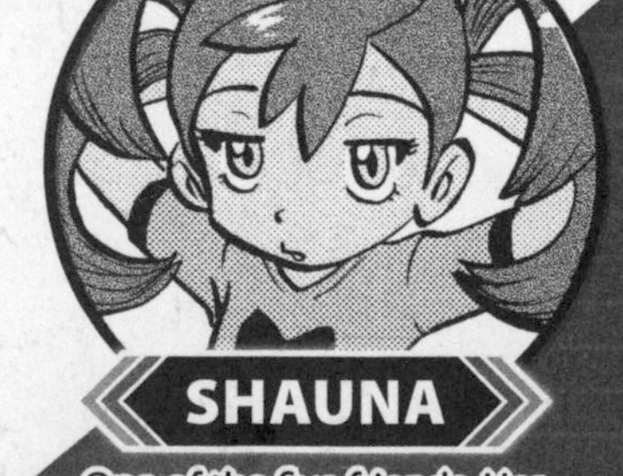

SHAUNA

One of the five friends. Her dream is to become a Furfrou Groomer. She is quick to speak her mind.

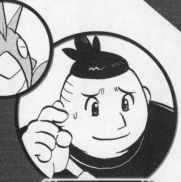

TIERNO

One of the five friends. A big boy with an even bigger heart. He is currently training to become a dancer.

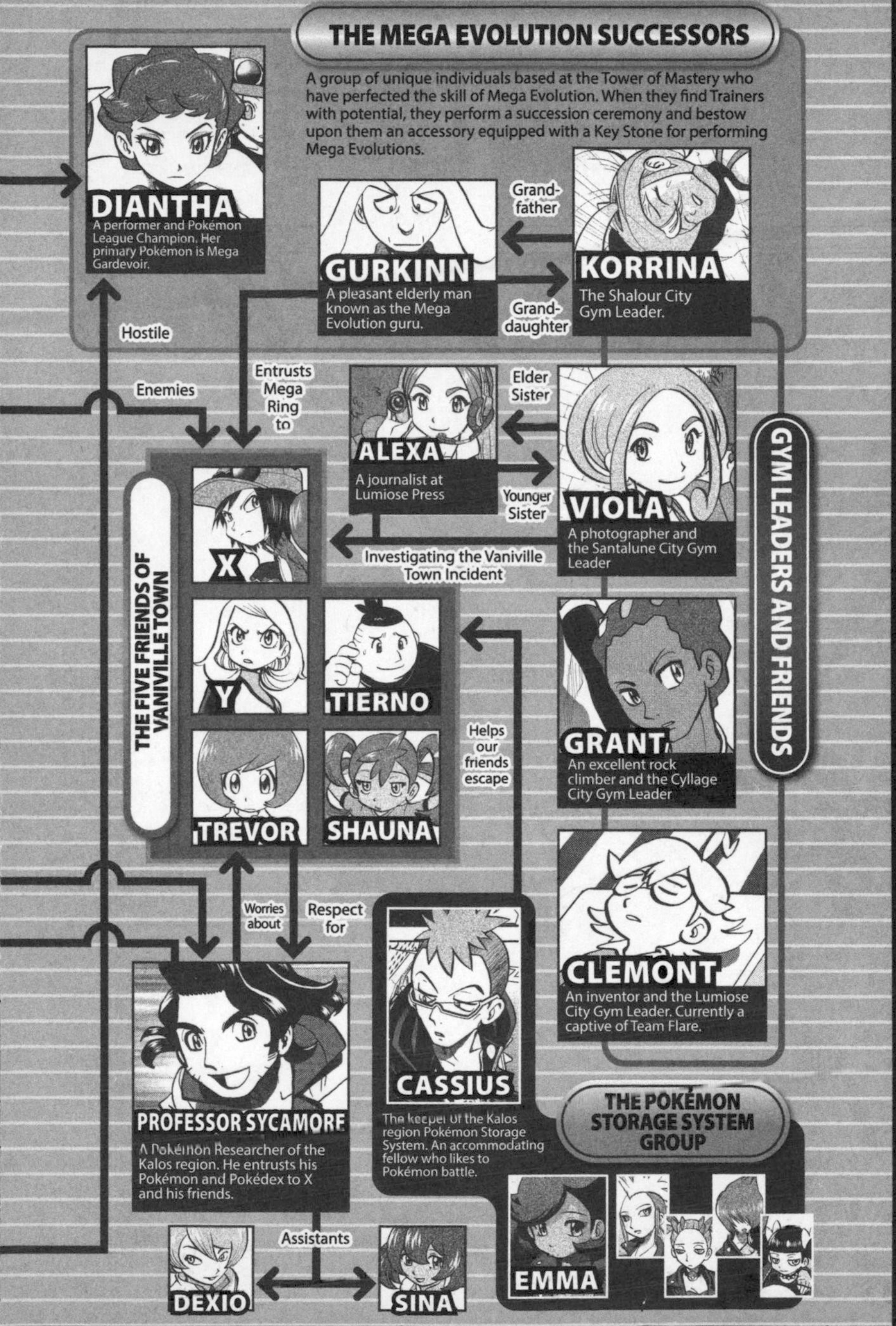
THE MEGA EVOLUTION SUCCESSORS
A group of unique individuals based at the Tower of Mastery who have perfected the skill of Mega Evolution. When they find Trainers with potential, they perform a succession ceremony and bestow upon them an accessory equipped with a Key Stone for performing Mega Evolutions.
DIANTHA
A performer and Pokémon League Champion. Her primary Pokémon is Mega Gardevoir.
Grand-father
KORRINA
The Shalour City Gym Leader.
GURKINN
A pleasant elderly man known as the Mega Evolution guru.
Grand-daughter
Hostile
Enemies
Entrusts Mega Ring to
ALEXA
A journalist at Lumiose Press
Elder Sister
Younger Sister
VIOLA
A photographer and the Santalune City Gym Leader
Investigating the Vaniville Town Incident
GYM LEADERS AND FRIENDS
THE FIVE FRIENDS OF VANIVILLE TOWN
X
Y
TIERNO
TREVOR
SHAUNA
GRANT
An excellent rock climber and the Cyllage City Gym Leader
Helps our friends escape
CLEMONT
An inventor and the Lumiose City Gym Leader. Currently a captive of Team Flare.
Worries about
Respect for
PROFESSOR SYCAMORE
A Pokémon Researcher of the Kalos region. He entrusts his Pokémon and Pokédex to X and his friends.
CASSIUS
The keeper of the Kalos region Pokémon Storage System. An accommodating fellow who likes to Pokémon battle.
THE POKÉMON STORAGE SYSTEM GROUP
EMMA
Assistants
DEXIO
SINA

CHARACTER CORRELATION CHART

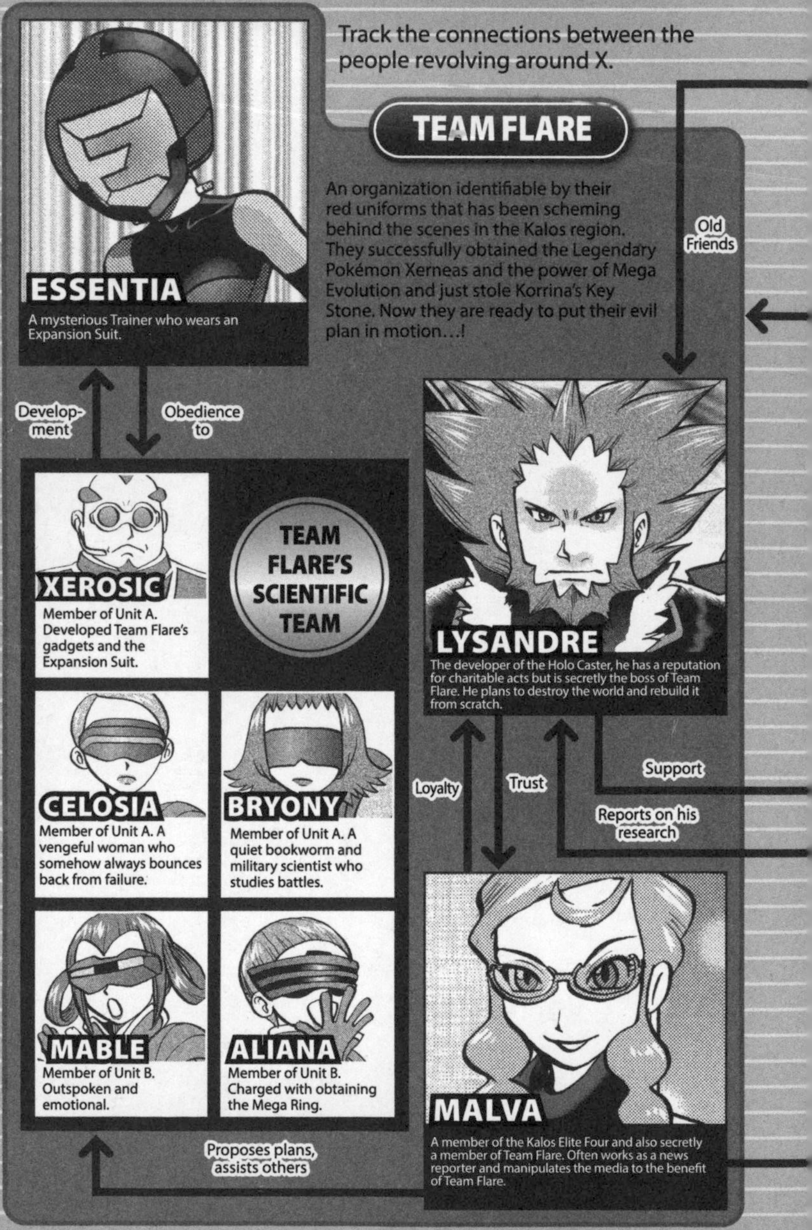

Track the connections between the people revolving around X.
TEAM FLARE
An organization identifiable by their red uniforms that has been scheming behind the scenes in the Kalos region. They successfully obtained the Legendary Pokémon Xerneas and the power of Mega Evolution and just stole Korrina's Key Stone. Now they are ready to put their evil plan in motion…!
ESSENTIA
A mysterious Trainer who wears an Expansion Suit.
Develop-ment
Obedience to
Old Friends
TEAM FLARE'S SCIENTIFIC TEAM
XEROSIC
Member of Unit A. Developed Team Flare's gadgets and the Expansion Suit.
CELOSIA
Member of Unit A. A vengeful woman who somehow always bounces back from failure.
BRYONY
Member of Unit A. A quiet bookworm and military scientist who studies battles.
MABLE
Member of Unit B. Outspoken and emotional.
ALIANA
Member of Unit B. Charged with obtaining the Mega Ring.
LYSANDRE
The developer of the Holo Caster, he has a reputation for charitable acts but is secretly the boss of Team Flare. He plans to destroy the world and rebuild it from scratch.
Loyalty
Trust
Support
Reports on his research
MALVA
A member of the Kalos Elite Four and also secretly a member of Team Flare. Often works as a news reporter and manipulates the media to the benefit of Team Flare.
Proposes plans, assists others

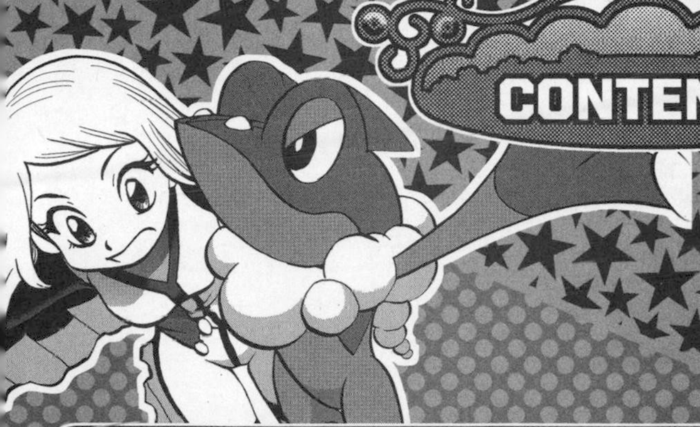

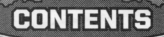

CONTENTS

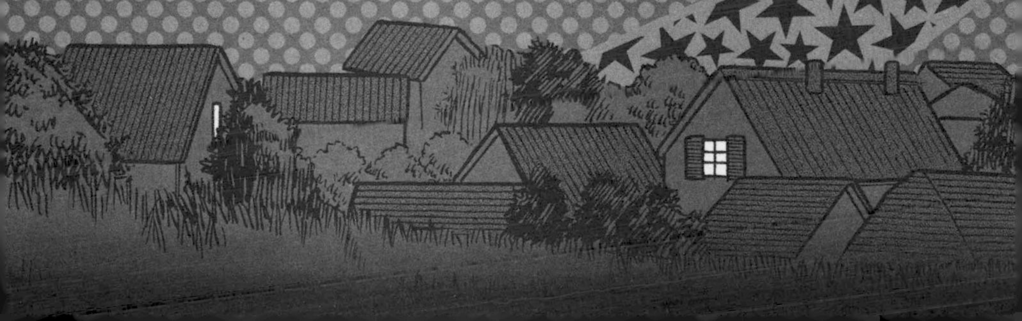

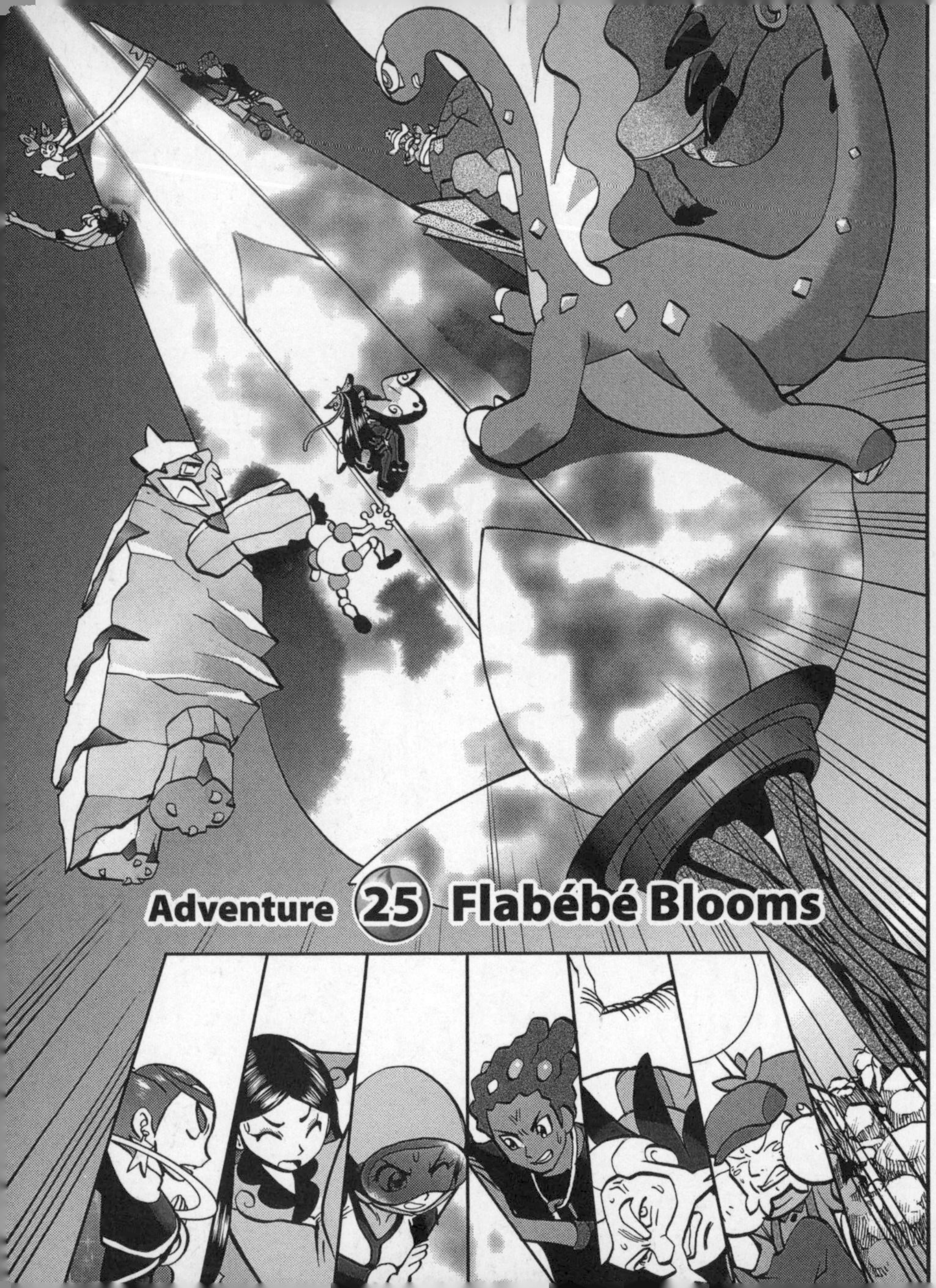
Adventure 25 Flabébé Blooms

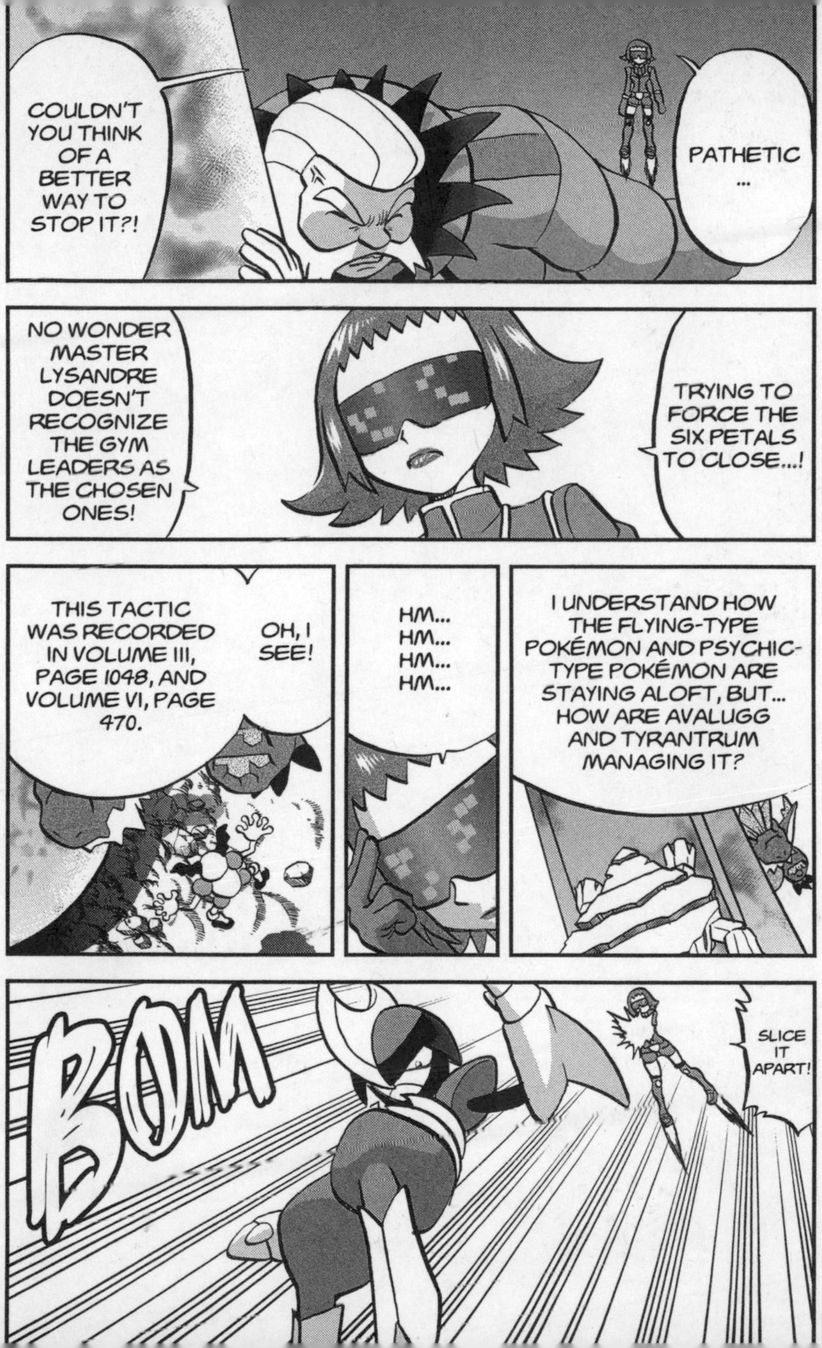
PATHETIC...
COULDN'T YOU THINK OF A BETTER WAY TO STOP IT?!
TRYING TO FORCE THE SIX PETALS TO CLOSE...!
NO WONDER MASTER LYSANDRE DOESN'T RECOGNIZE THE GYM LEADERS AS THE CHOSEN ONES!
I UNDERSTAND HOW THE FLYING-TYPE POKÉMON AND PSYCHIC-TYPE POKÉMON ARE STAYING ALOFT, BUT... HOW ARE AVALUGG AND TYRANTRUM MANAGING IT?
HM... HM... HM... HM...
OH, I SEE!
THIS TACTIC WAS RECORDED IN VOLUME III, PAGE 1048, AND VOLUME VI, PAGE 470.
SLICE IT APART!
BOM

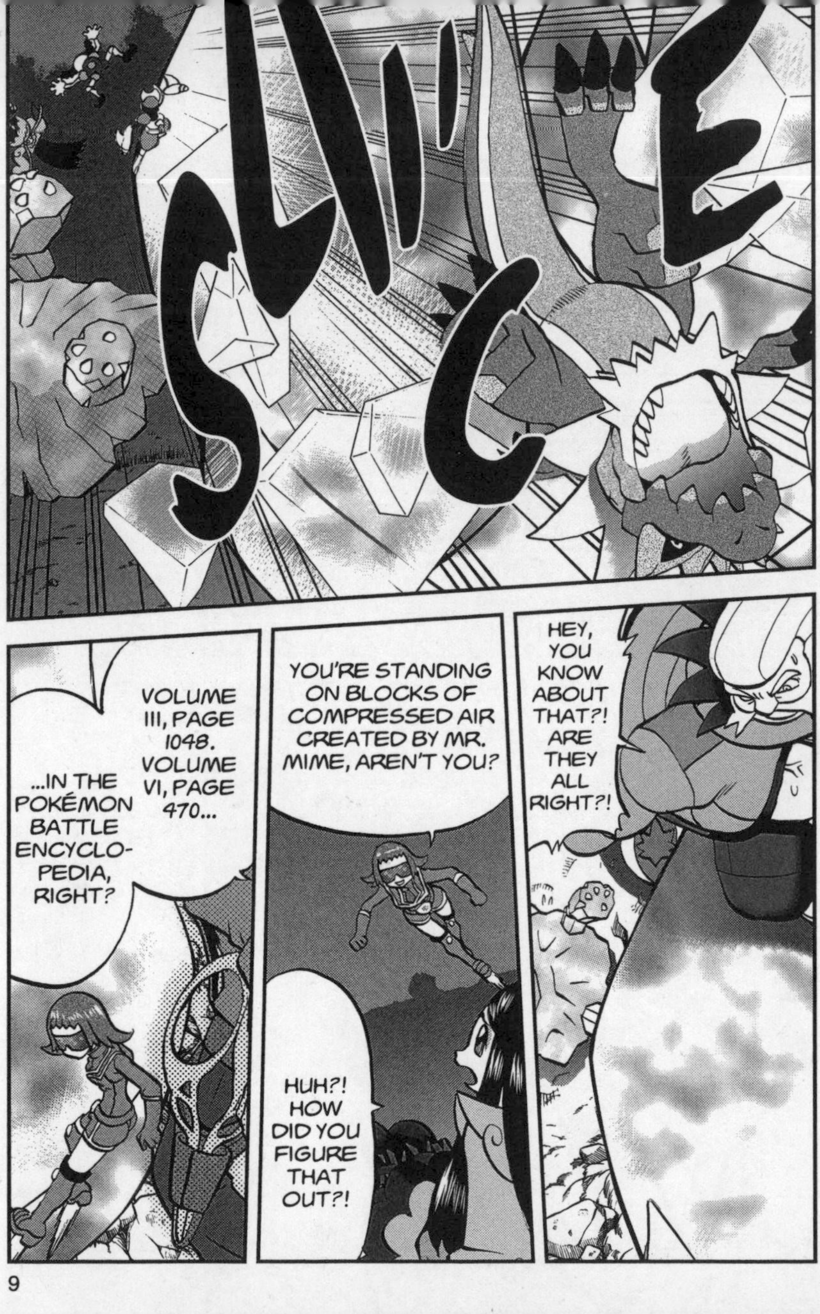
SLIICE
HEY, YOU KNOW ABOUT THAT?! ARE THEY ALL RIGHT?!
YOU'RE STANDING ON BLOCKS OF COMPRESSED AIR CREATED BY MR. MIME, AREN'T YOU?
HUH?! HOW DID YOU FIGURE THAT OUT?!
VOLUME III, PAGE 1048. VOLUME VI, PAGE 470...
...IN THE POKÉMON BATTLE ENCYCLOPEDIA, RIGHT?

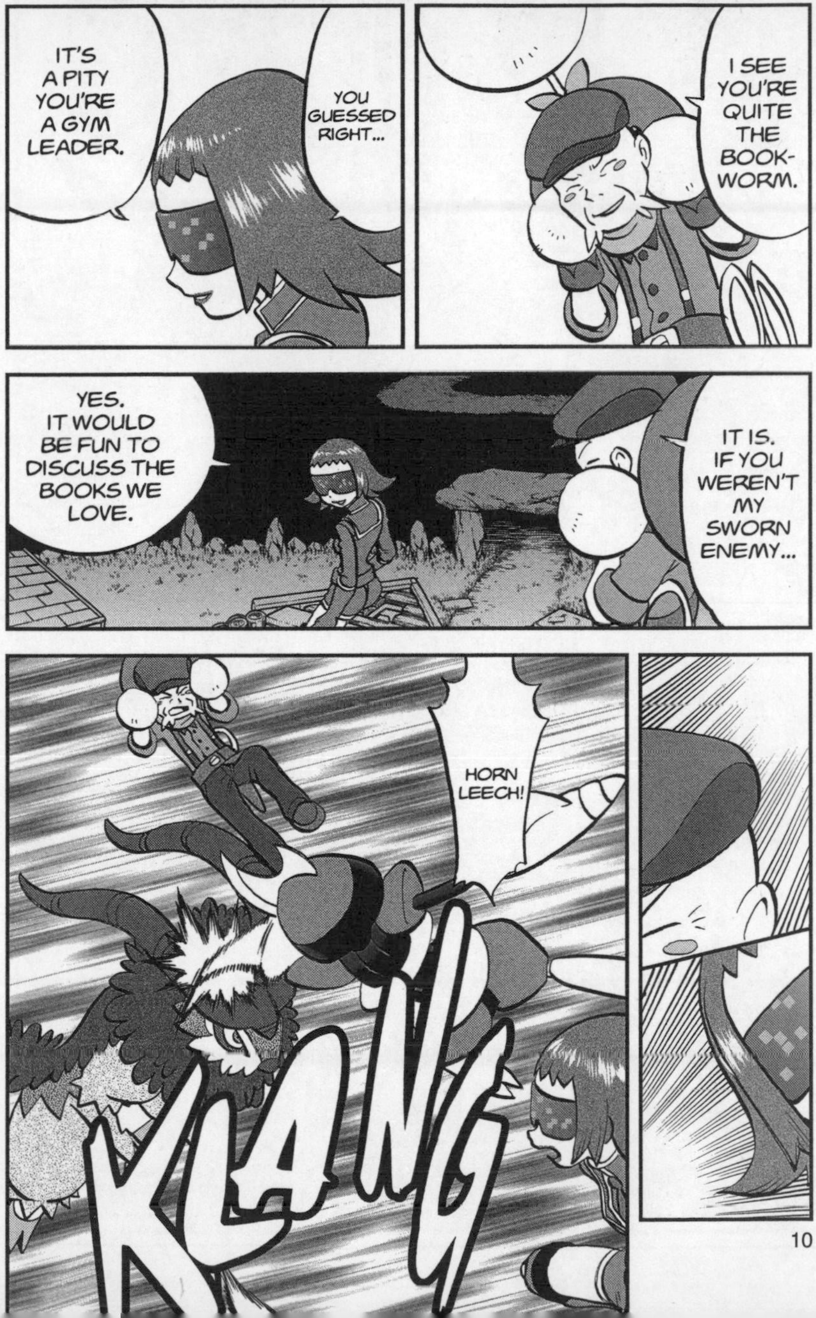
I SEE YOU'RE QUITE THE BOOKWORM.
YOU GUESSED RIGHT...
IT'S A PITY YOU'RE A GYM LEADER.
IT IS. IF YOU WEREN'T MY SWORN ENEMY...
YES. IT WOULD BE FUN TO DISCUSS THE BOOKS WE LOVE.
HORN LEECH!
KLANG

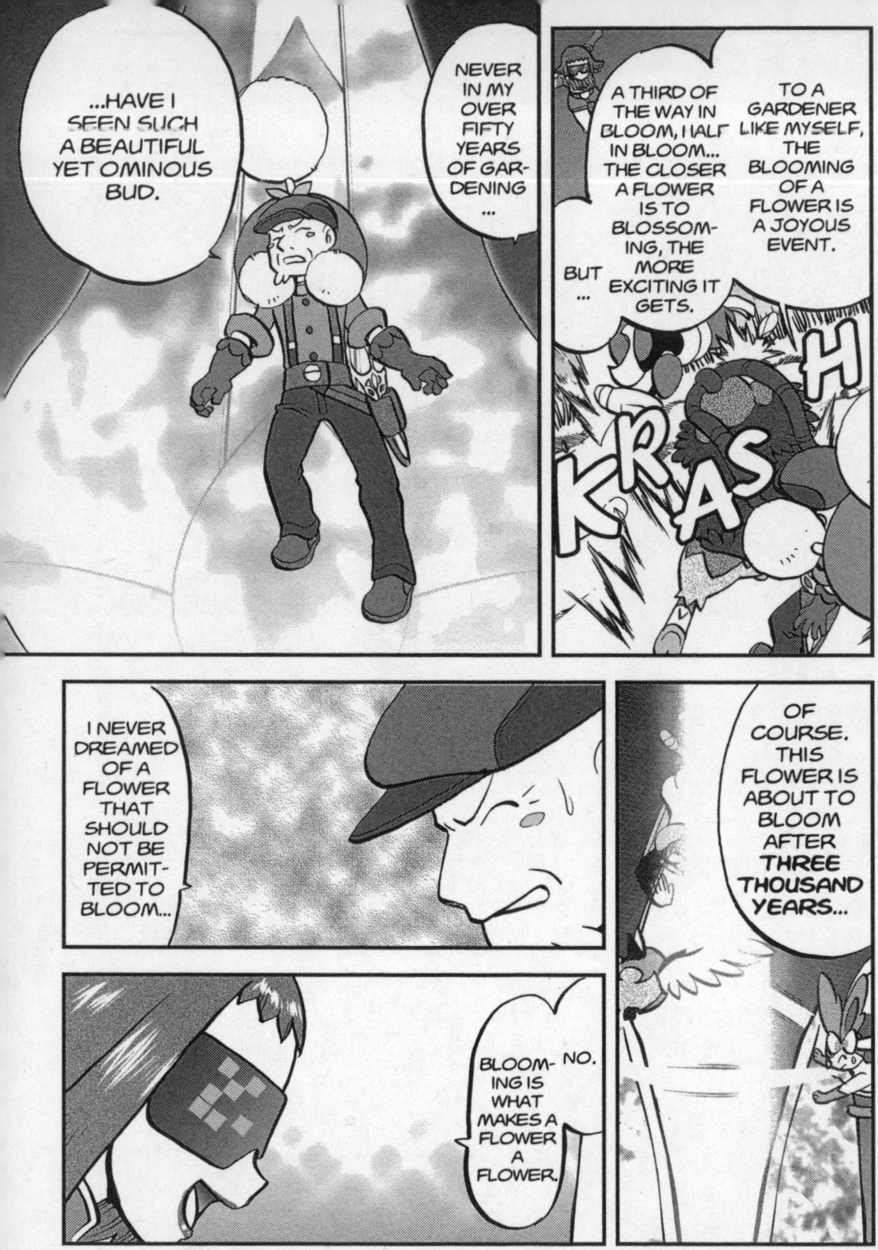
TO A GARDENER LIKE MYSELF, THE BLOOMING OF A FLOWER IS A JOYOUS EVENT.
A THIRD OF THE WAY IN BLOOM, HALF IN BLOOM... THE CLOSER A FLOWER IS TO BLOSSOMING, THE MORE EXCITING IT GETS.
BUT ...
KRASH
NEVER IN MY OVER FIFTY YEARS OF GARDENING ...
...HAVE I SEEN SUCH A BEAUTIFUL YET OMINOUS BUD.
OF COURSE. THIS FLOWER IS ABOUT TO BLOOM AFTER THREE THOUSAND YEARS...
I NEVER DREAMED OF A FLOWER THAT SHOULD NOT BE PERMITTED TO BLOOM...
NO.
BLOOMING IS WHAT MAKES A FLOWER A FLOWER.

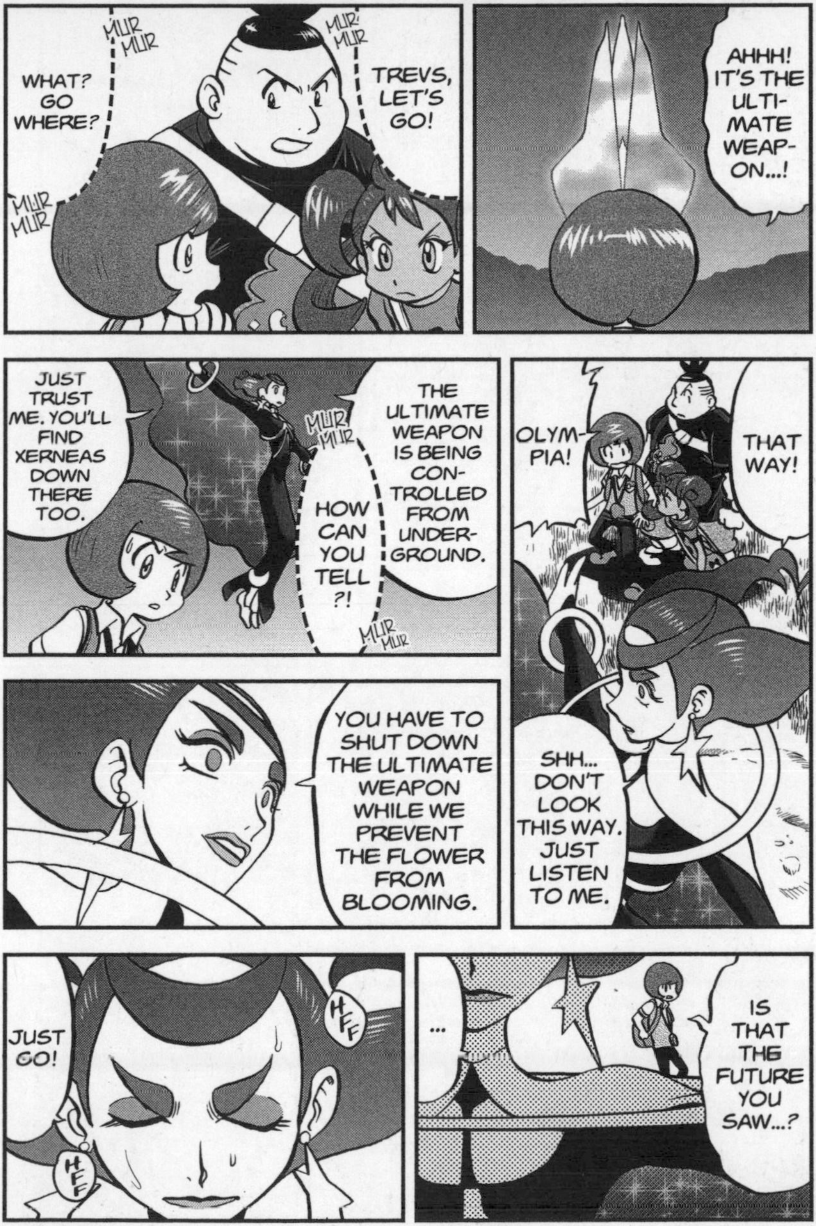
AHHH! IT'S THE ULTIMATE WEAPON...!
MUR MUR
TREVS, LET'S GO!
MUR MUR
WHAT? GO WHERE?
MUR MUR
THAT WAY!
OLYMPIA!
SHH... DON'T LOOK THIS WAY. JUST LISTEN TO ME.
THE ULTIMATE WEAPON IS BEING CONTROLLED FROM UNDERGROUND.
MUR MUR
HOW CAN YOU TELL?!
JUST TRUST ME. YOU'LL FIND XERNEAS DOWN THERE TOO.
MUR MUR
YOU HAVE TO SHUT DOWN THE ULTIMATE WEAPON WHILE WE PREVENT THE FLOWER FROM BLOOMING.
IS THAT THE FUTURE YOU SAW...?
...
HFF
JUST GO!
HFF

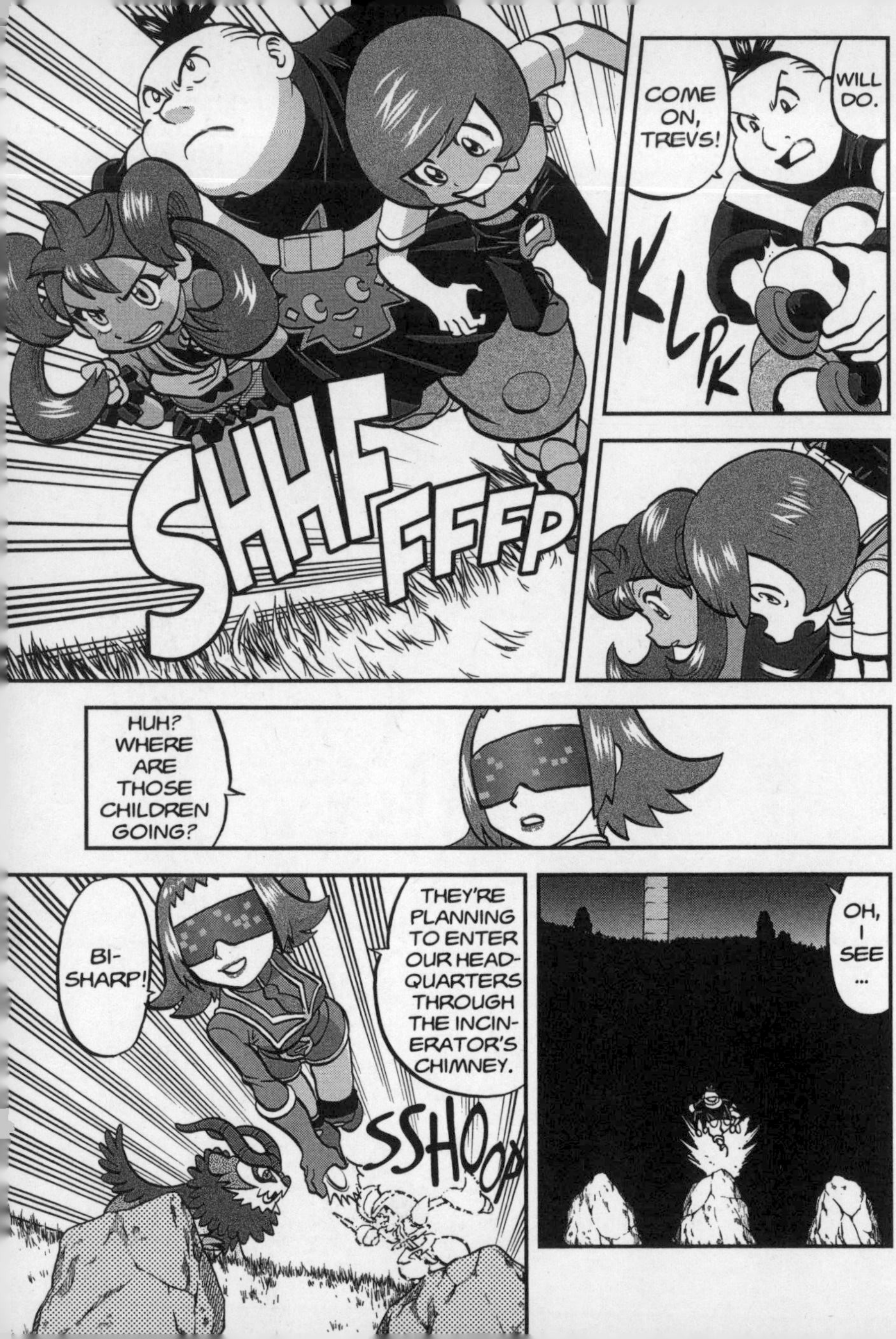
WILL DO.
COME ON, TREVS!
KLPK
SHHFFFFP
HUH? WHERE ARE THOSE CHILDREN GOING?
OH, I SEE ...
THEY'RE PLANNING TO ENTER OUR HEADQUARTERS THROUGH THE INCINERATOR'S CHIMNEY.
BI-SHARP!
SSHOOP

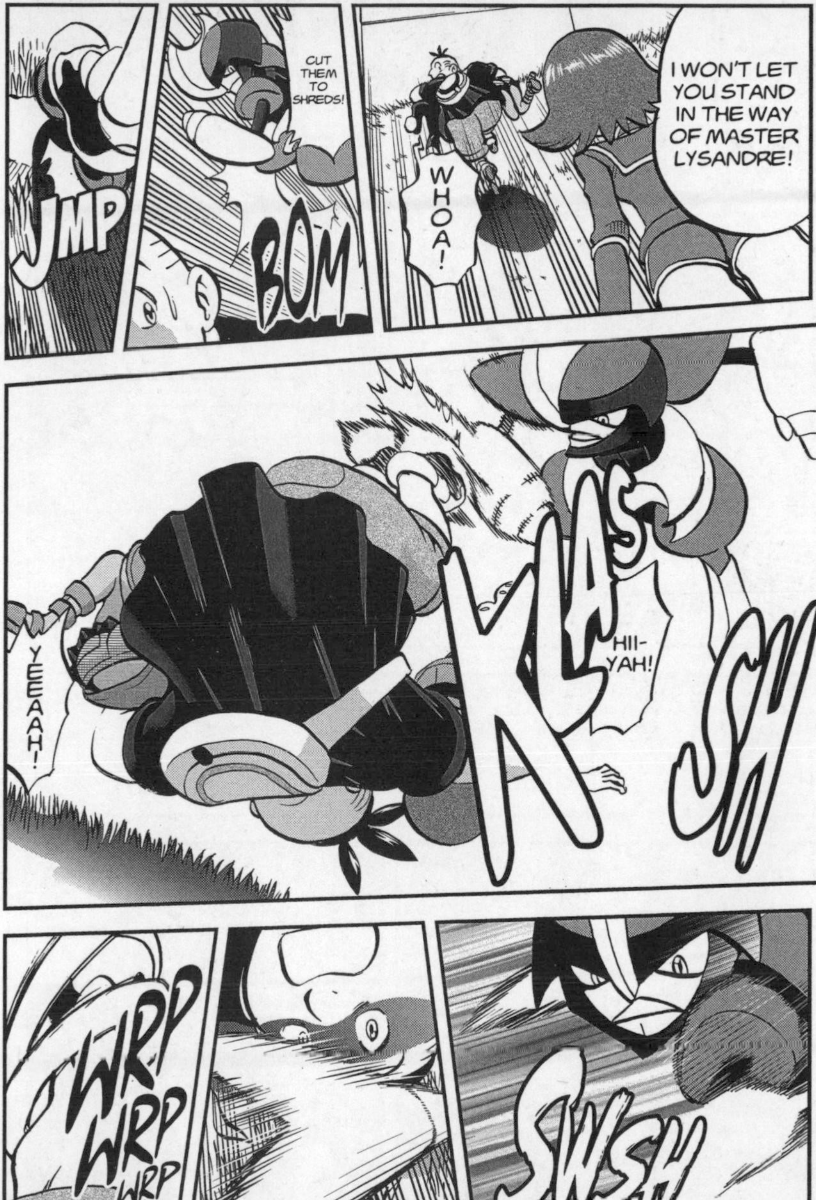
I WON'T LET YOU STAND IN THE WAY OF MASTER LYSANDRE!
WHOA!
CUT THEM TO SHREDS!
BOM
JMP
KASSH
HII-YAH!
YEEAAAH!
SWSH
WRP WRP WRP

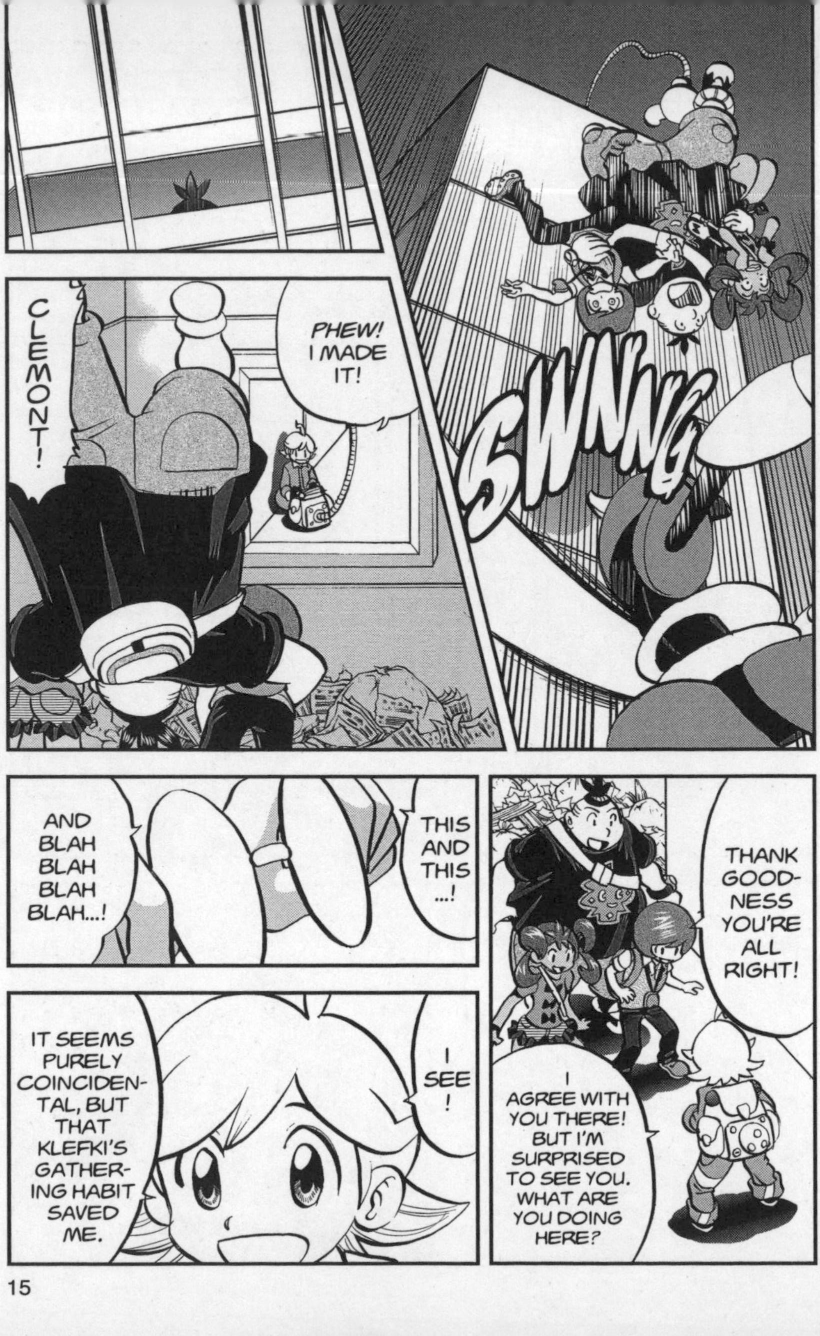
SWNNG
PHEW! I MADE IT!
CLEMONT!
THANK GOODNESS YOU'RE ALL RIGHT!
I AGREE WITH YOU THERE! BUT I'M SURPRISED TO SEE YOU. WHAT ARE YOU DOING HERE?
THIS AND THIS...!
AND BLAH BLAH BLAH BLAH...!
I SEE!
IT SEEMS PURELY COINCIDENTAL, BUT THAT KLEFKI'S GATHERING HABIT SAVED ME.

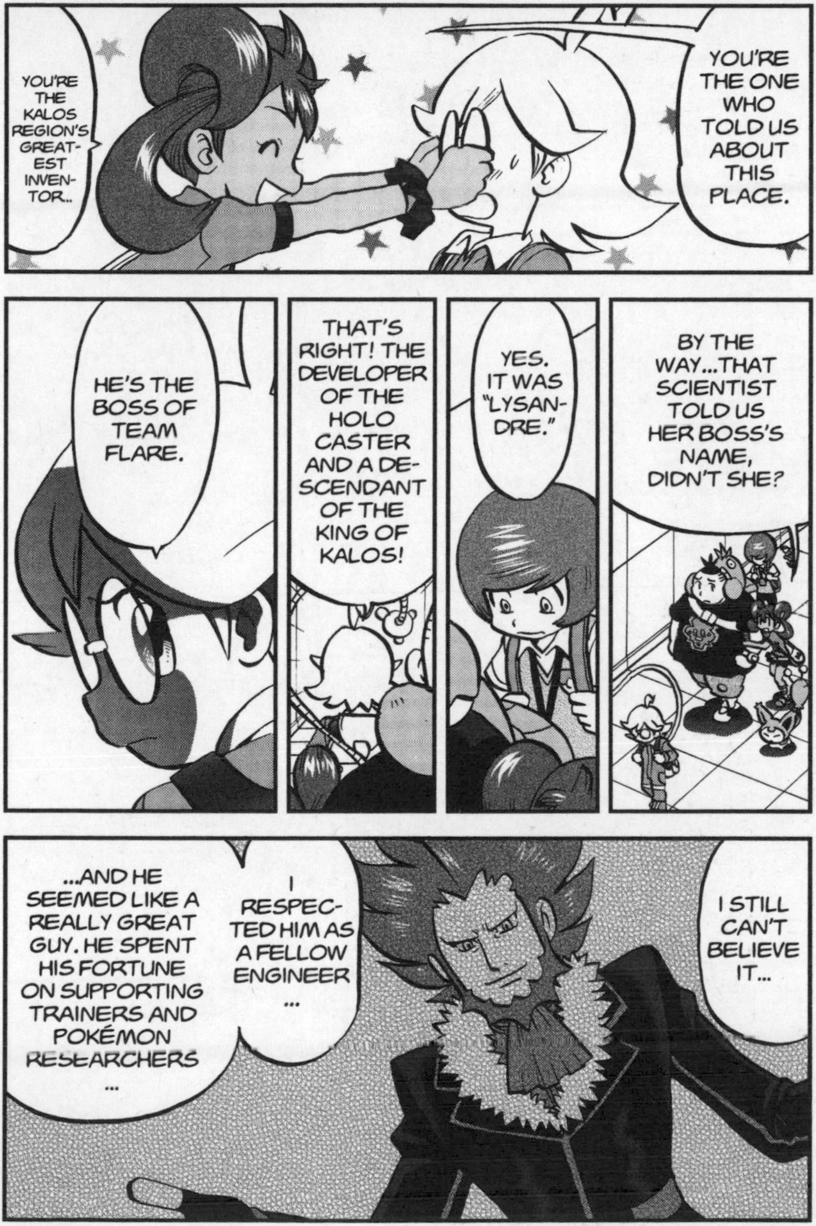
YOU'RE THE ONE WHO TOLD US ABOUT THIS PLACE.
YOU'RE THE KALOS REGION'S GREAT-EST INVEN-TOR...
BY THE WAY...THAT SCIENTIST TOLD US HER BOSS'S NAME, DIDN'T SHE?
YES. IT WAS "LYSAN-DRE."
THAT'S RIGHT! THE DEVELOPER OF THE HOLO CASTER AND A DE-SCENDANT OF THE KING OF KALOS!
HE'S THE BOSS OF TEAM FLARE.
I STILL CAN'T BELIEVE IT...
I RESPEC-TED HIM AS A FELLOW ENGINEER ...
...AND HE SEEMED LIKE A REALLY GREAT GUY. HE SPENT HIS FORTUNE ON SUPPORTING TRAINERS AND POKÉMON RESEARCHERS ...

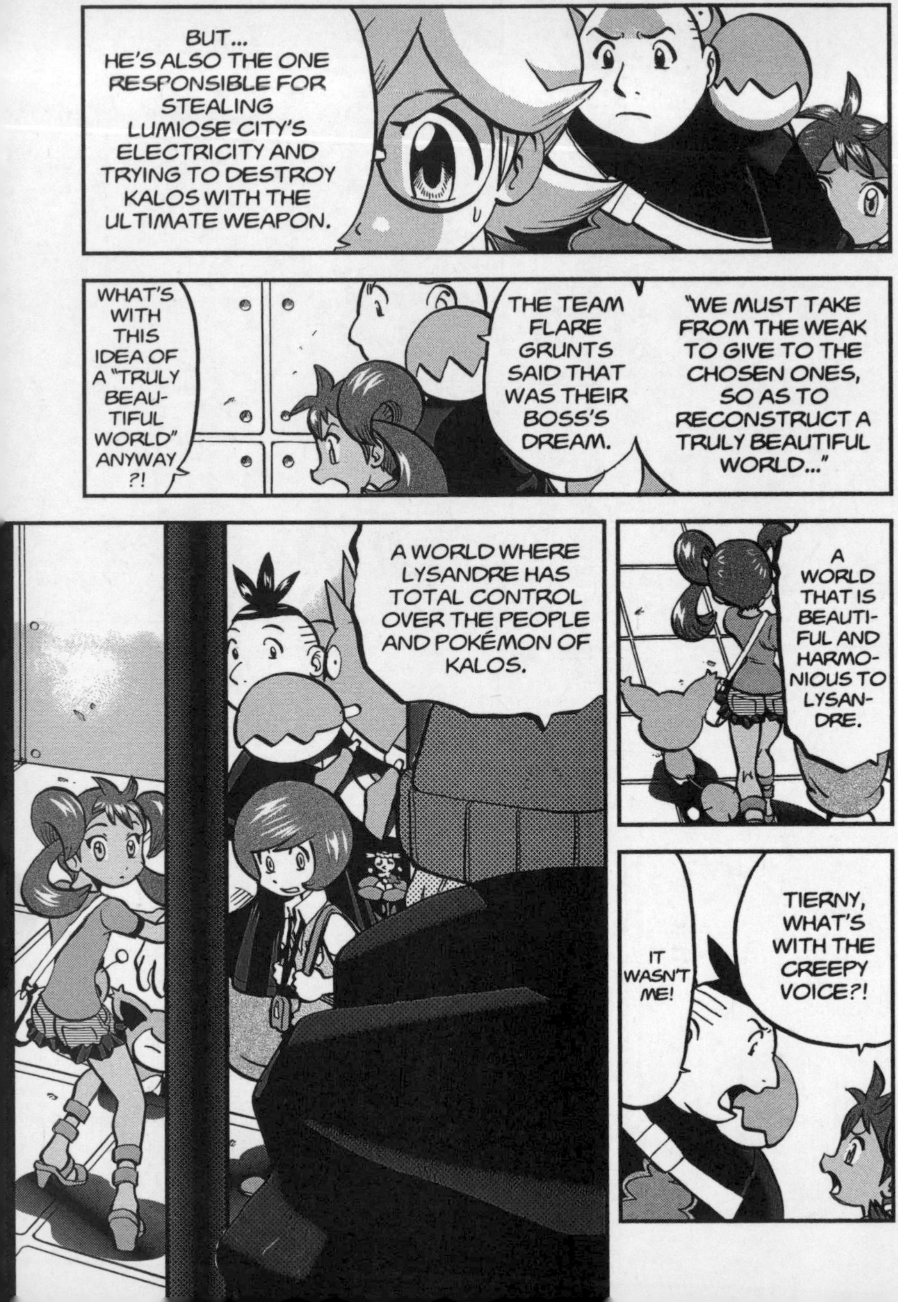
BUT... HE'S ALSO THE ONE RESPONSIBLE FOR STEALING LUMIOSE CITY'S ELECTRICITY AND TRYING TO DESTROY KALOS WITH THE ULTIMATE WEAPON.
"WE MUST TAKE FROM THE WEAK TO GIVE TO THE CHOSEN ONES, SO AS TO RECONSTRUCT A TRULY BEAUTIFUL WORLD..."
THE TEAM FLARE GRUNTS SAID THAT WAS THEIR BOSS'S DREAM.
WHAT'S WITH THIS IDEA OF A "TRULY BEAUTIFUL WORLD" ANYWAY?!
A WORLD THAT IS BEAUTIFUL AND HARMONIOUS TO LYSANDRE.
TIERNY, WHAT'S WITH THE CREEPY VOICE?!
IT WASN'T ME!
A WORLD WHERE LYSANDRE HAS TOTAL CONTROL OVER THE PEOPLE AND POKÉMON OF KALOS.

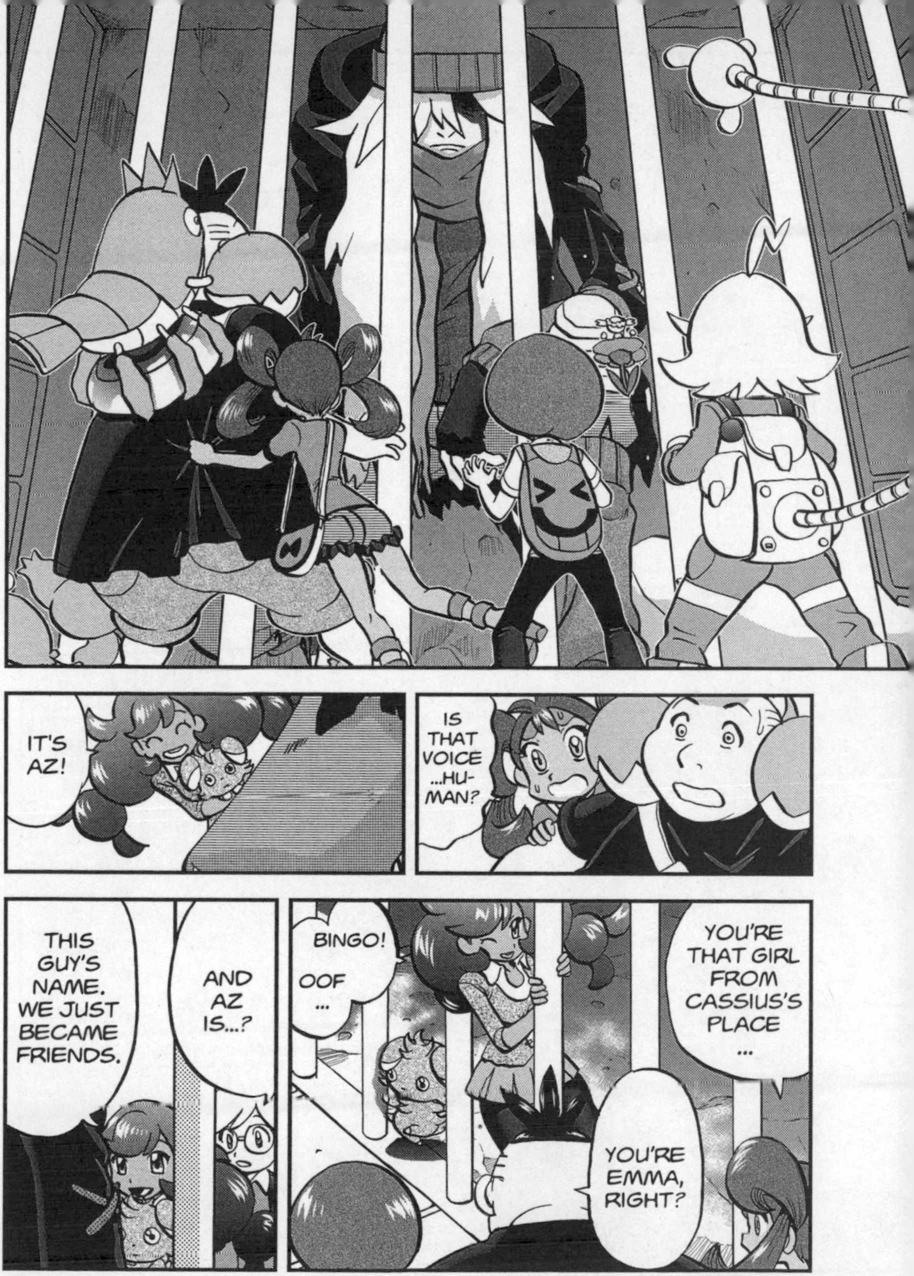
IS THAT VOICE ...HU-MAN?
IT'S AZ!
YOU'RE THAT GIRL FROM CASSIUS'S PLACE ...
YOU'RE EMMA, RIGHT?
BINGO!
OOF ...
AND AZ IS...?
THIS GUY'S NAME. WE JUST BECAME FRIENDS.

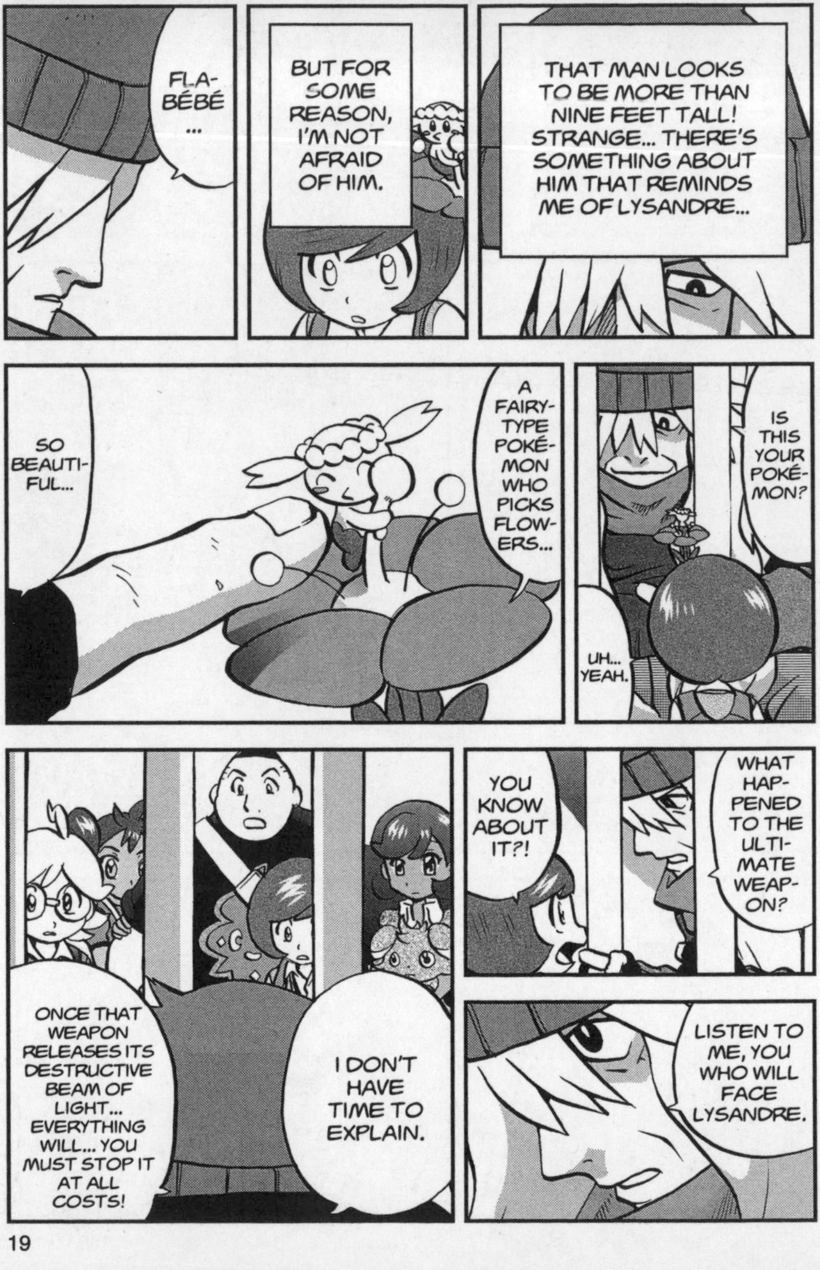
THAT MAN LOOKS TO BE MORE THAN NINE FEET TALL! STRANGE... THERE'S SOMETHING ABOUT HIM THAT REMINDS ME OF LYSANDRE...
BUT FOR SOME REASON, I'M NOT AFRAID OF HIM.
FLA-BÉBÉ...
IS THIS YOUR POKÉMON?
UH... YEAH.
A FAIRY-TYPE POKÉMON WHO PICKS FLOWERS...
SO BEAUTIFUL...
WHAT HAPPENED TO THE ULTIMATE WEAPON?
YOU KNOW ABOUT IT?!
LISTEN TO ME, YOU WHO WILL FACE LYSANDRE.
I DON'T HAVE TIME TO EXPLAIN.
ONCE THAT WEAPON RELEASES ITS DESTRUCTIVE BEAM OF LIGHT... EVERYTHING WILL... YOU MUST STOP IT AT ALL COSTS!

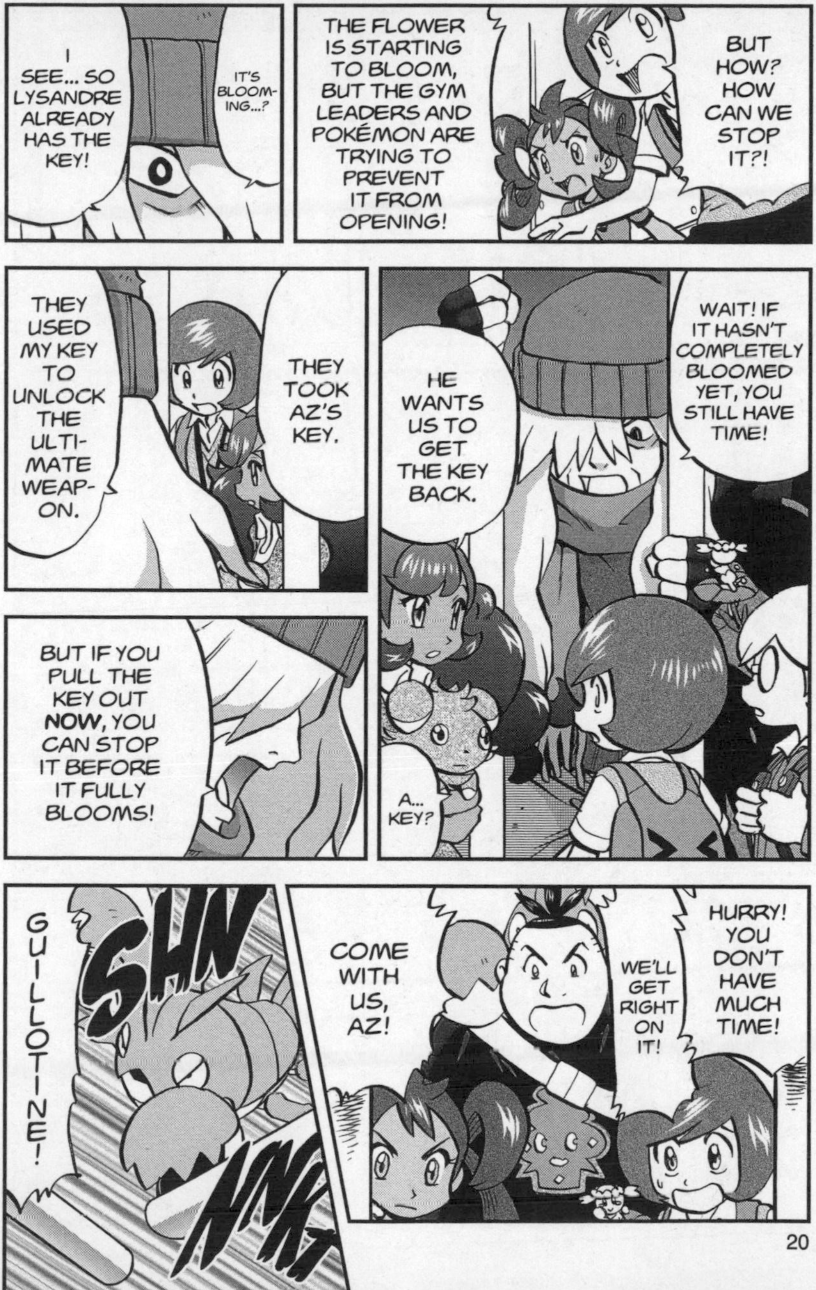
BUT HOW? HOW CAN WE STOP IT?!
THE FLOWER IS STARTING TO BLOOM, BUT THE GYM LEADERS AND POKÉMON ARE TRYING TO PREVENT IT FROM OPENING!
IT'S BLOOMING...?
I SEE... SO LYSANDRE ALREADY HAS THE KEY!
WAIT! IF IT HASN'T COMPLETELY BLOOMED YET, YOU STILL HAVE TIME!
HE WANTS US TO GET THE KEY BACK.
A... KEY?
THEY TOOK AZ'S KEY.
THEY USED MY KEY TO UNLOCK THE ULTIMATE WEAPON.
BUT IF YOU PULL THE KEY OUT **NOW**, YOU CAN STOP IT BEFORE IT FULLY BLOOMS!
HURRY! YOU DON'T HAVE MUCH TIME!
WE'LL GET RIGHT ON IT!
COME WITH US, AZ!
GUILLOTINE!
SHNNNK

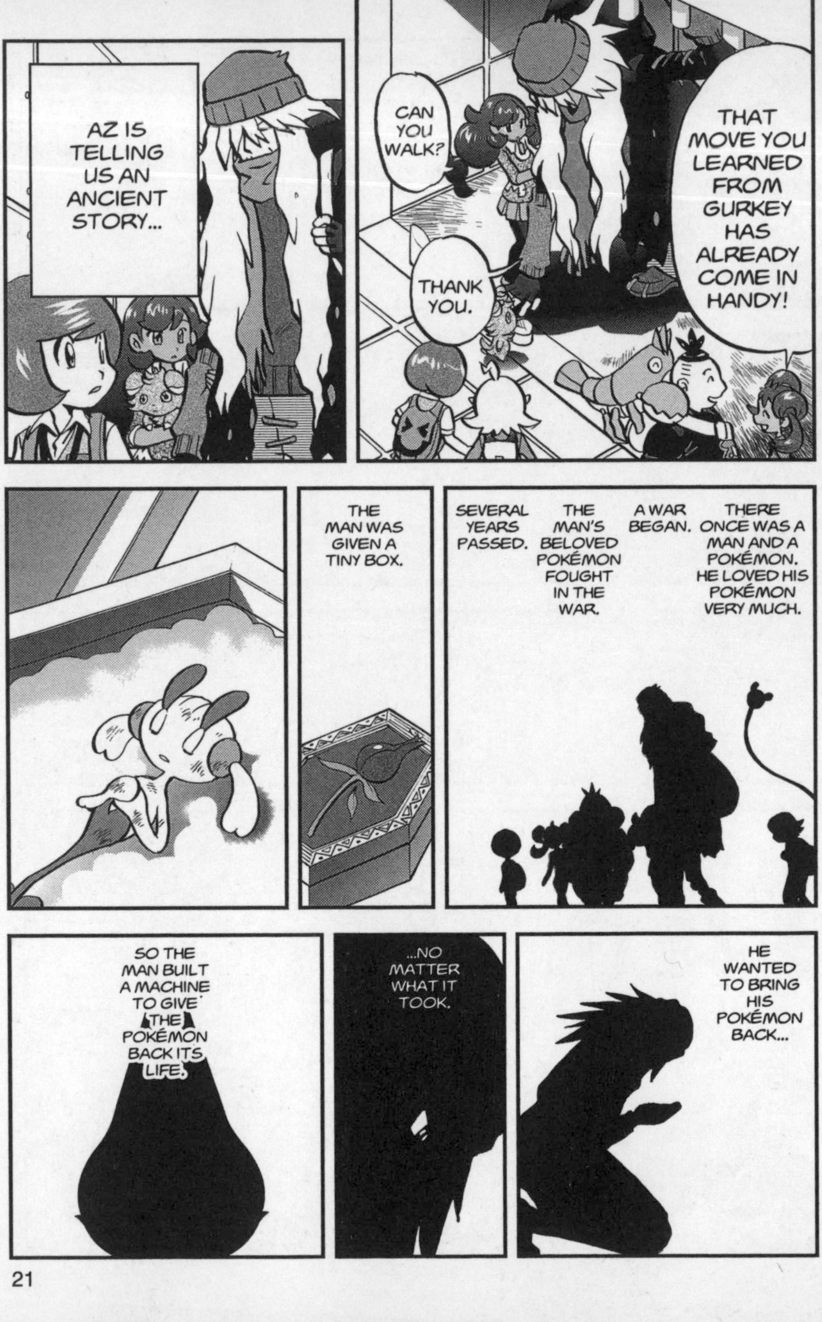
THAT MOVE YOU LEARNED FROM GURKEY HAS ALREADY COME IN HANDY!
CAN YOU WALK?
THANK YOU.
AZ IS TELLING US AN ANCIENT STORY...
THERE ONCE WAS A MAN AND A POKéMON. HE LOVED HIS POKéMON VERY MUCH.
A WAR BEGAN.
THE MAN'S BELOVED POKéMON FOUGHT IN THE WAR.
SEVERAL YEARS PASSED.
THE MAN WAS GIVEN A TINY BOX.
HE WANTED TO BRING HIS POKéMON BACK...
...NO MATTER WHAT IT TOOK.
SO THE MAN BUILT A MACHINE TO GIVE THE POKéMON BACK ITS LIFE.

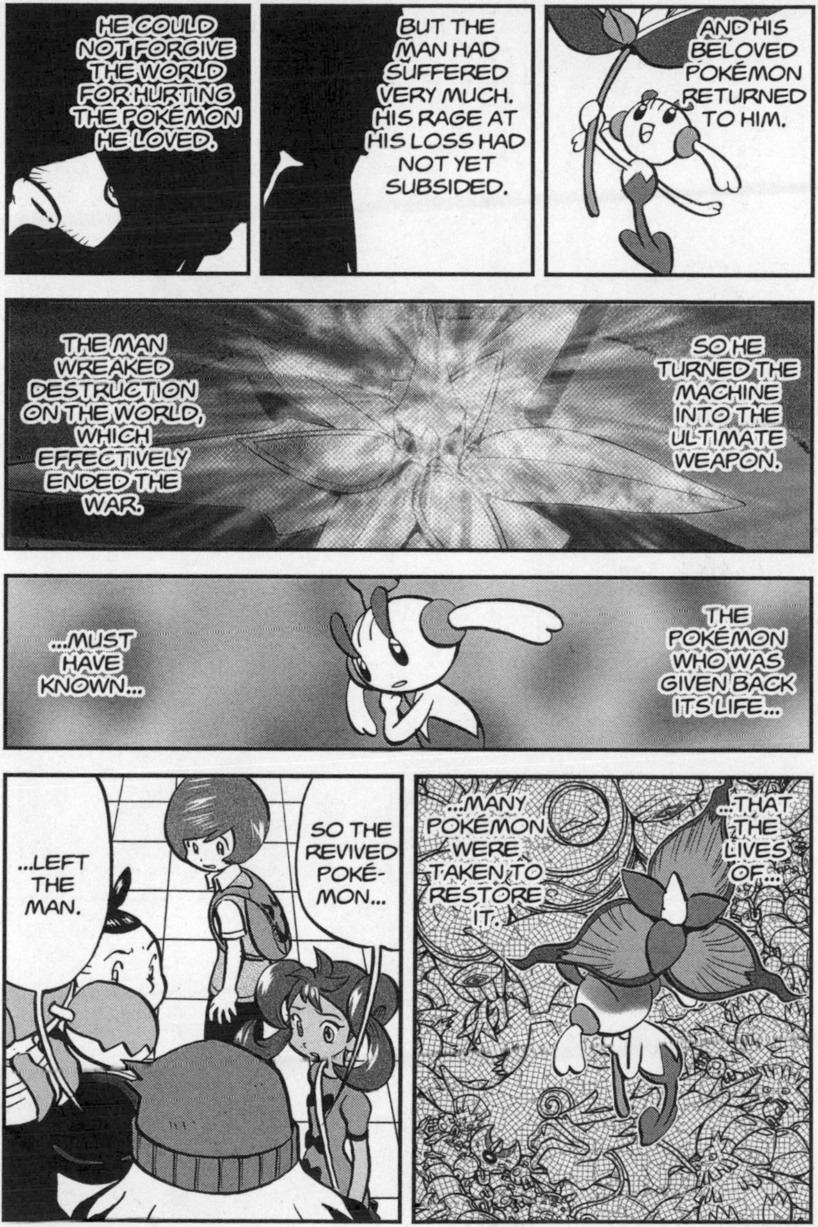
AND HIS BELOVED POKÉMON RETURNED TO HIM.
BUT THE MAN HAD SUFFERED VERY MUCH. HIS RAGE AT HIS LOSS HAD NOT YET SUBSIDED.
HE COULD NOT FORGIVE THE WORLD FOR HURTING THE POKÉMON HE LOVED.
SO HE TURNED THE MACHINE INTO THE ULTIMATE WEAPON.
THE MAN WREAKED DESTRUCTION ON THE WORLD, WHICH EFFECTIVELY ENDED THE WAR.
THE POKÉMON WHO WAS GIVEN BACK ITS LIFE...
...MUST HAVE KNOWN...
...THAT THE LIVES OF...
...MANY POKÉMON WERE TAKEN TO RESTORE IT.
SO THE REVIVED POKÉ-MON...
...LEFT THE MAN.

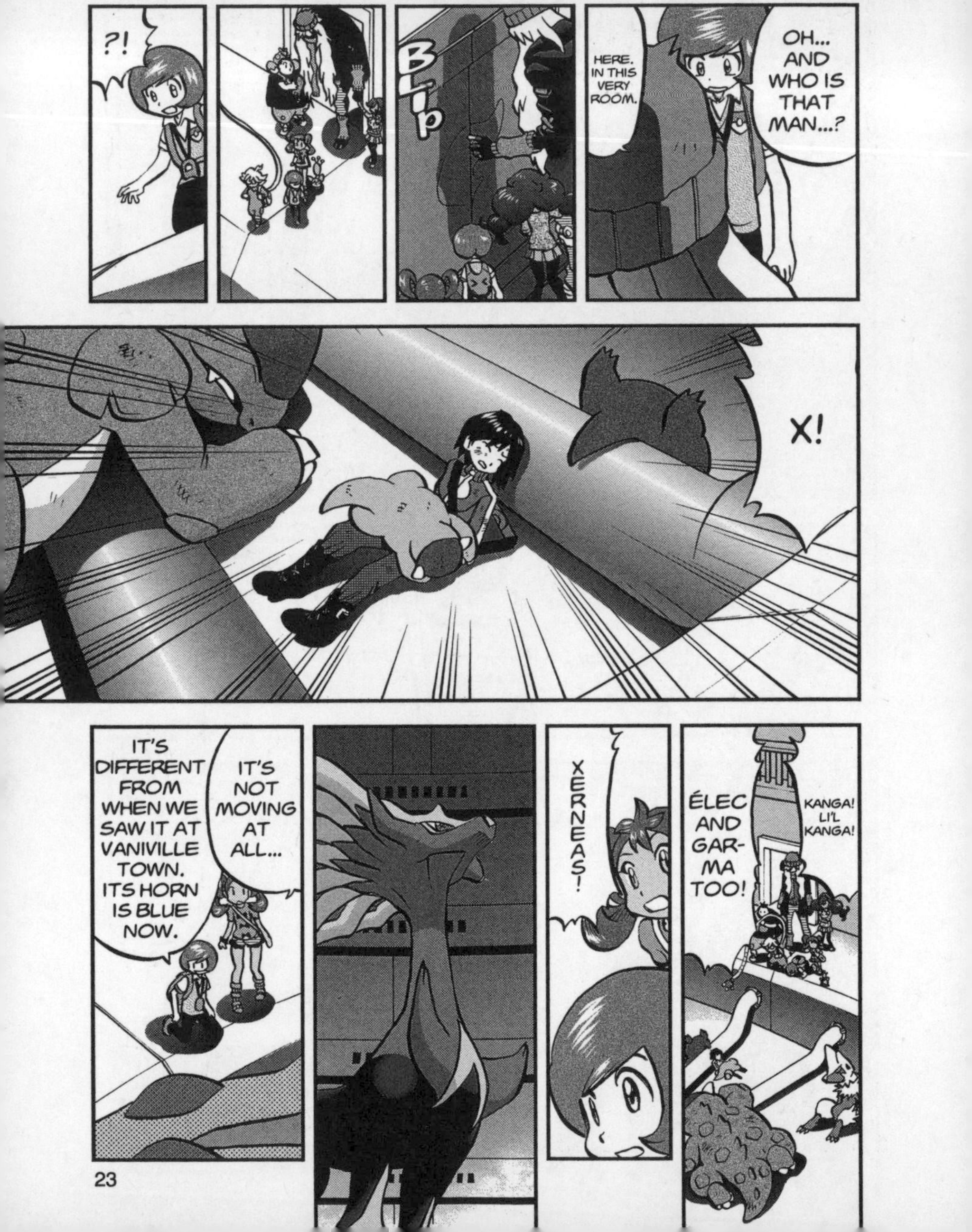
OH... AND WHO IS THAT MAN...?
HERE. IN THIS VERY ROOM.
BLIP
?!
X!
KANGA! LI'L KANGA!
ÉLEC AND GAR-MA TOO!
XERNEAS!
IT'S NOT MOVING AT ALL...
IT'S DIFFERENT FROM WHEN WE SAW IT AT VANIVILLE TOWN. ITS HORN IS BLUE NOW.

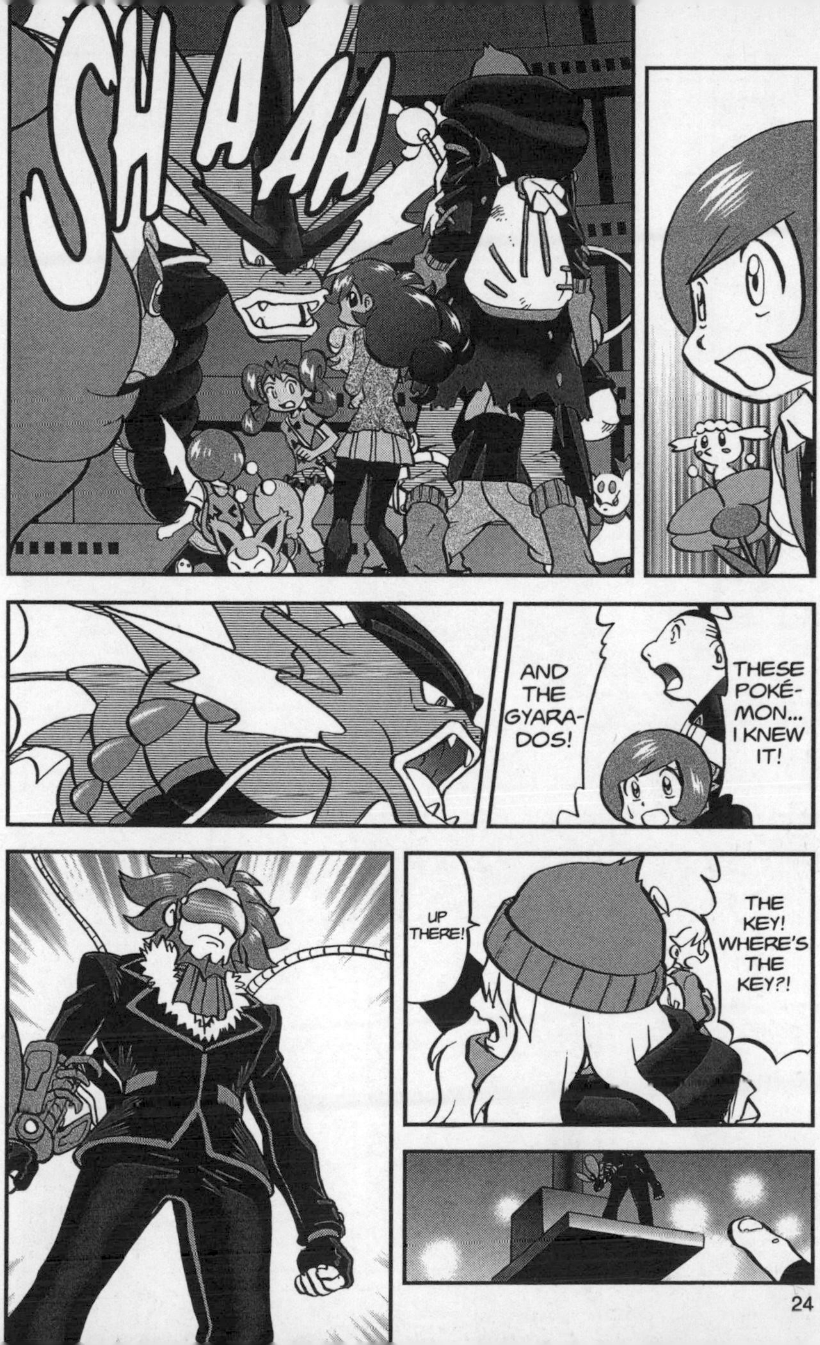
SHAAAA
THESE POKÉMON... I KNEW IT!
AND THE GYARADOS!
THE KEY! WHERE'S THE KEY?!
UP THERE!

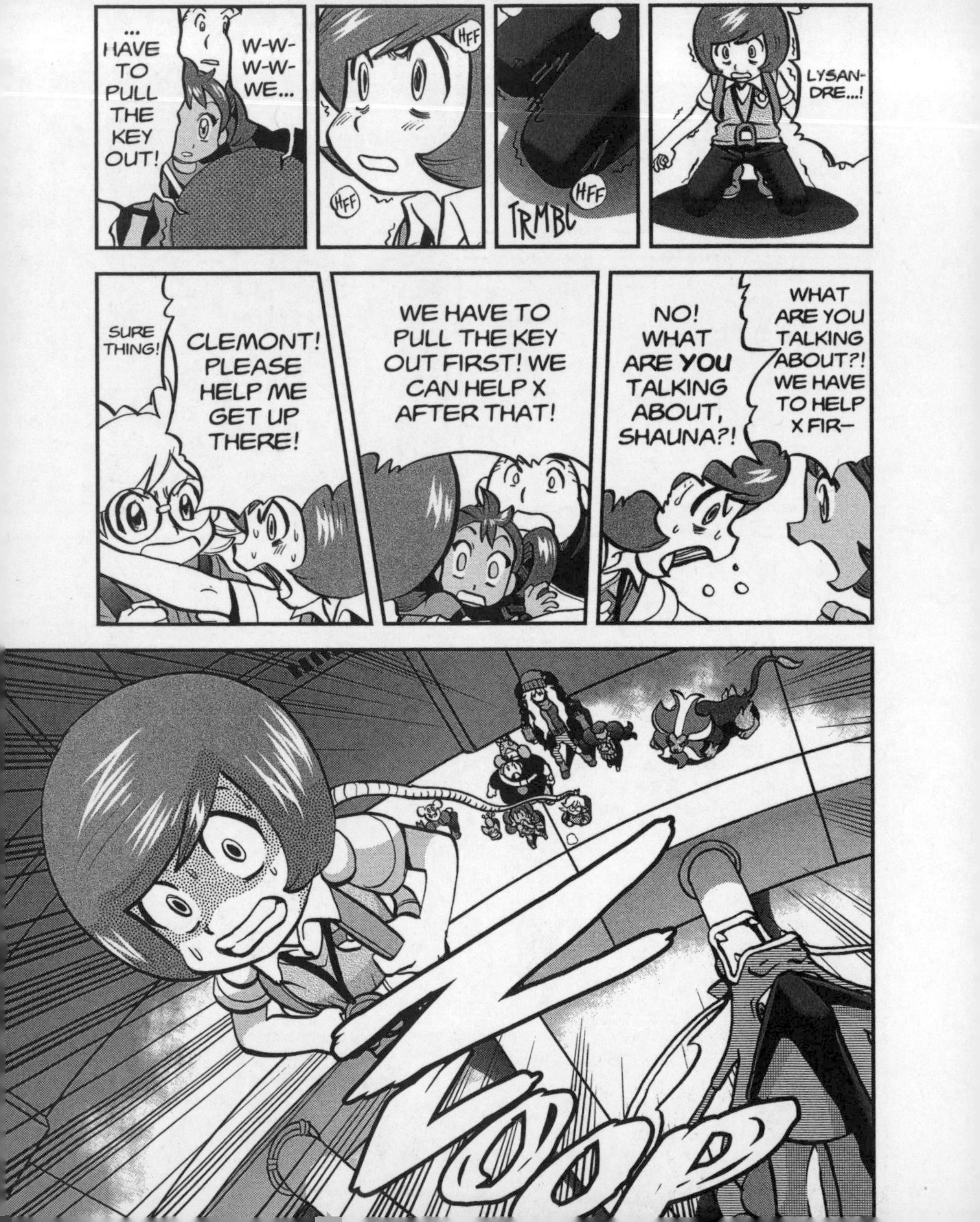
LYSANDRE...!
HFF
TRMBL
HFF
HFF
HFF
W-W-W-W-WE...
... HAVE TO PULL THE KEY OUT!
WHAT ARE YOU TALKING ABOUT?! WE HAVE TO HELP X FIR—
NO! WHAT ARE **YOU** TALKING ABOUT, SHAUNA?!
WE HAVE TO PULL THE KEY OUT FIRST! WE CAN HELP X AFTER THAT!
CLEMONT! PLEASE HELP ME GET UP THERE!
SURE THING!
ZOOP

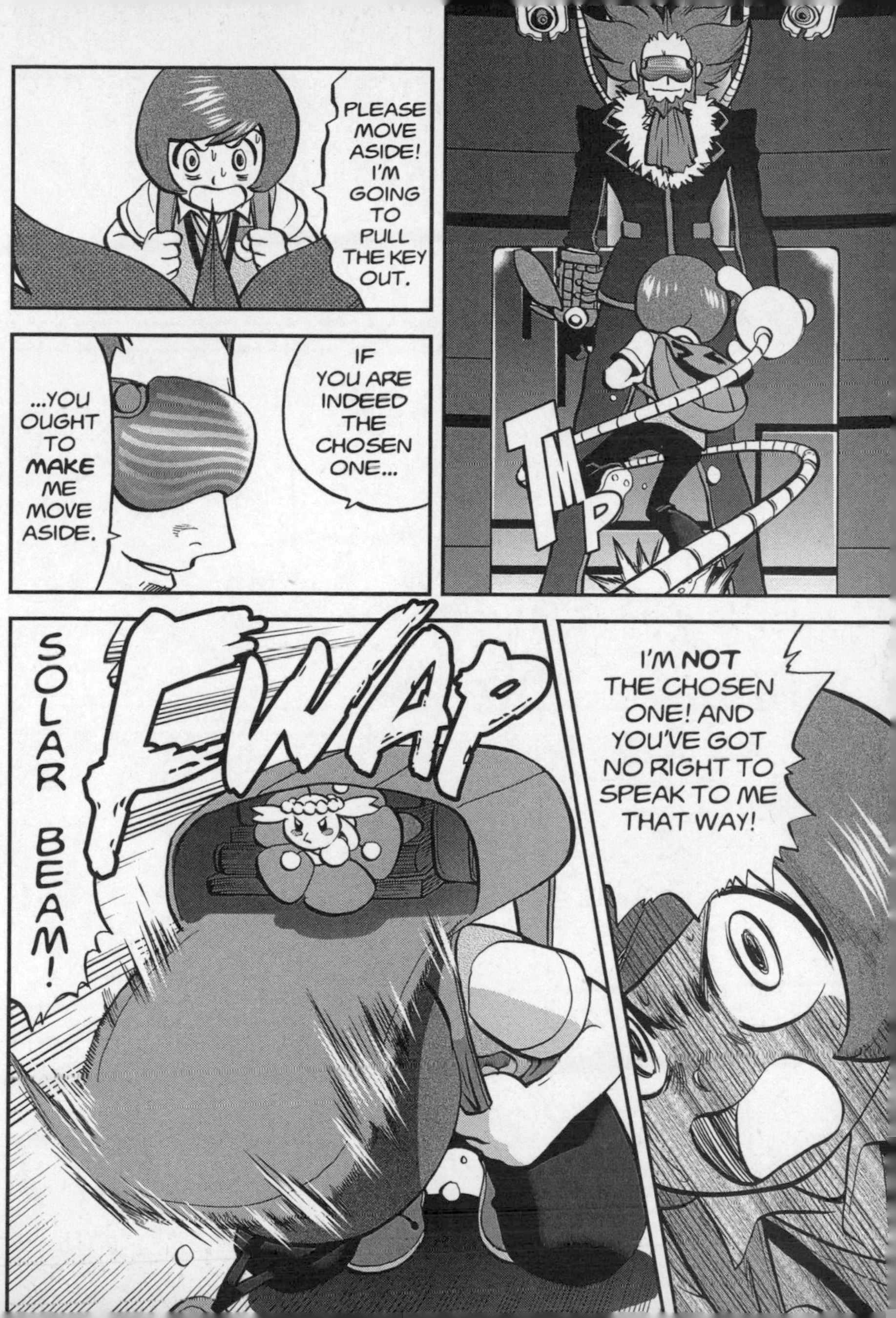
TMP
PLEASE MOVE ASIDE! I'M GOING TO PULL THE KEY OUT.
IF YOU ARE INDEED THE CHOSEN ONE...
...YOU OUGHT TO MAKE ME MOVE ASIDE.
I'M NOT THE CHOSEN ONE! AND YOU'VE GOT NO RIGHT TO SPEAK TO ME THAT WAY!
FWAP
SOLAR BEAM!

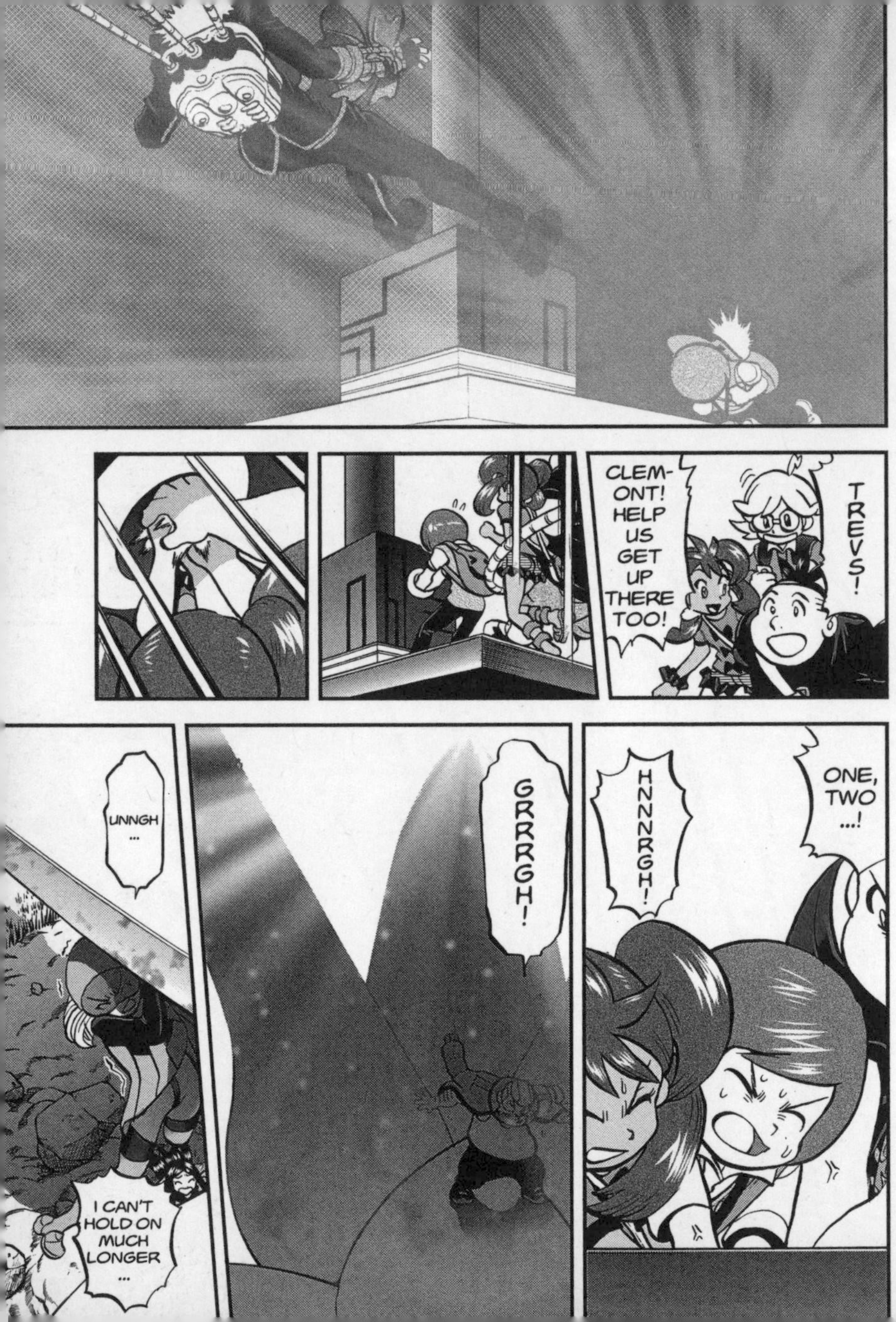
TREVS!
CLEM-ONT! HELP US GET UP THERE TOO!
ONE, TWO ...!
HNNNRGH!
GRRRGH!
UNNGH ...
I CAN'T HOLD ON MUCH LONGER ...

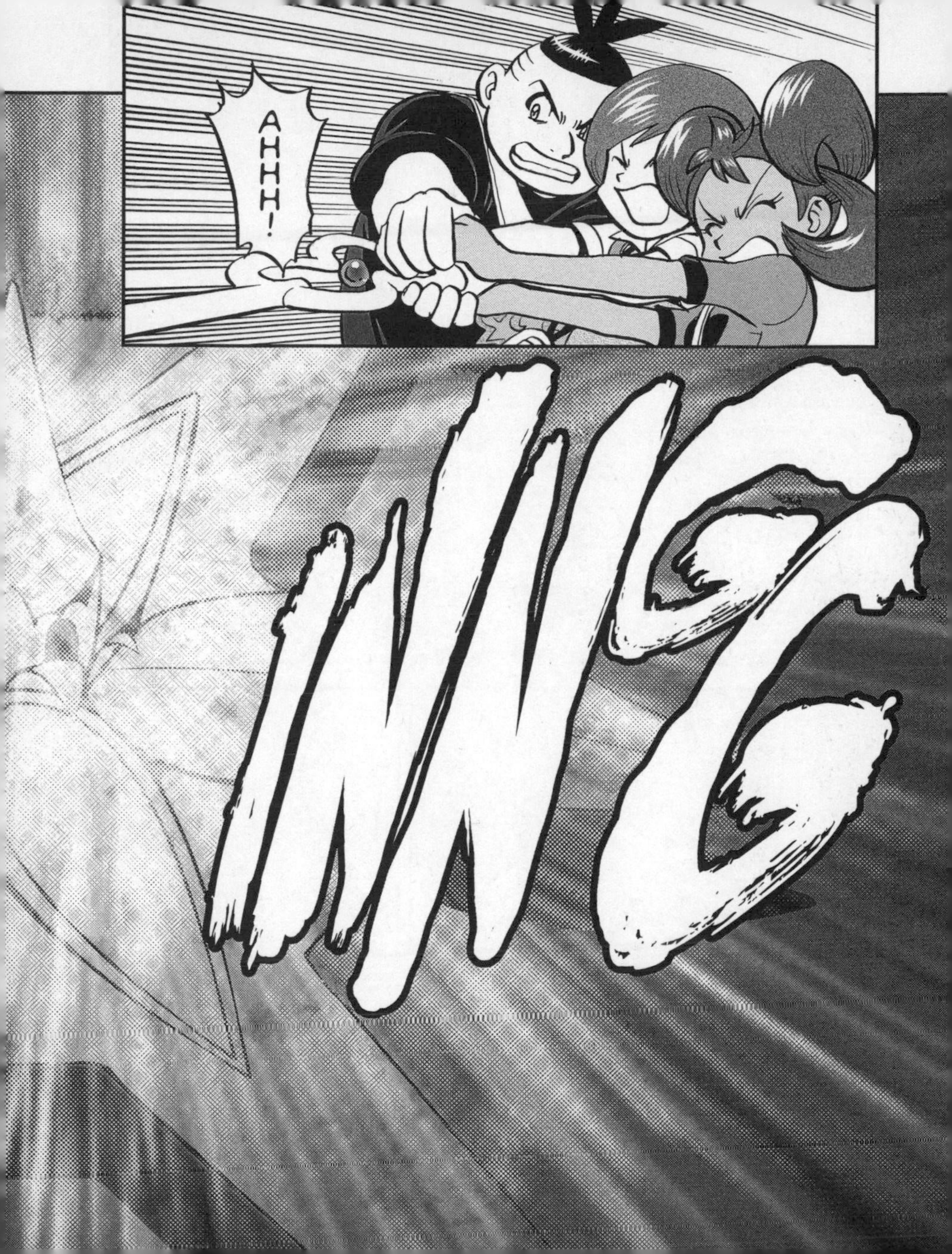
AHHH!

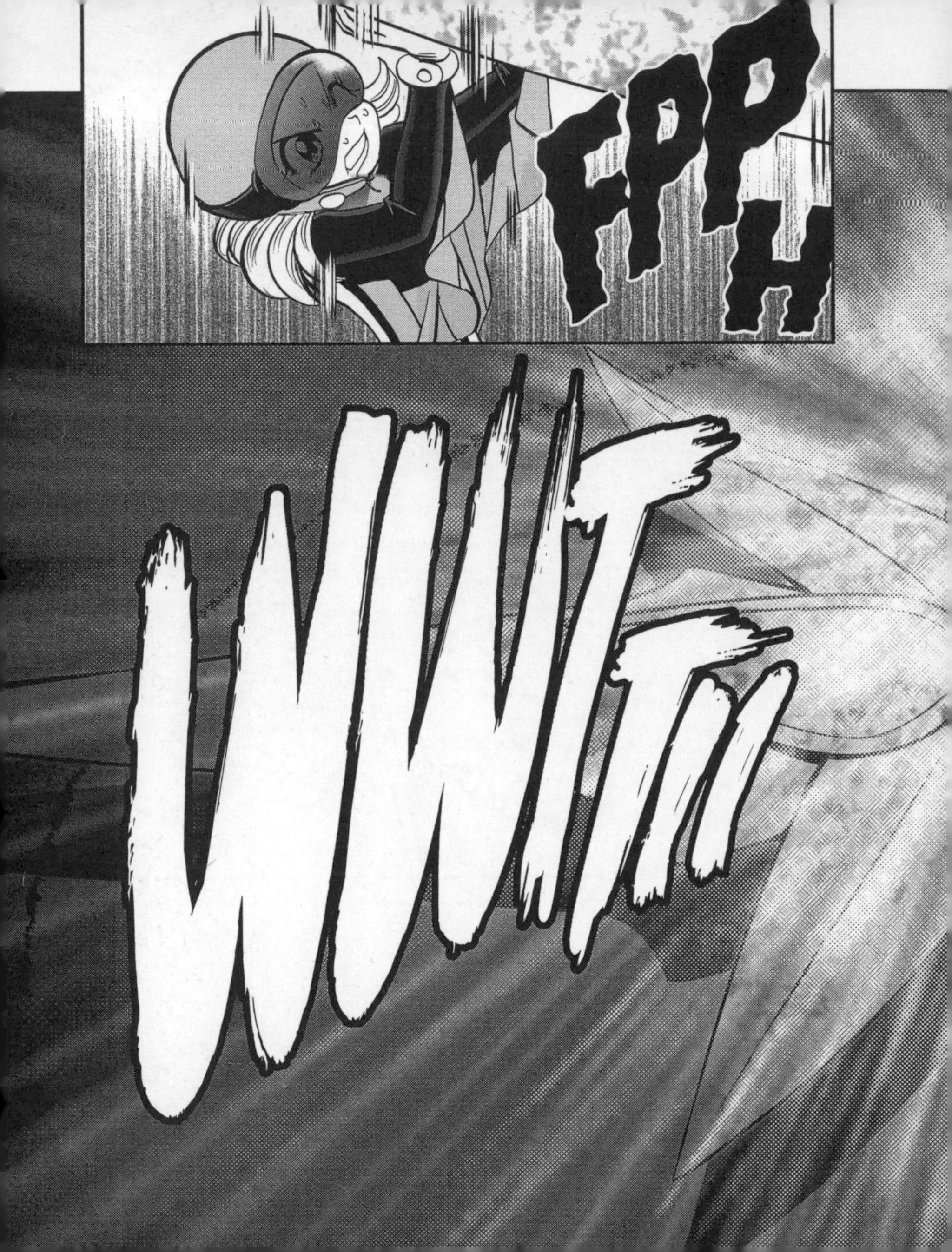
FPPA

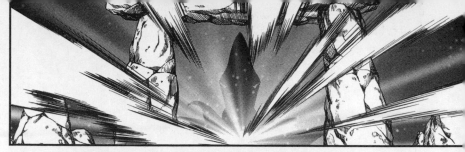

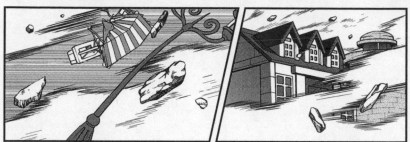

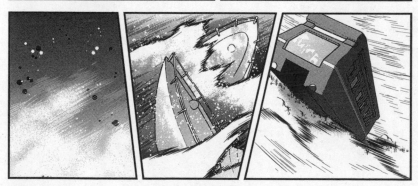

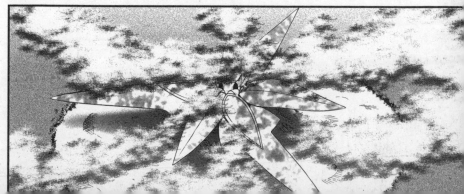

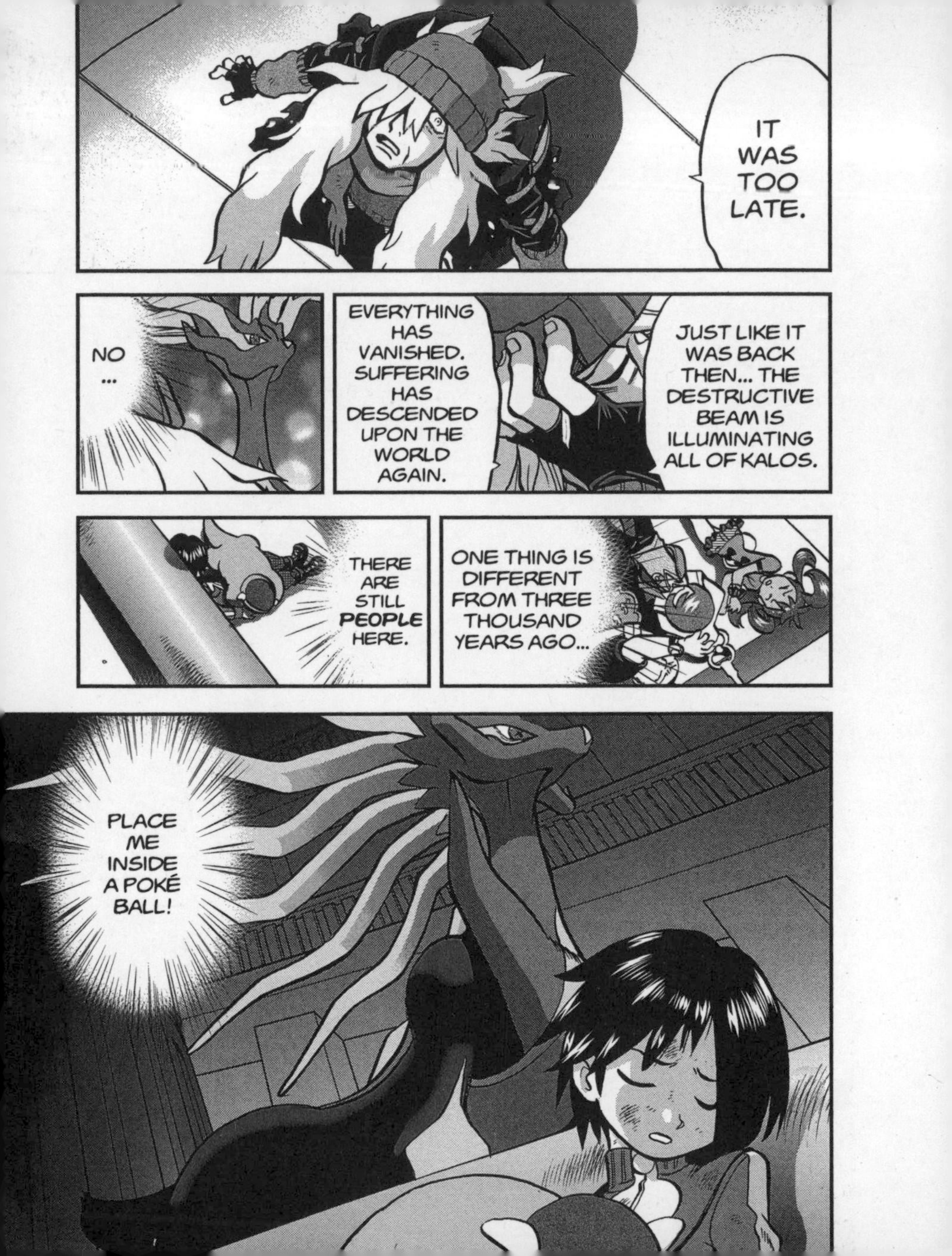
IT WAS TOO LATE.
JUST LIKE IT WAS BACK THEN... THE DESTRUCTIVE BEAM IS ILLUMINATING ALL OF KALOS.
EVERYTHING HAS VANISHED. SUFFERING HAS DESCENDED UPON THE WORLD AGAIN.
NO ...
ONE THING IS DIFFERENT FROM THREE THOUSAND YEARS AGO...
THERE ARE STILL **PEOPLE** HERE.
PLACE ME INSIDE A POKÉ BALL!

Current Location

Geosenge Town

A town lined with mysterious stones and encircled by strange ruins of old.

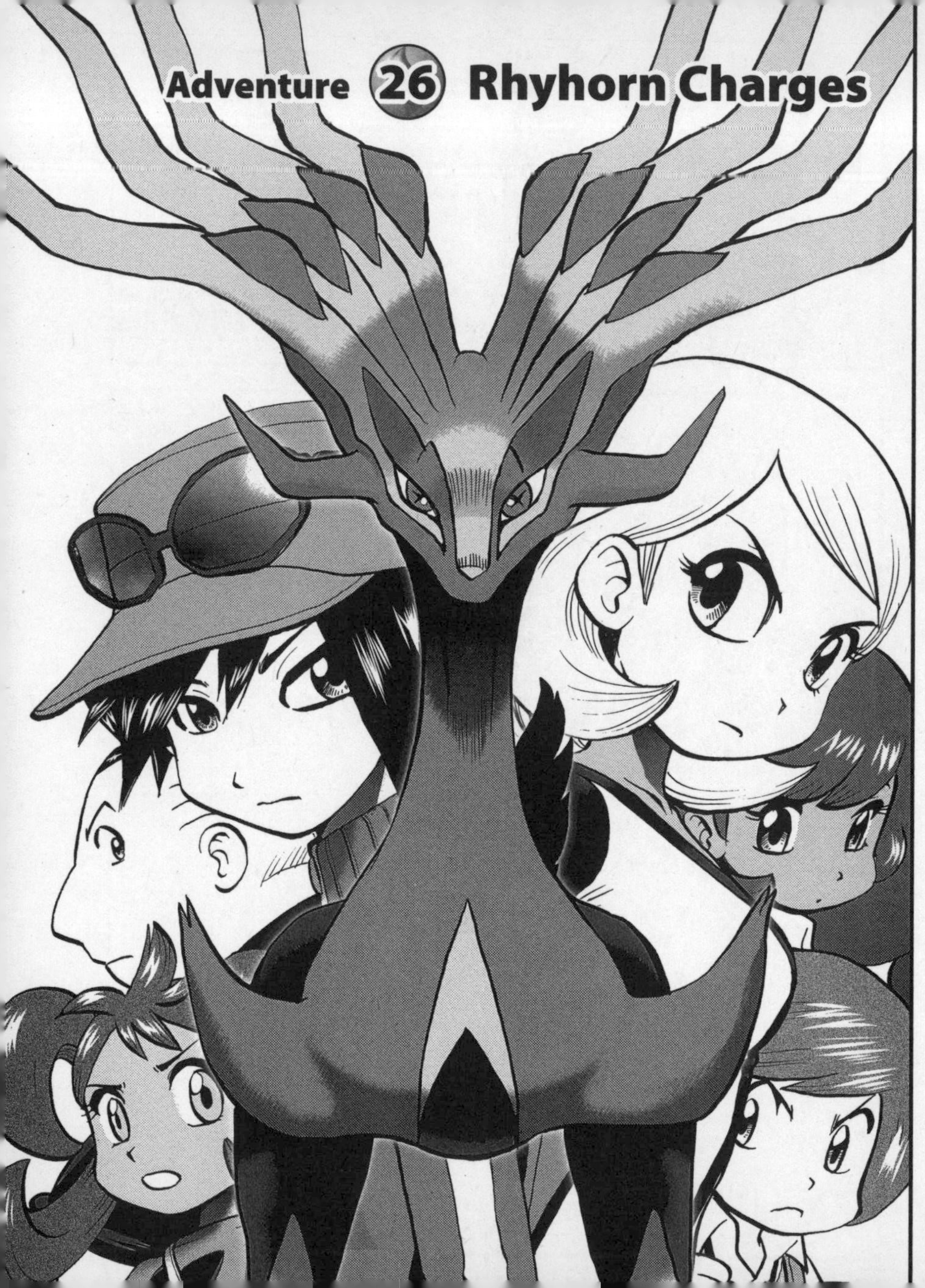
Adventure 26 Rhyhorn Charges

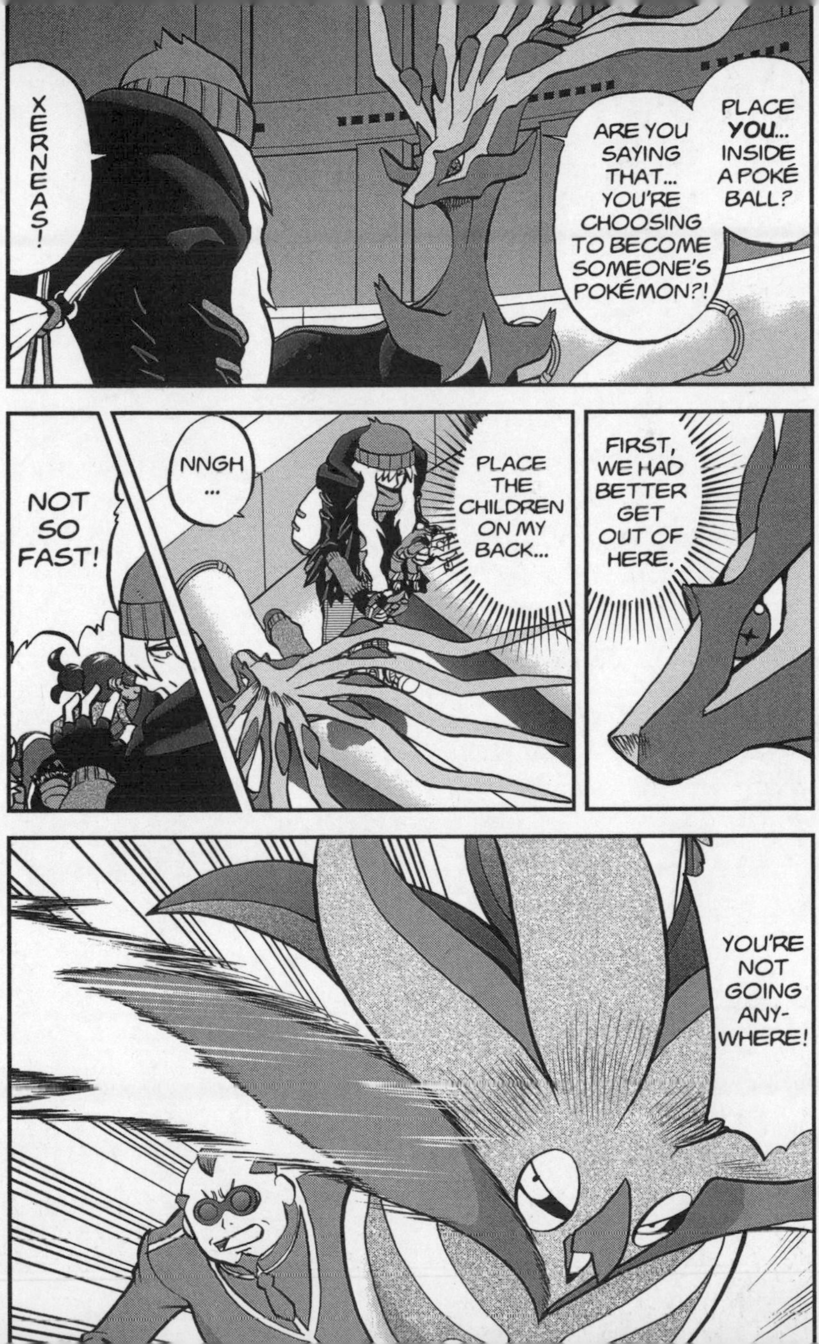
PLACE **YOU**... INSIDE A POKÉ BALL?
ARE YOU SAYING THAT... YOU'RE CHOOSING TO BECOME SOMEONE'S POKÉMON?!
XERNEAS!
FIRST, WE HAD BETTER GET OUT OF HERE.
PLACE THE CHILDREN ON MY BACK...
NNGH...
NOT SO FAST!
YOU'RE NOT GOING ANY-WHERE!

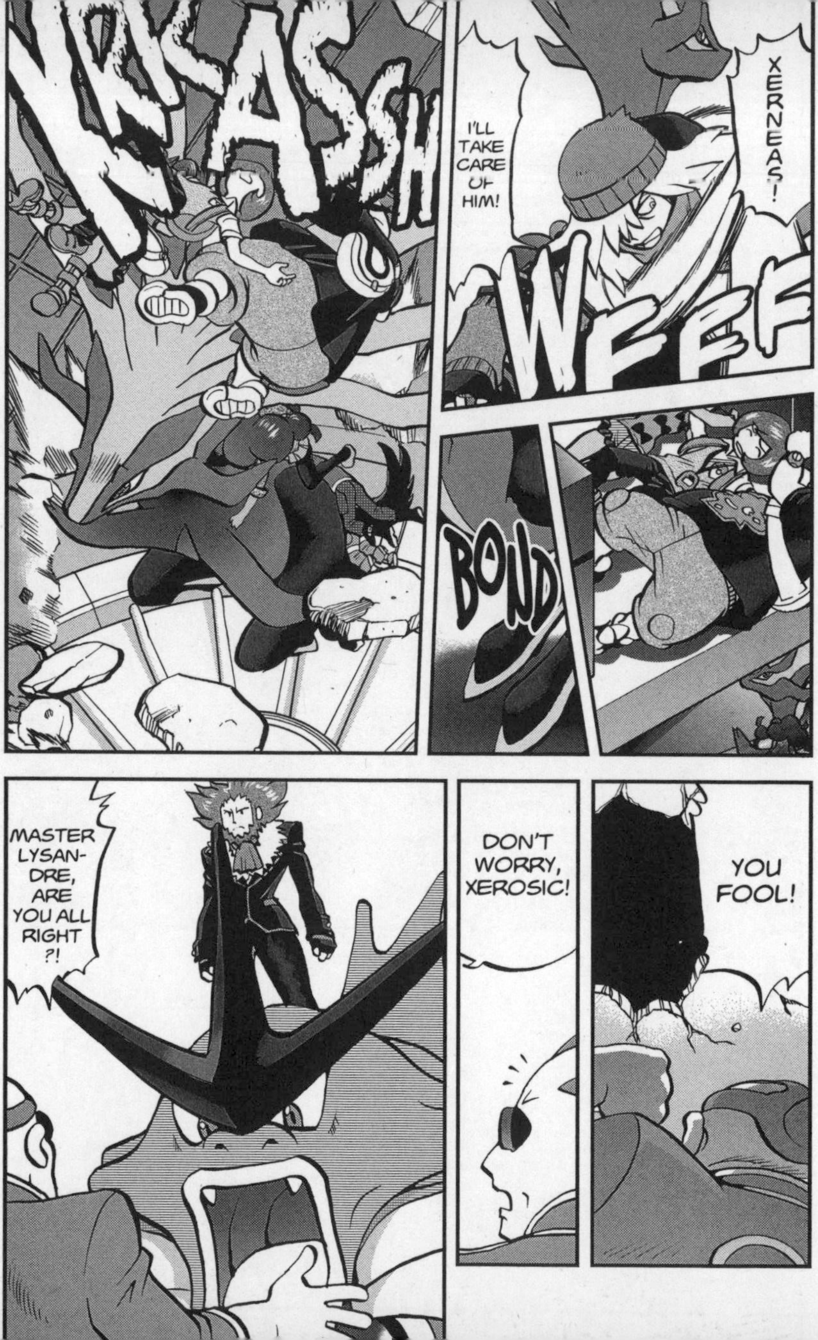
XERNEAS!
I'LL TAKE CARE OF HIM!
WFFF
BOND
YOU FOOL!
DON'T WORRY, XEROSIC!
MASTER LYSANDRE, ARE YOU ALL RIGHT?!

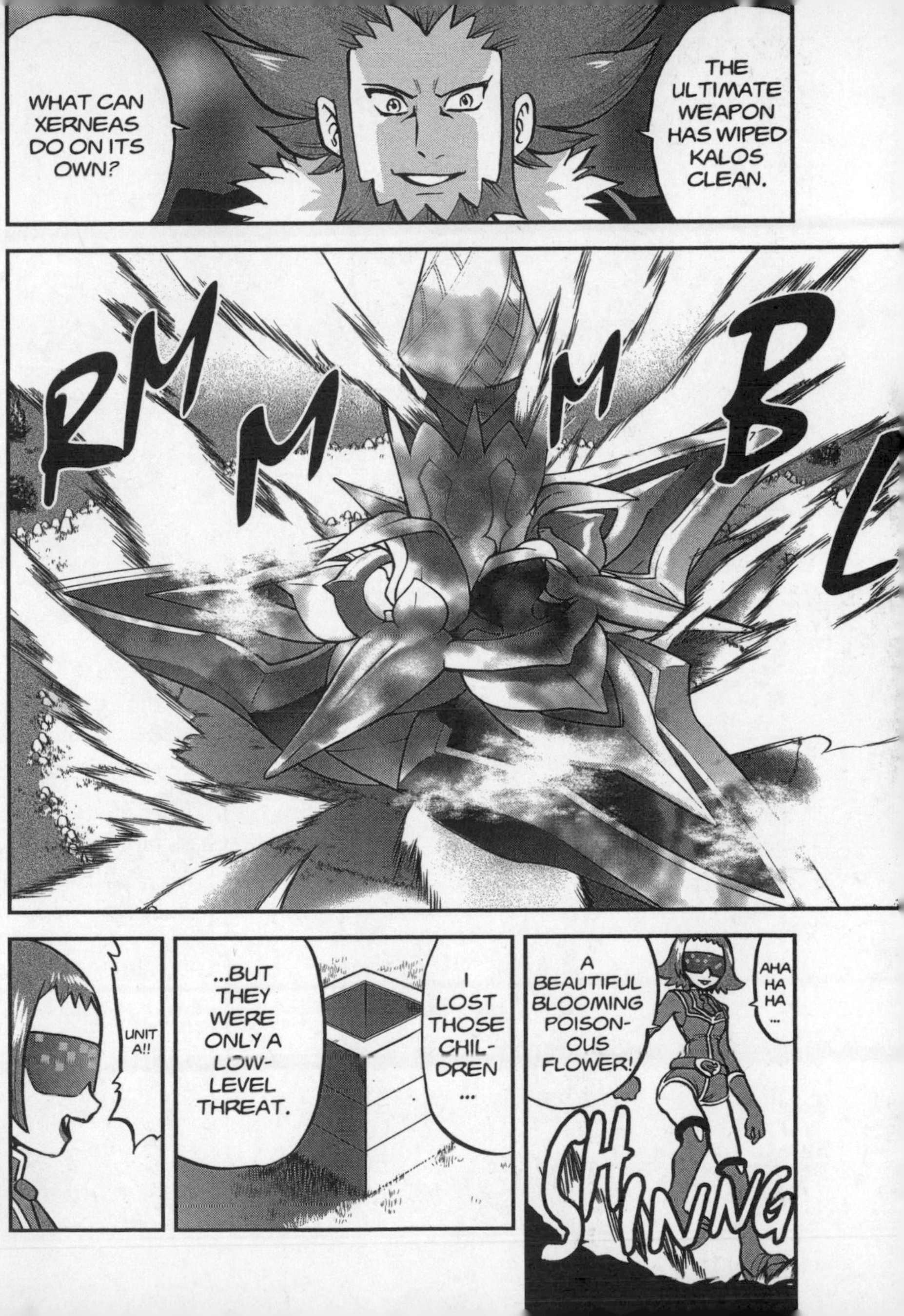
THE ULTIMATE WEAPON HAS WIPED KALOS CLEAN.
WHAT CAN XERNEAS DO ON ITS OWN?
RMMMBL
AHA HA HA ...
A BEAUTIFUL BLOOMING POISON-OUS FLOWER!
SHINING
I LOST THOSE CHIL-DREN ...
...BUT THEY WERE ONLY A LOW-LEVEL THREAT.
UNIT A!!

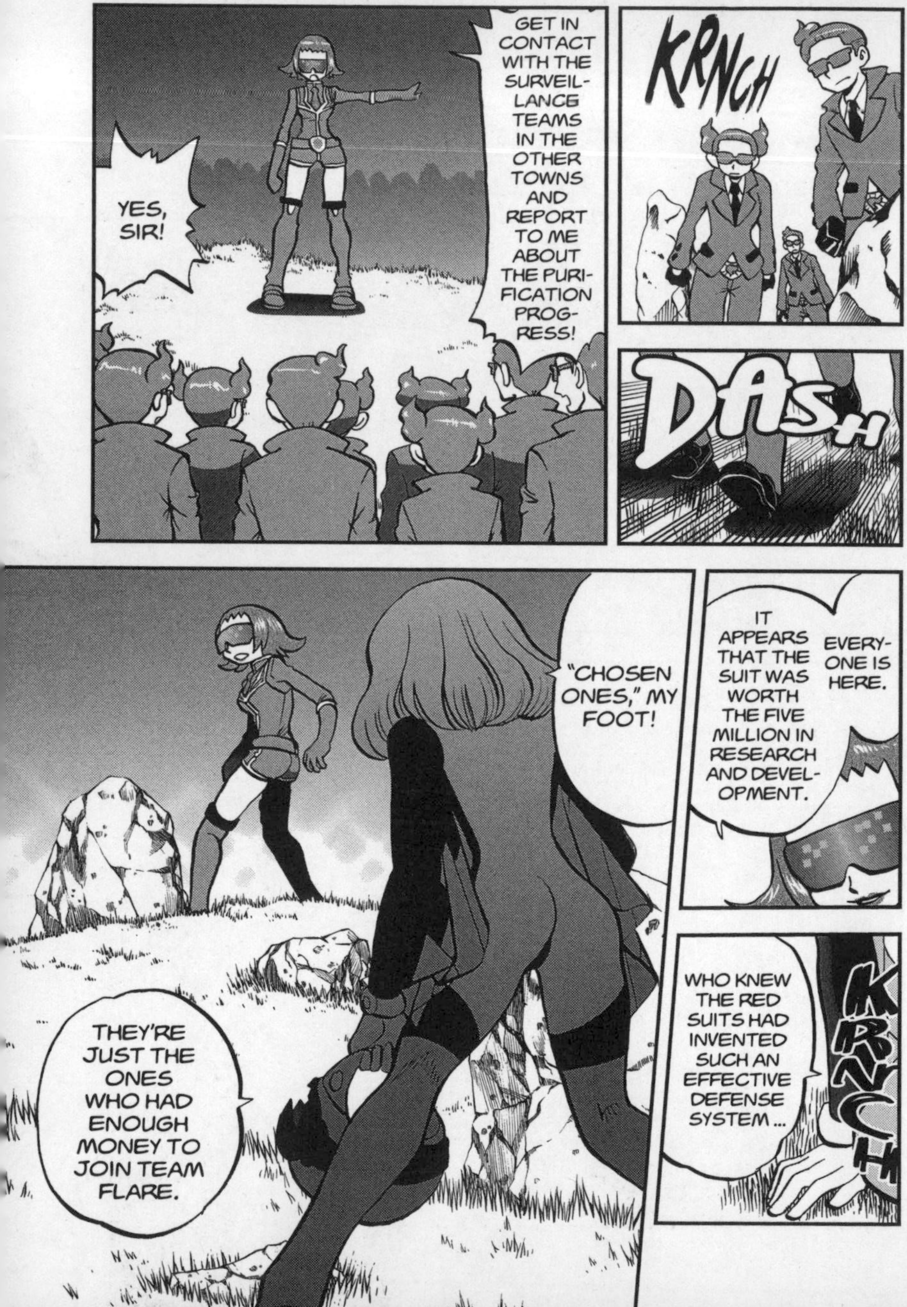
KRNCH
DASH
GET IN CONTACT WITH THE SURVEIL-LANCE TEAMS IN THE OTHER TOWNS AND REPORT TO ME ABOUT THE PURI-FICATION PROG-RESS!
YES, SIR!
EVERY-ONE IS HERE.
IT APPEARS THAT THE SUIT WAS WORTH THE FIVE MILLION IN RESEARCH AND DEVEL-OPMENT.
WHO KNEW THE RED SUITS HAD INVENTED SUCH AN EFFECTIVE DEFENSE SYSTEM ...
KRNCH
"CHOSEN ONES," MY FOOT!
THEY'RE JUST THE ONES WHO HAD ENOUGH MONEY TO JOIN TEAM FLARE.

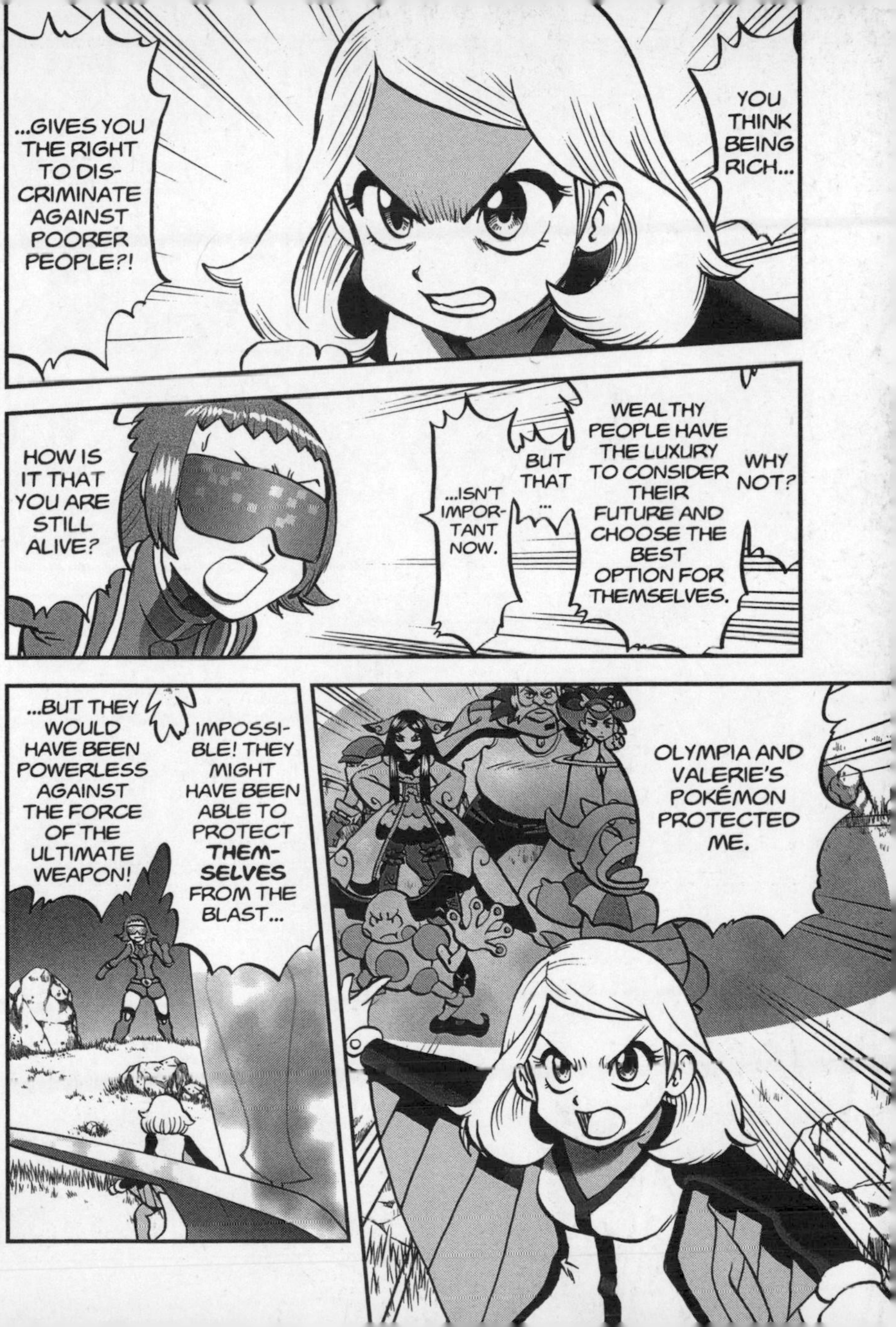
YOU THINK BEING RICH...
...GIVES YOU THE RIGHT TO DISCRIMINATE AGAINST POORER PEOPLE?!
WHY NOT?
WEALTHY PEOPLE HAVE THE LUXURY TO CONSIDER THEIR FUTURE AND CHOOSE THE BEST OPTION FOR THEMSELVES.
BUT THAT ...
...ISN'T IMPORTANT NOW.
HOW IS IT THAT YOU ARE STILL ALIVE?
OLYMPIA AND VALERIE'S POKÉMON PROTECTED ME.
IMPOSSIBLE! THEY MIGHT HAVE BEEN ABLE TO PROTECT **THEMSELVES** FROM THE BLAST...
...BUT THEY WOULD HAVE BEEN POWERLESS AGAINST THE FORCE OF THE ULTIMATE WEAPON!

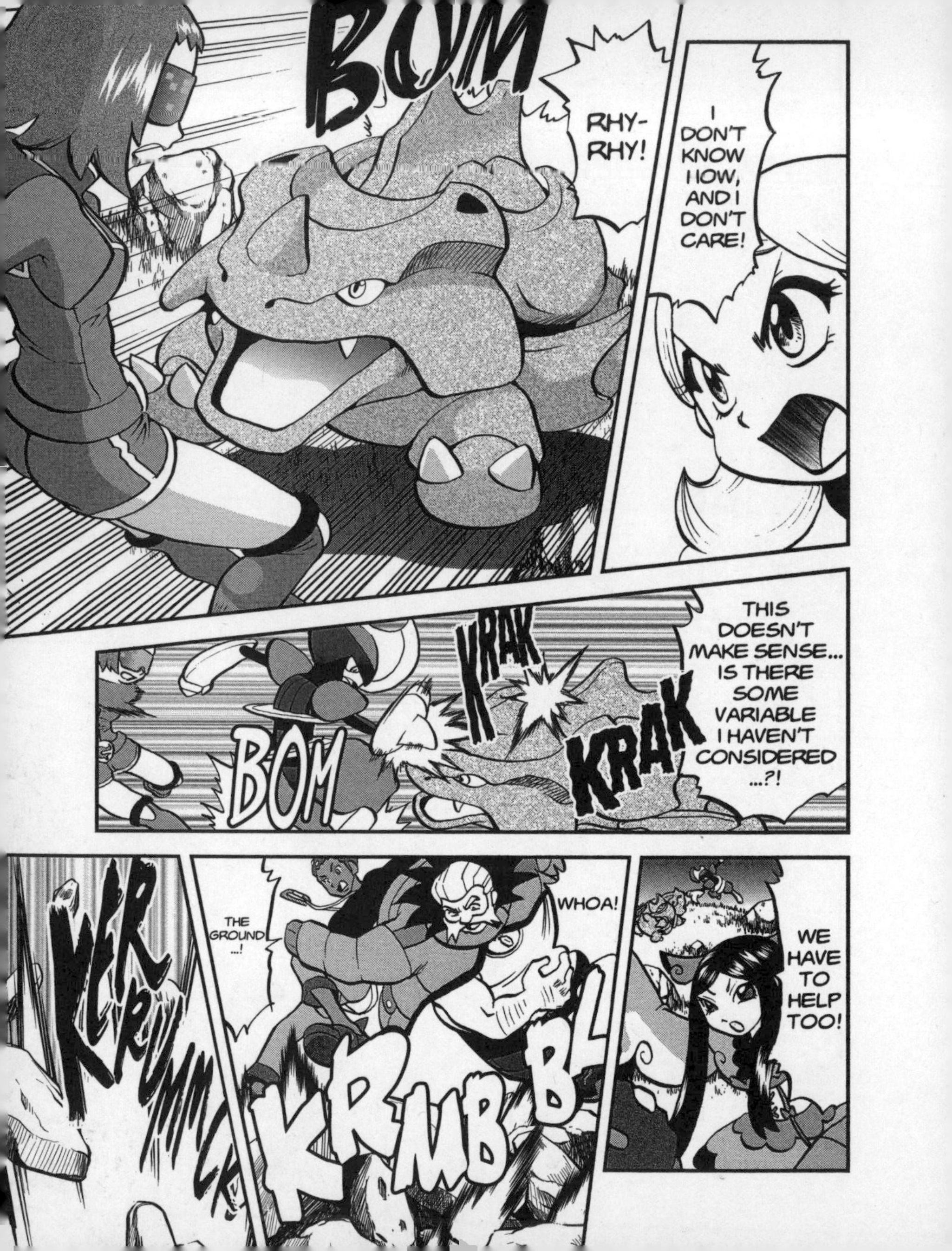
I DON'T KNOW HOW, AND I DON'T CARE!
BOM
RHY-RHY!
THIS DOESN'T MAKE SENSE... IS THERE SOME VARIABLE I HAVEN'T CONSIDERED ...?!
KRAK
KRAK
BOM
WE HAVE TO HELP TOO!
WHOA!
THE GROUND ...!
BL
KRMB

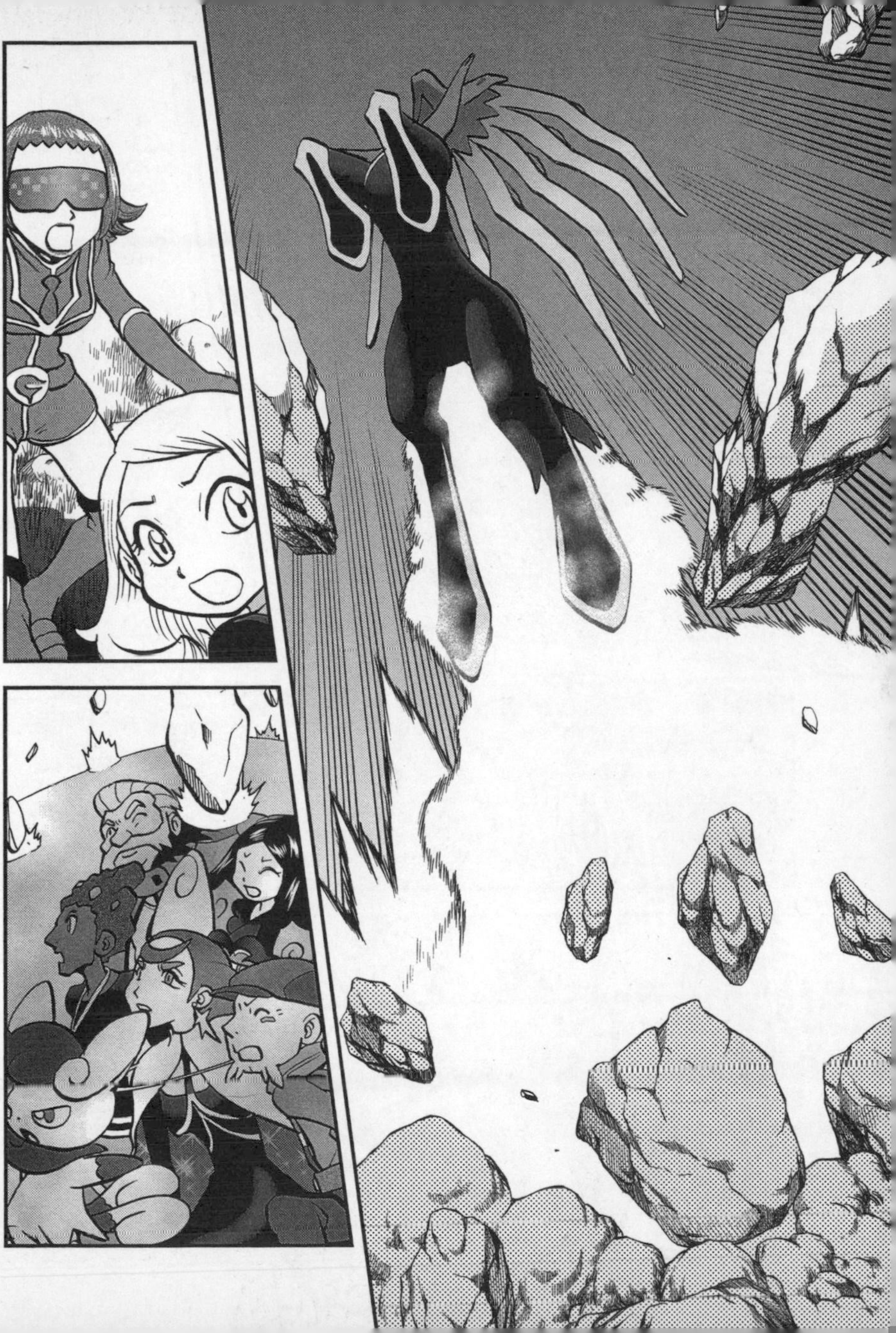

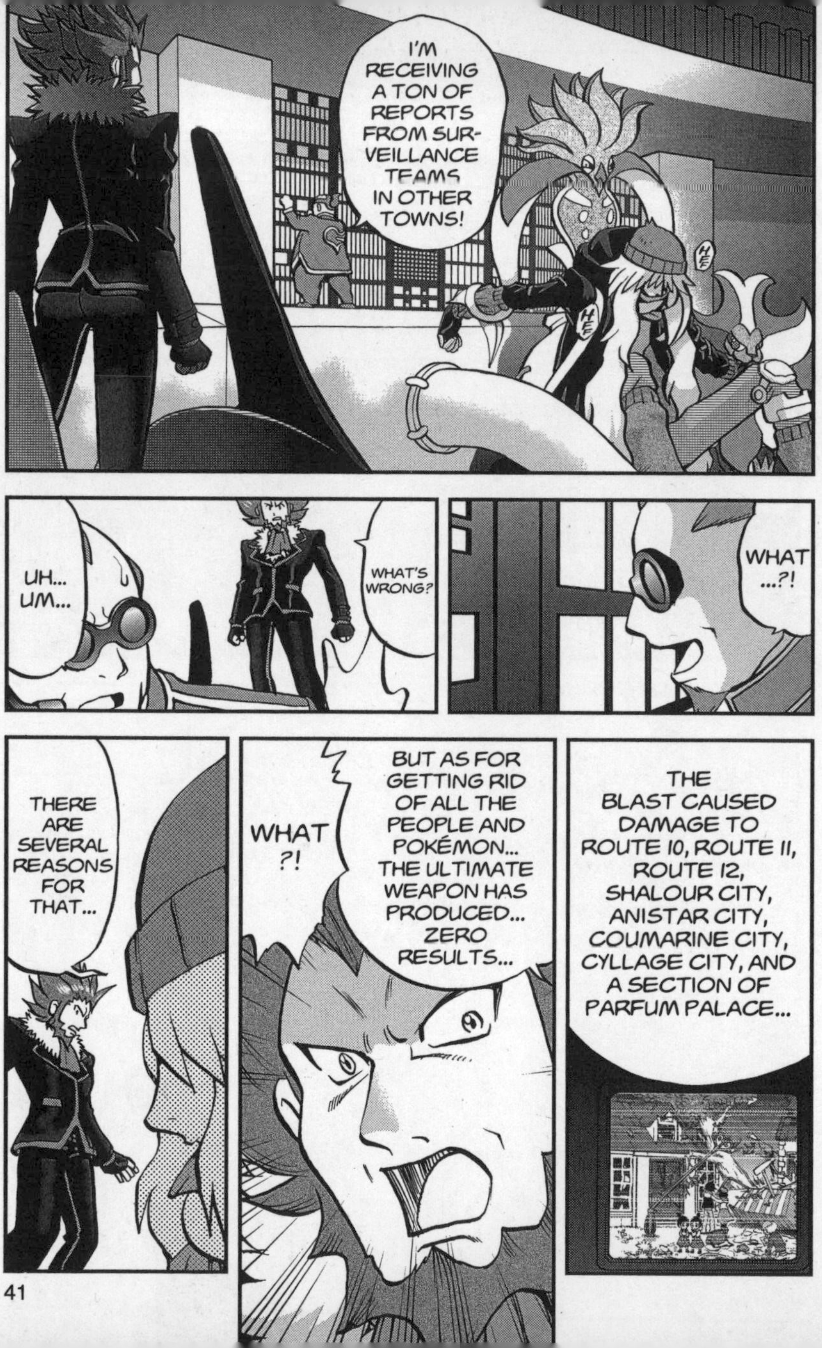
I'M RECEIVING A TON OF REPORTS FROM SUR-VEILLANCE TEAMS IN OTHER TOWNS!
HE
HE
WHAT ...?!
WHAT'S WRONG?
UH... UM...
THE BLAST CAUSED DAMAGE TO ROUTE 10, ROUTE 11, ROUTE 12, SHALOUR CITY, ANISTAR CITY, COUMARINE CITY, CYLLAGE CITY, AND A SECTION OF PARFUM PALACE...
BUT AS FOR GETTING RID OF ALL THE PEOPLE AND POKÉMON... THE ULTIMATE WEAPON HAS PRODUCED... ZERO RESULTS...
WHAT ?!
THERE ARE SEVERAL REASONS FOR THAT...

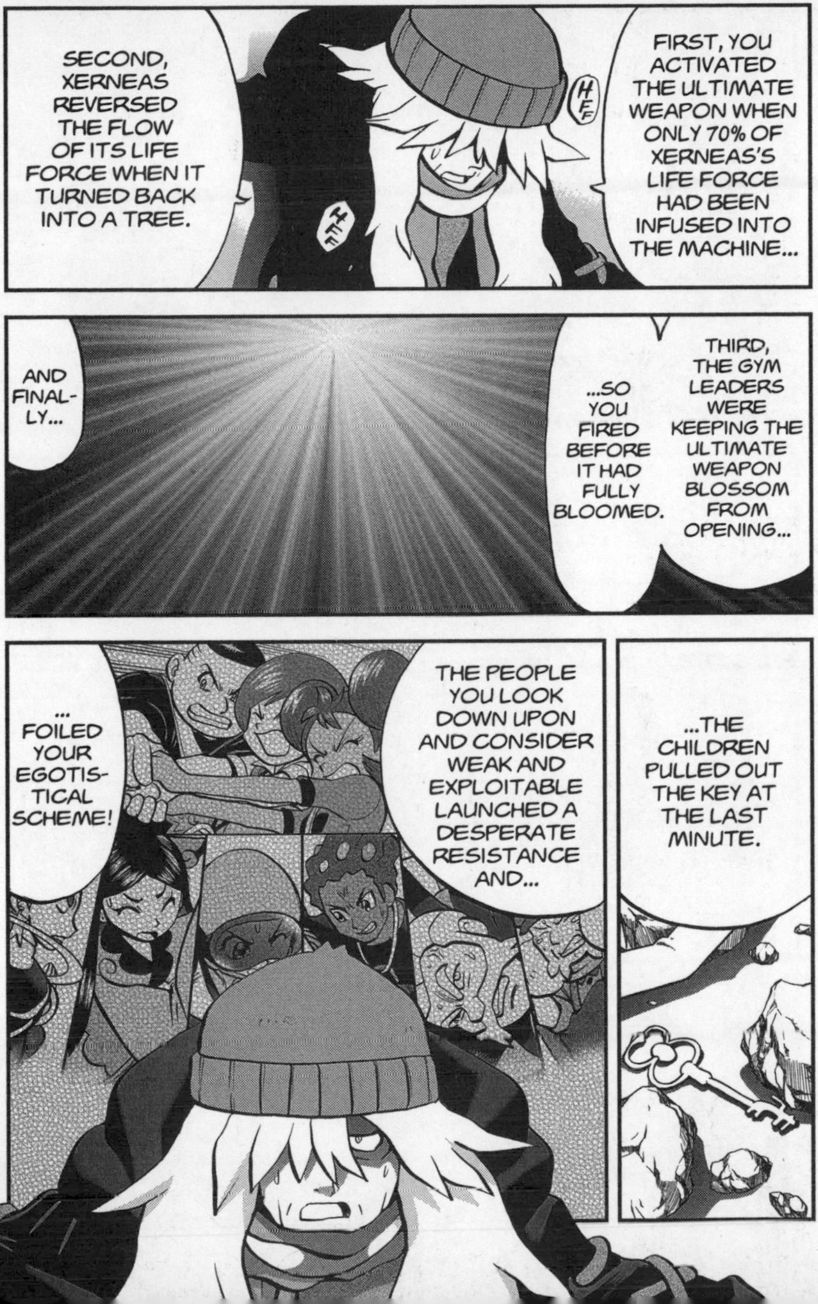
FIRST, YOU ACTIVATED THE ULTIMATE WEAPON WHEN ONLY 70% OF XERNEAS'S LIFE FORCE HAD BEEN INFUSED INTO THE MACHINE...
HFF
HFF
SECOND, XERNEAS REVERSED THE FLOW OF ITS LIFE FORCE WHEN IT TURNED BACK INTO A TREE.
THIRD, THE GYM LEADERS WERE KEEPING THE ULTIMATE WEAPON BLOSSOM FROM OPENING...
...SO YOU FIRED BEFORE IT HAD FULLY BLOOMED.
AND FINAL-LY...
...THE CHILDREN PULLED OUT THE KEY AT THE LAST MINUTE.
THE PEOPLE YOU LOOK DOWN UPON AND CONSIDER WEAK AND EXPLOITABLE LAUNCHED A DESPERATE RESISTANCE AND...
...FOILED YOUR EGOTIS-TICAL SCHEME!

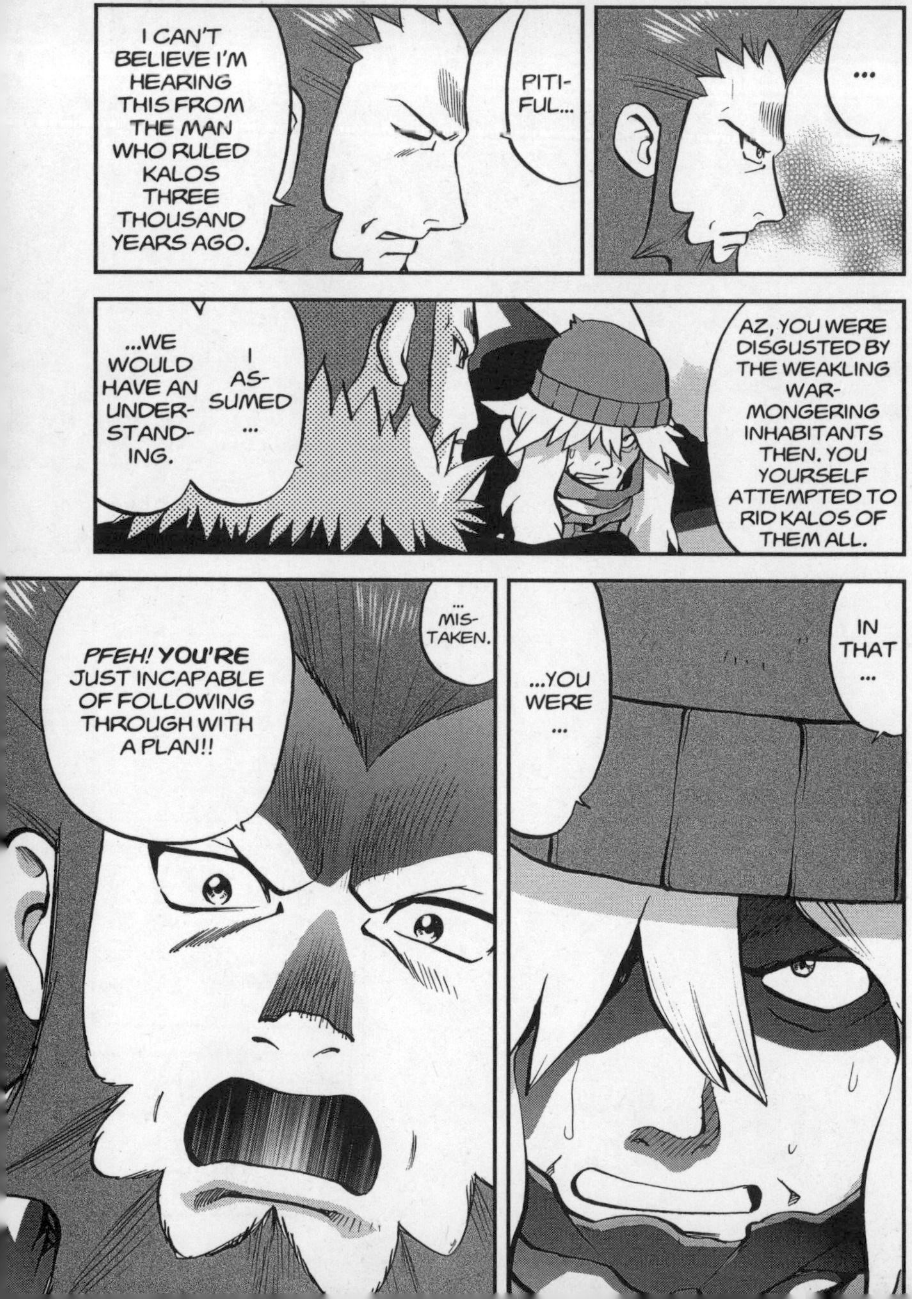
...
PITI-FUL...
I CAN'T BELIEVE I'M HEARING THIS FROM THE MAN WHO RULED KALOS THREE THOUSAND YEARS AGO.
AZ, YOU WERE DISGUSTED BY THE WEAKLING WAR-MONGERING INHABITANTS THEN. YOU YOURSELF ATTEMPTED TO RID KALOS OF THEM ALL.
I AS-SUMED...
...WE WOULD HAVE AN UNDER-STAND-ING.
IN THAT...
...YOU WERE...
...MIS-TAKEN.
PFEH! **YOU'RE** JUST INCAPABLE OF FOLLOWING THROUGH WITH A PLAN!!

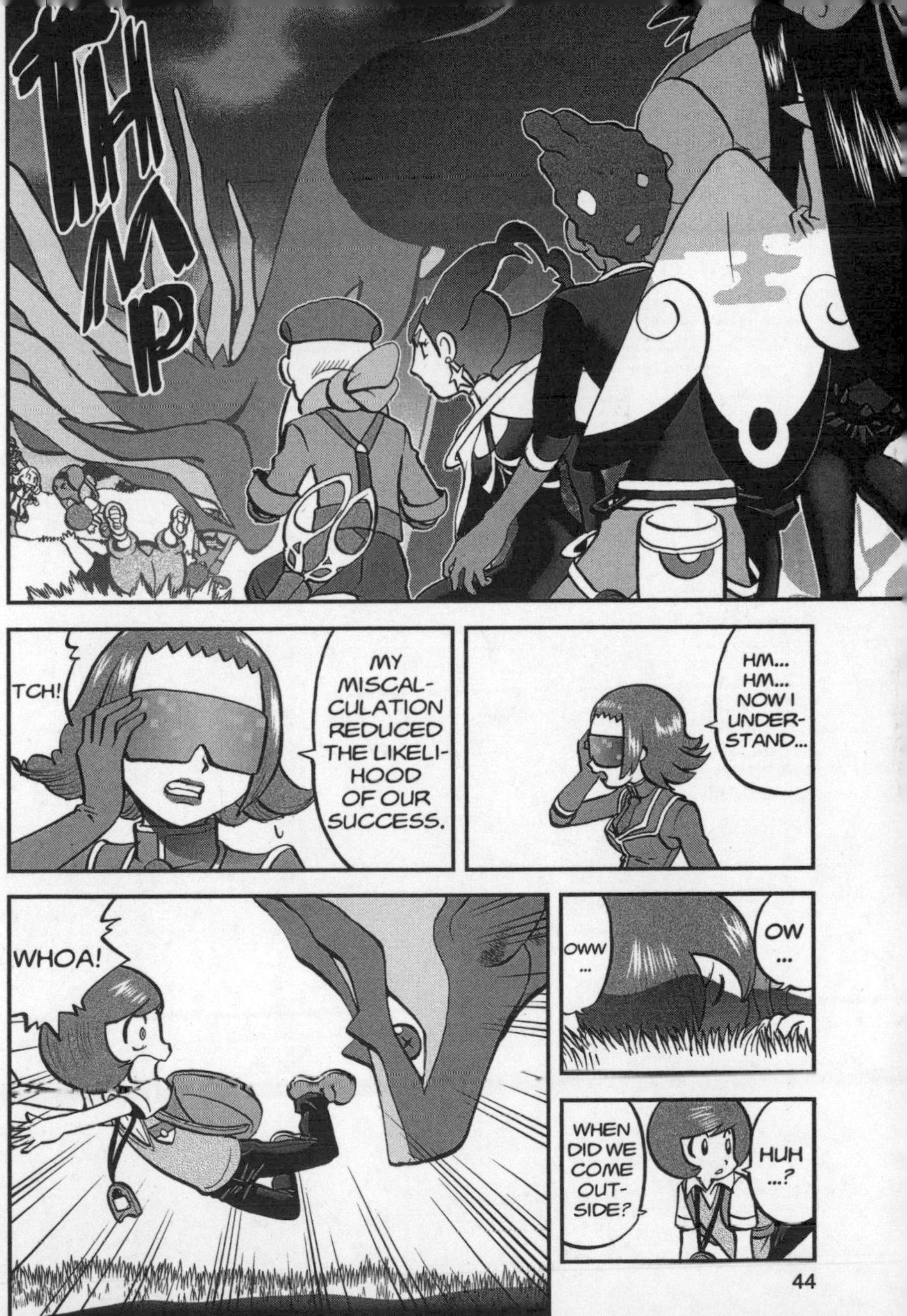
THMP
HM... HM... NOW I UNDERSTAND...
MY MISCALCULATION REDUCED THE LIKELIHOOD OF OUR SUCCESS.
TCH!
OW ...
OWW ...
HUH ...?
WHEN DID WE COME OUTSIDE?
WHOA!

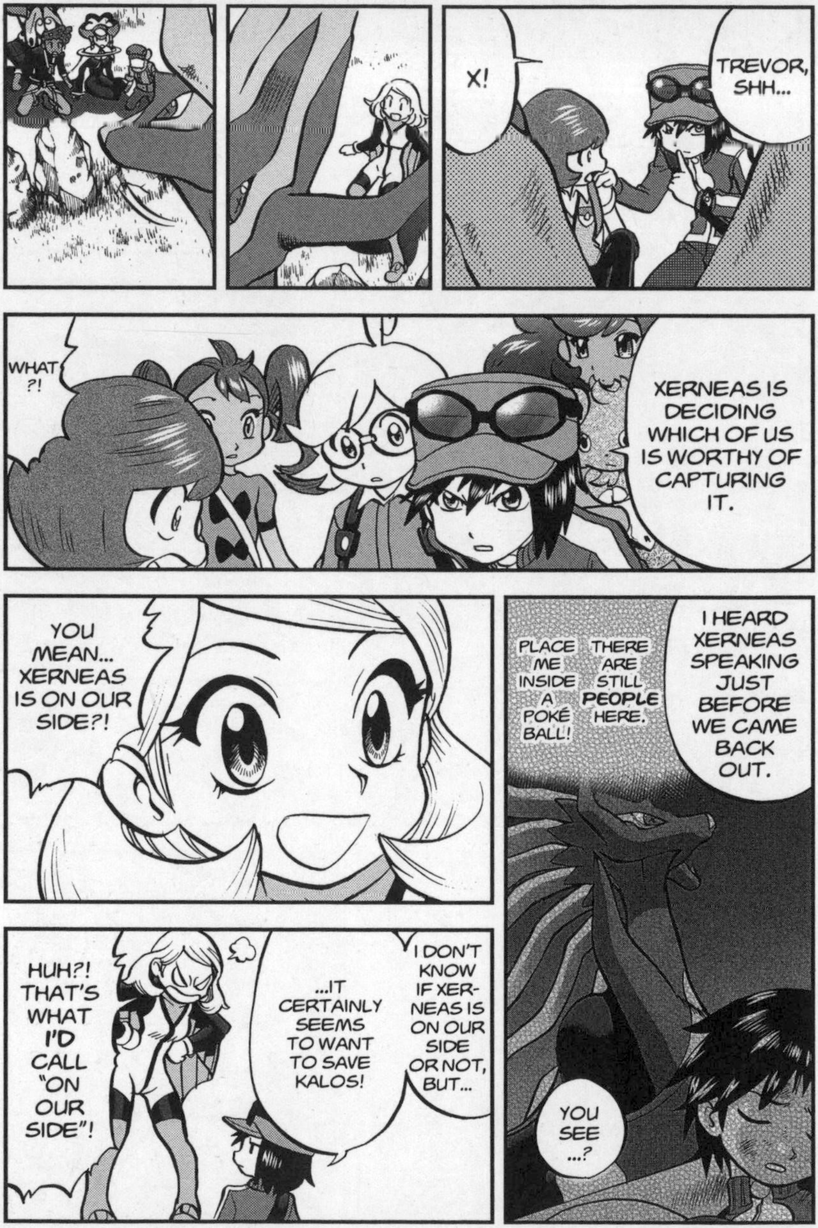
TREVOR, SHH...
X!
XERNEAS IS DECIDING WHICH OF US IS WORTHY OF CAPTURING IT.
WHAT?!
I HEARD XERNEAS SPEAKING JUST BEFORE WE CAME BACK OUT.
THERE ARE STILL PEOPLE HERE.
PLACE ME INSIDE A POKÉ BALL!
YOU SEE ...?
YOU MEAN... XERNEAS IS ON OUR SIDE?!
I DON'T KNOW IF XER-NEAS IS ON OUR SIDE OR NOT, BUT...
...IT CERTAINLY SEEMS TO WANT TO SAVE KALOS!
HUH?! THAT'S WHAT I'D CALL "ON OUR SIDE"!

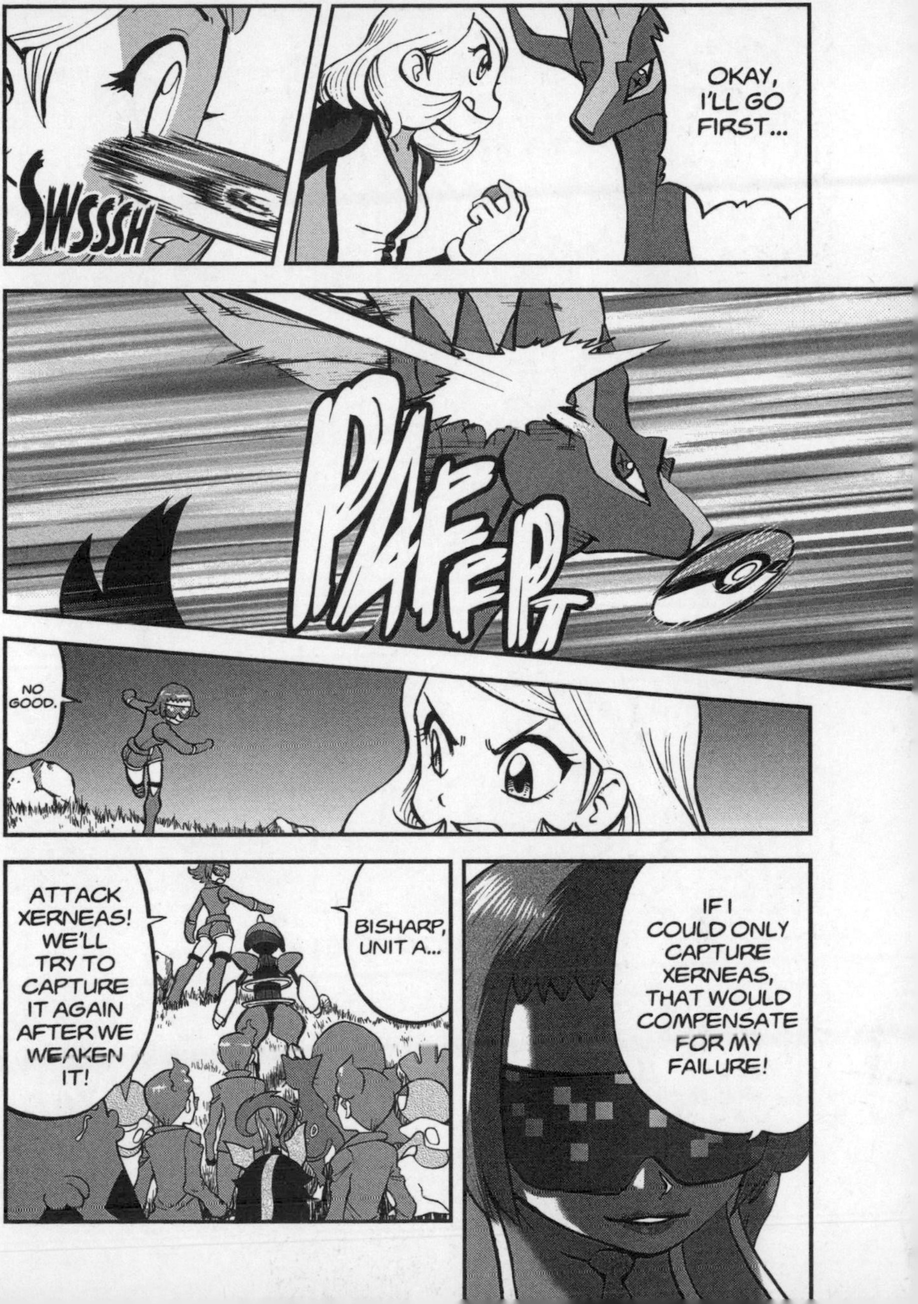
OKAY, I'LL GO FIRST...
SWSSSH
PAFFPT
NO GOOD.
IF I COULD ONLY CAPTURE XERNEAS, THAT WOULD COMPENSATE FOR MY FAILURE!
BISHARP, UNIT A...
ATTACK XERNEAS! WE'LL TRY TO CAPTURE IT AGAIN AFTER WE WEAKEN IT!

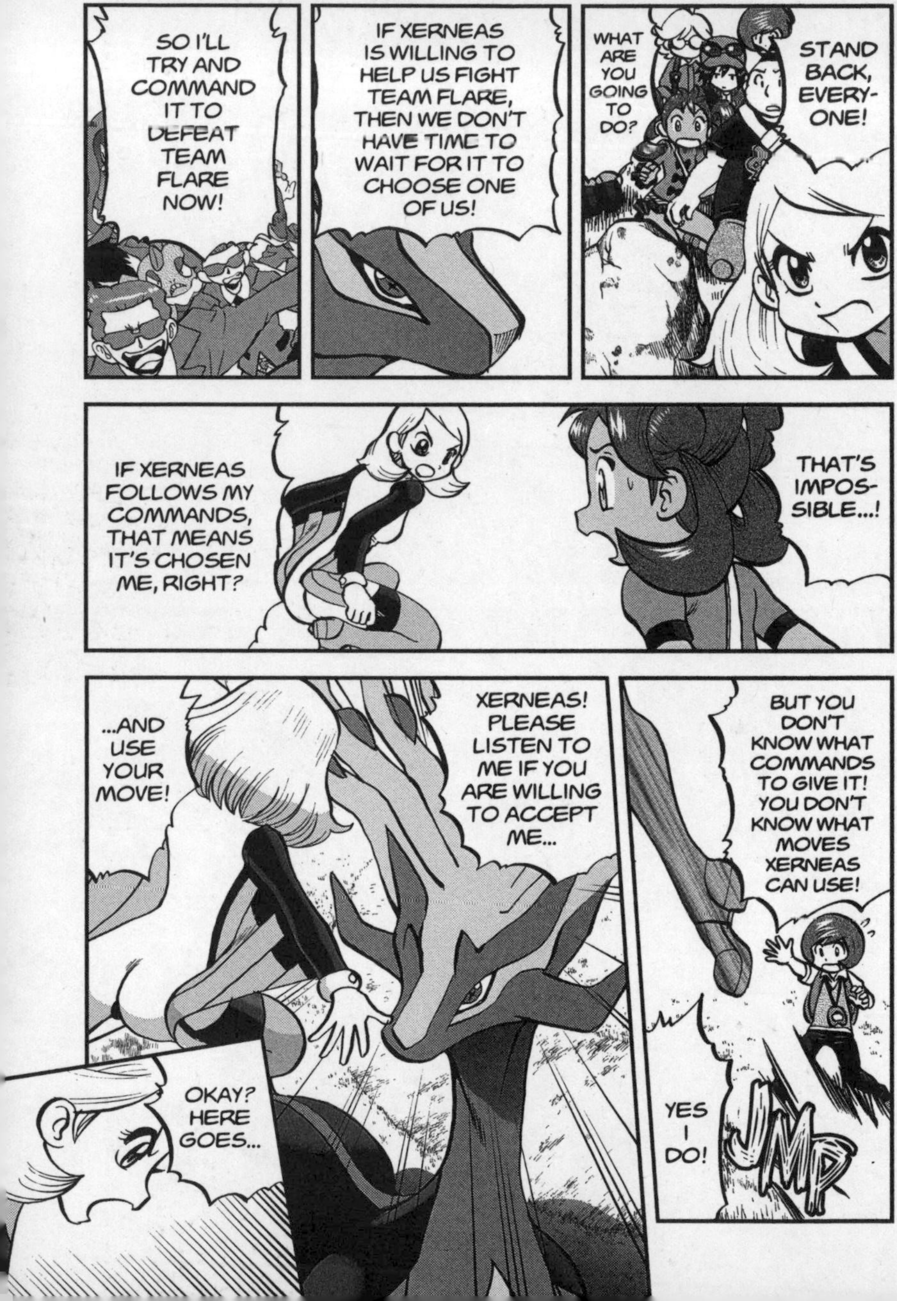
STAND BACK, EVERY-ONE!
WHAT ARE YOU GOING TO DO?
IF XERNEAS IS WILLING TO HELP US FIGHT TEAM FLARE, THEN WE DON'T HAVE TIME TO WAIT FOR IT TO CHOOSE ONE OF US!
SO I'LL TRY AND COMMAND IT TO DEFEAT TEAM FLARE NOW!
THAT'S IMPOS-SIBLE...!
IF XERNEAS FOLLOWS MY COMMANDS, THAT MEANS IT'S CHOSEN ME, RIGHT?
BUT YOU DON'T KNOW WHAT COMMANDS TO GIVE IT! YOU DON'T KNOW WHAT MOVES XERNEAS CAN USE!
YES I DO!
JMP
XERNEAS! PLEASE LISTEN TO ME IF YOU ARE WILLING TO ACCEPT ME...
...AND USE YOUR MOVE!
OKAY? HERE GOES...

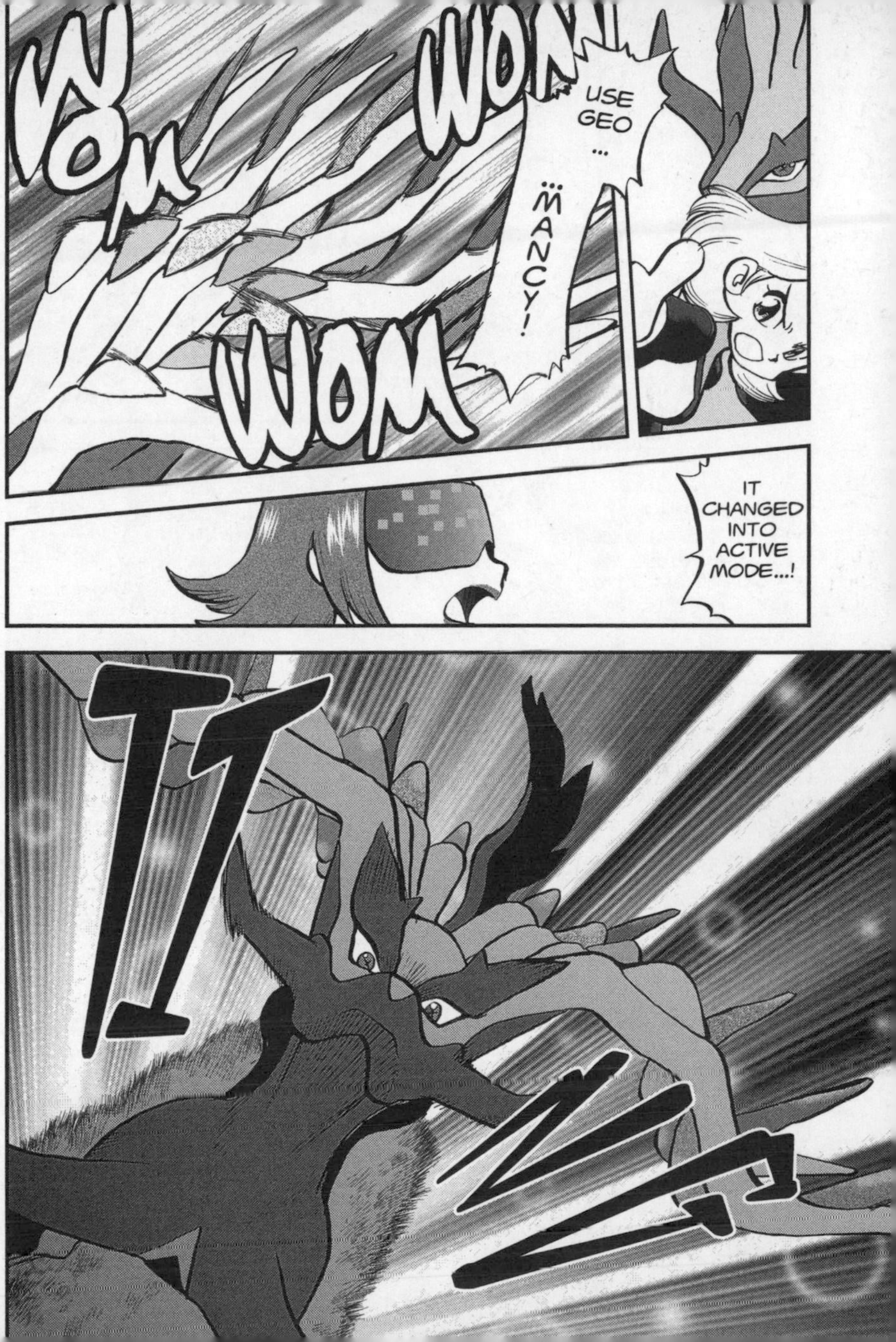
WOM
USE GEO ... ...MANCY!
WOM
WOM
IT CHANGED INTO ACTIVE MODE...!

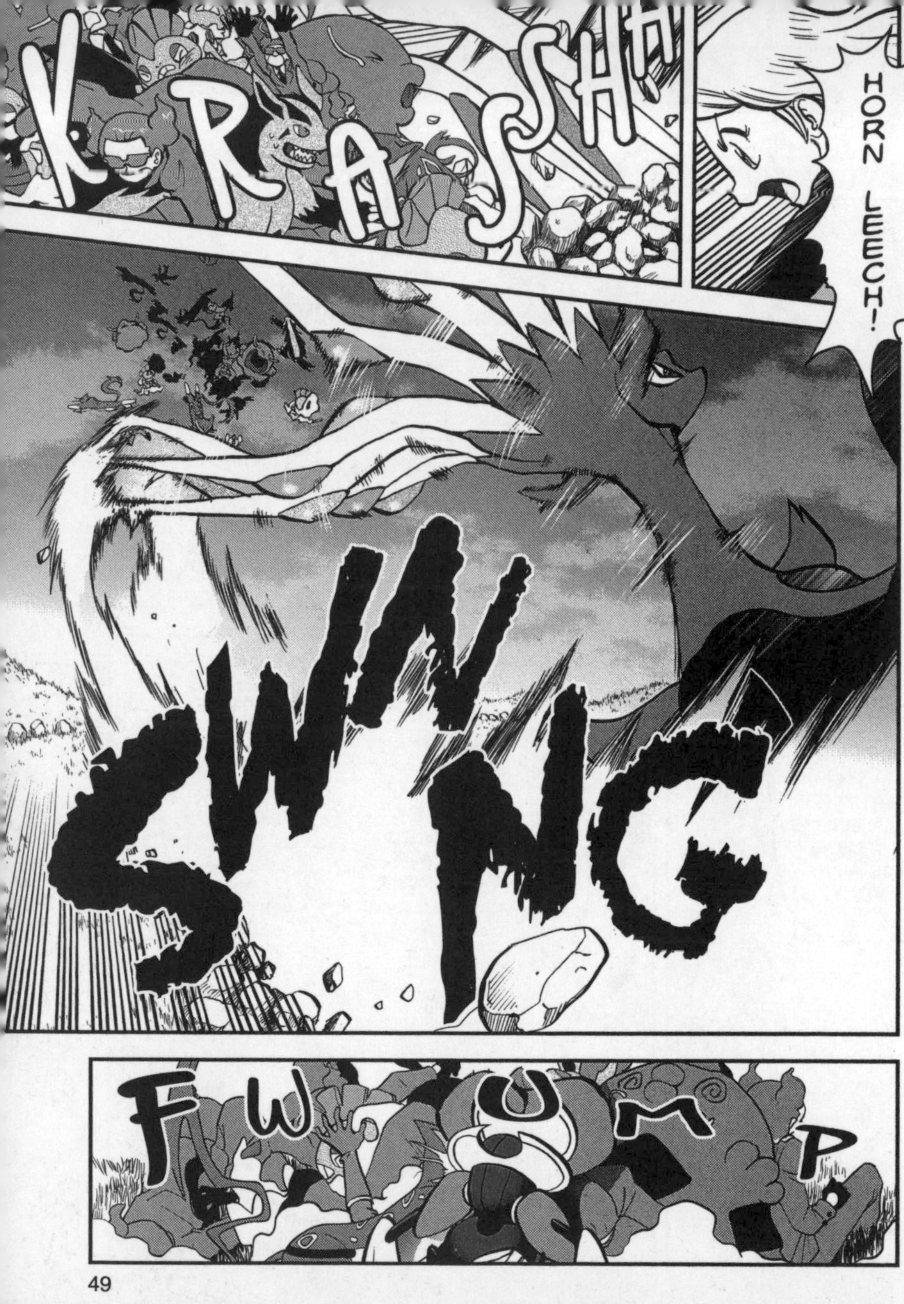
HORN LEECH!
KRASH!!
SWING
FWUMP

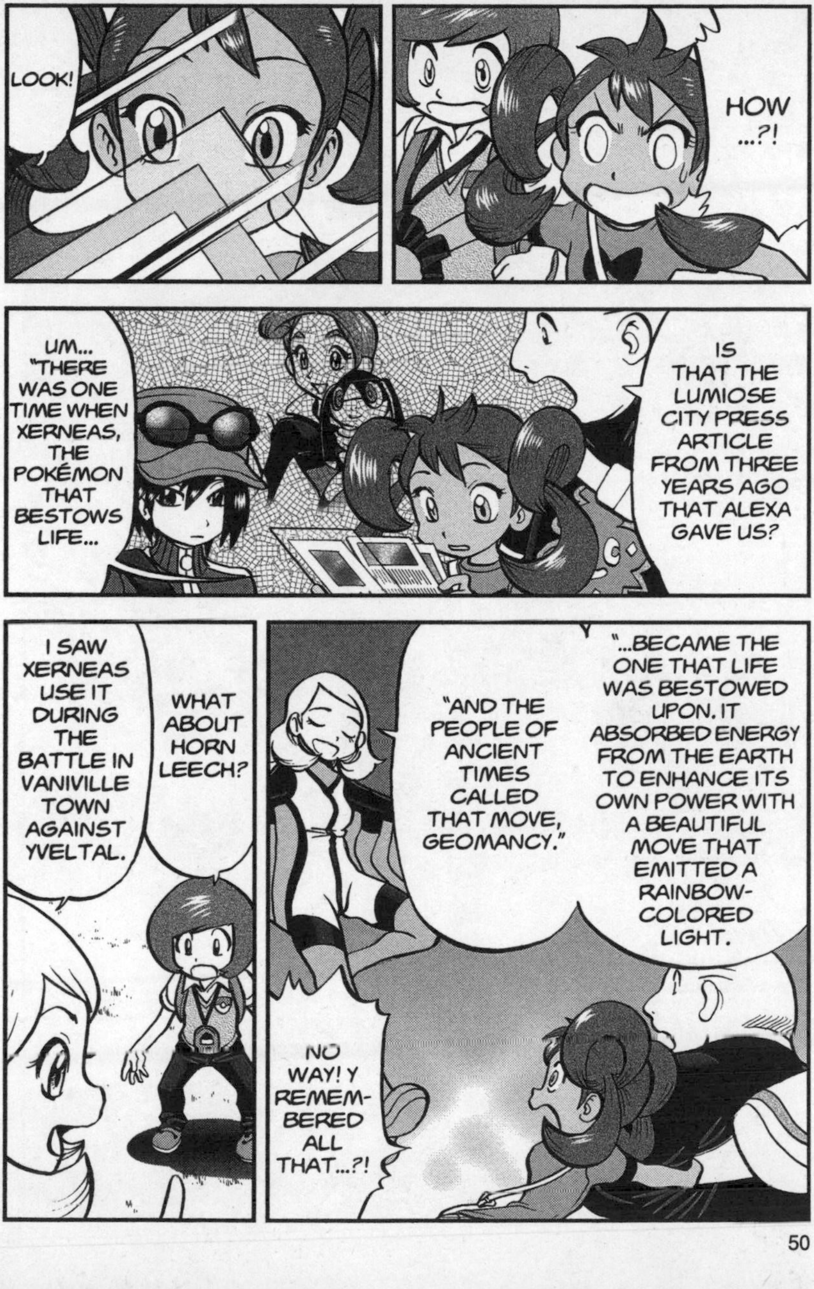
HOW ...?!
LOOK!
IS THAT THE LUMIOSE CITY PRESS ARTICLE FROM THREE YEARS AGO THAT ALEXA GAVE US?
UM... "THERE WAS ONE TIME WHEN XERNEAS, THE POKÉMON THAT BESTOWS LIFE...
"...BECAME THE ONE THAT LIFE WAS BESTOWED UPON. IT ABSORBED ENERGY FROM THE EARTH TO ENHANCE ITS OWN POWER WITH A BEAUTIFUL MOVE THAT EMITTED A RAINBOW-COLORED LIGHT.
"AND THE PEOPLE OF ANCIENT TIMES CALLED THAT MOVE, GEOMANCY."
NO WAY! Y REMEM-BERED ALL THAT...?!
WHAT ABOUT HORN LEECH?
I SAW XERNEAS USE IT DURING THE BATTLE IN VANIVILLE TOWN AGAINST YVELTAL.

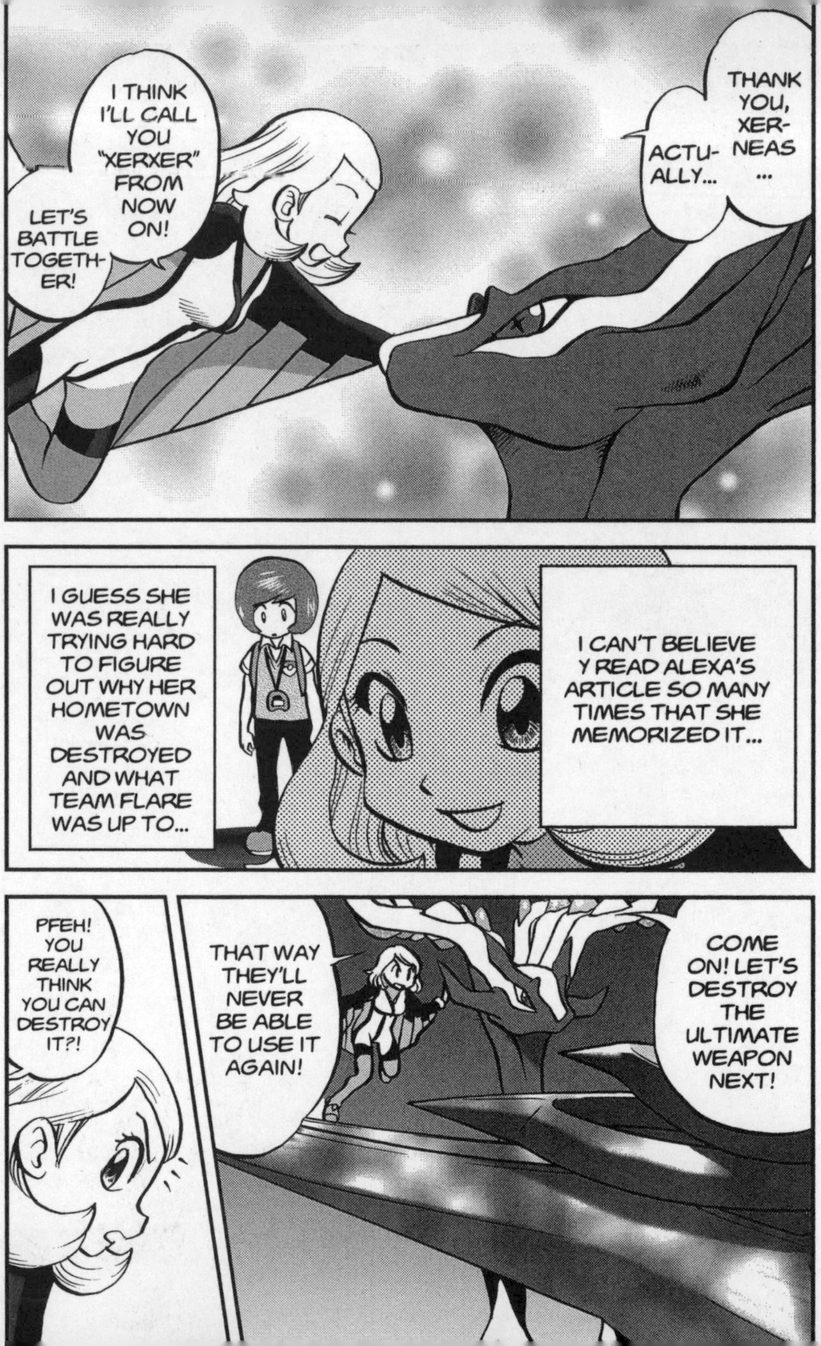
THANK YOU, XERNEAS...
ACTUALLY...
I THINK I'LL CALL YOU "XERXER" FROM NOW ON!
LET'S BATTLE TOGETHER!
I CAN'T BELIEVE Y READ ALEXA'S ARTICLE SO MANY TIMES THAT SHE MEMORIZED IT...
I GUESS SHE WAS REALLY TRYING HARD TO FIGURE OUT WHY HER HOMETOWN WAS DESTROYED AND WHAT TEAM FLARE WAS UP TO...
COME ON! LET'S DESTROY THE ULTIMATE WEAPON NEXT!
THAT WAY THEY'LL NEVER BE ABLE TO USE IT AGAIN!
PFEH! YOU REALLY THINK YOU CAN DESTROY IT?!

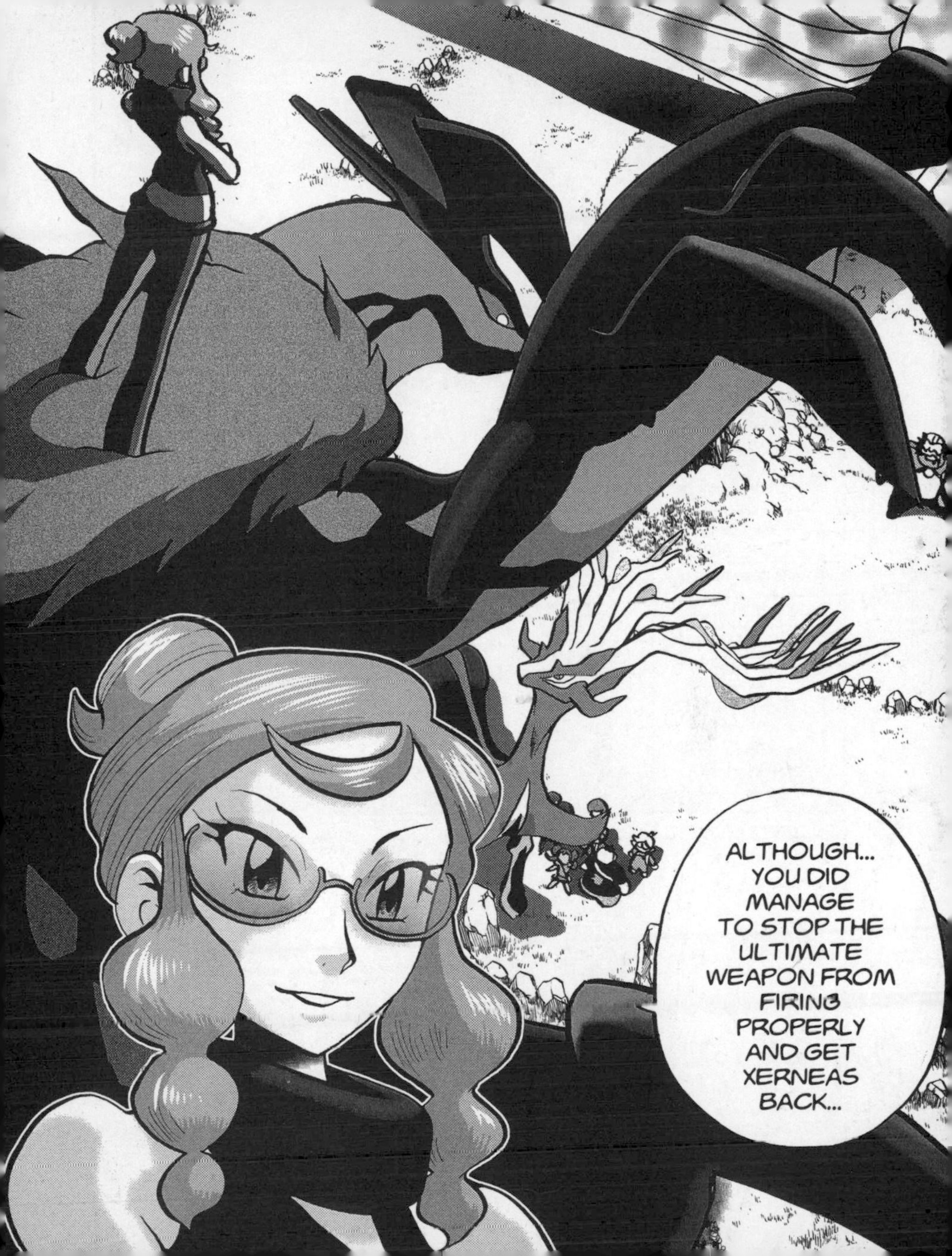
ALTHOUGH... YOU DID MANAGE TO STOP THE ULTIMATE WEAPON FROM FIRING PROPERLY AND GET XERNEAS BACK...

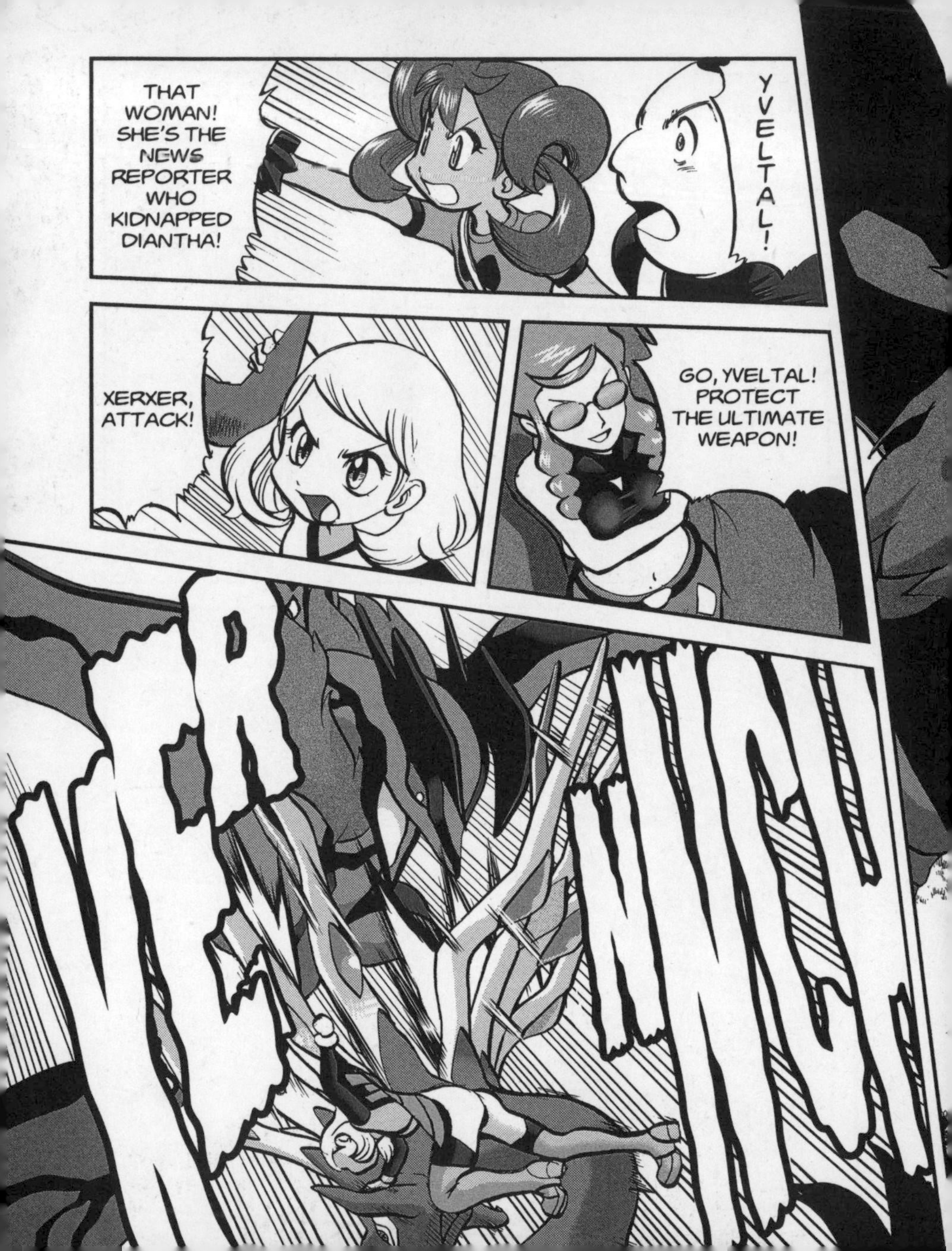
YVELTAL!
THAT WOMAN! SHE'S THE NEWS REPORTER WHO KIDNAPPED DIANTHA!
GO, YVELTAL! PROTECT THE ULTIMATE WEAPON!
XERXER, ATTACK!

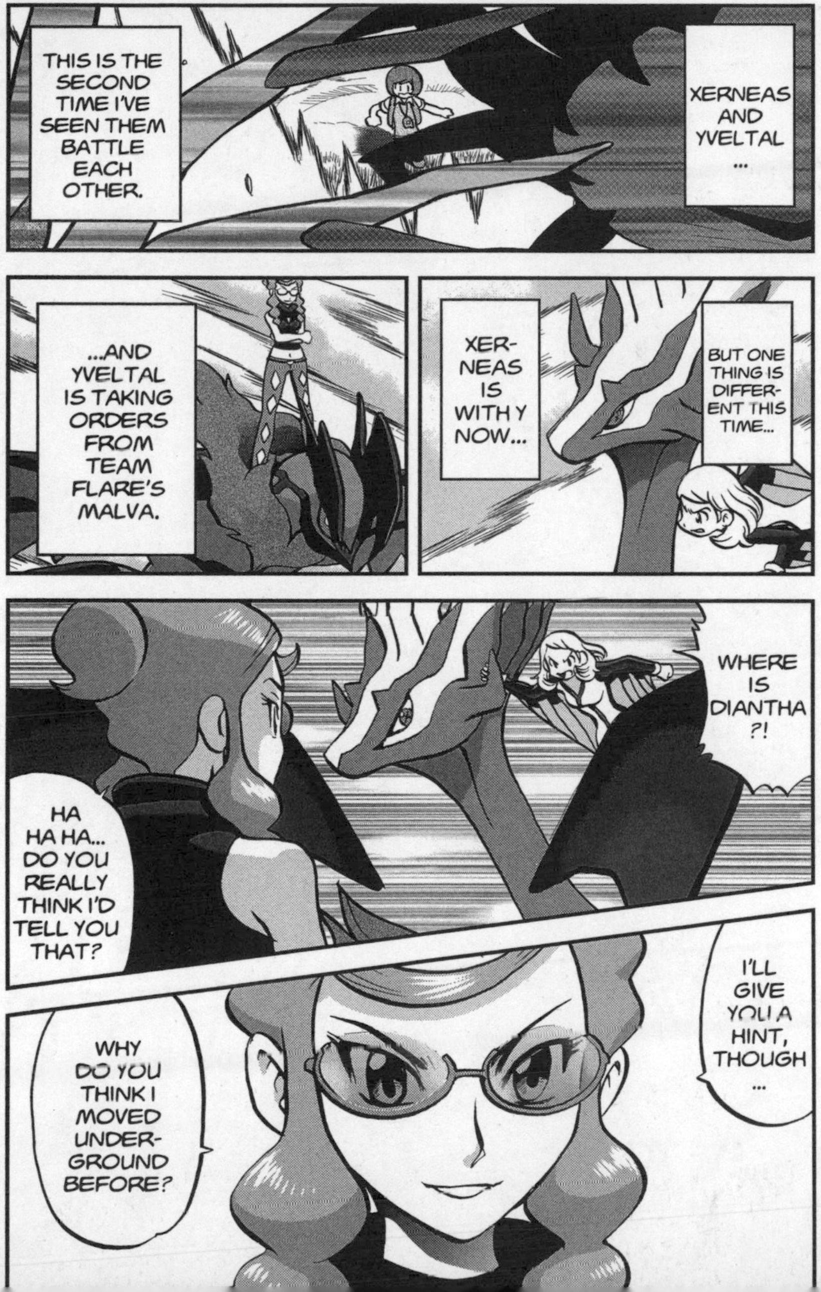
XERNEAS AND YVELTAL...
THIS IS THE SECOND TIME I'VE SEEN THEM BATTLE EACH OTHER.
BUT ONE THING IS DIFFERENT THIS TIME...
XERNEAS IS WITH Y NOW...
...AND YVELTAL IS TAKING ORDERS FROM TEAM FLARE'S MALVA.
WHERE IS DIANTHA?!
HA HA HA... DO YOU REALLY THINK I'D TELL YOU THAT?
I'LL GIVE YOU A HINT, THOUGH...
WHY DO YOU THINK I MOVED UNDERGROUND BEFORE?

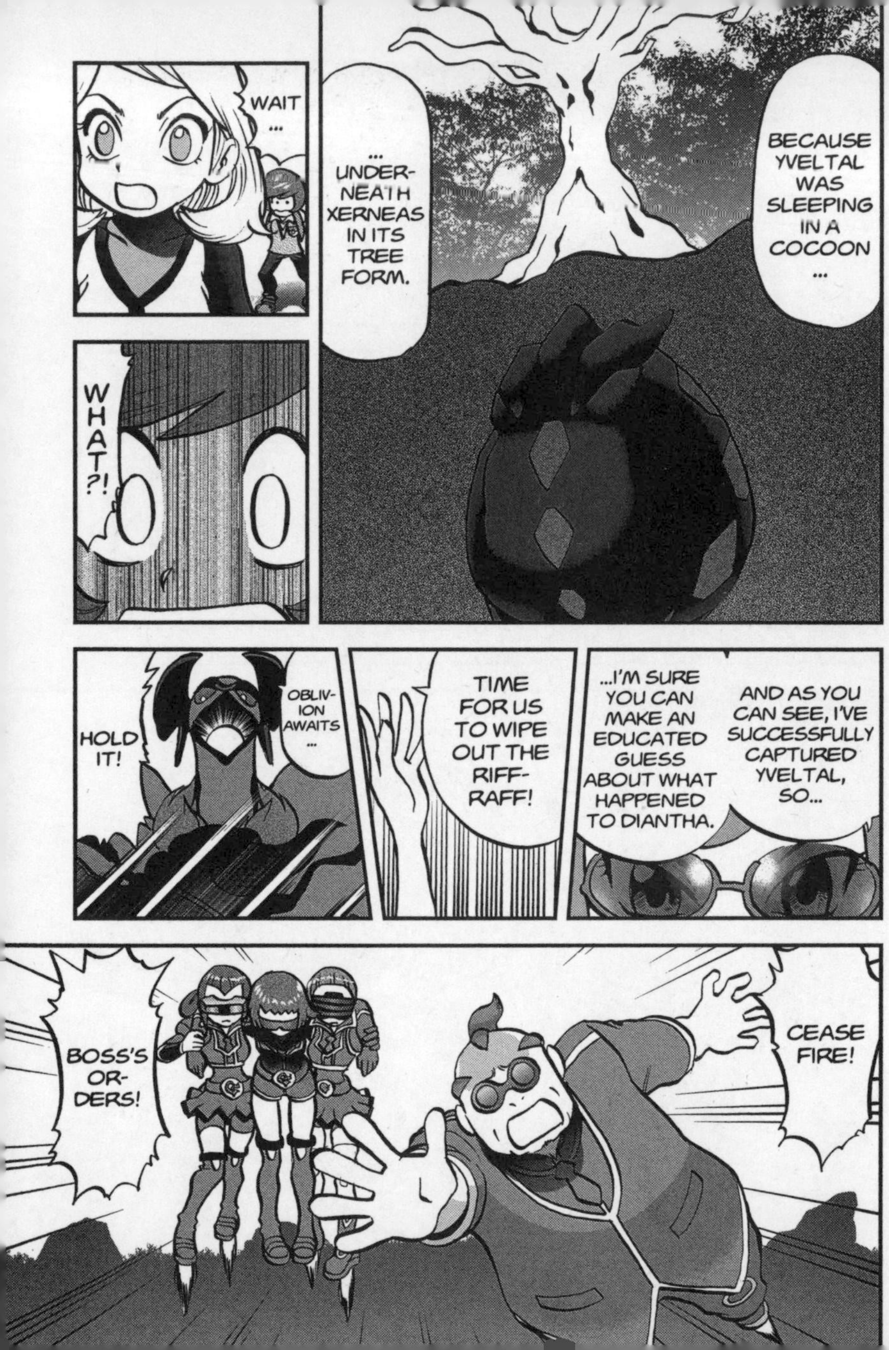
BECAUSE YVELTAL WAS SLEEPING IN A COCOON ...
... UNDER-NEATH XERNEAS IN ITS TREE FORM.
WAIT ...
WHAT?!
AND AS YOU CAN SEE, I'VE SUCCESSFULLY CAPTURED YVELTAL, SO...
...I'M SURE YOU CAN MAKE AN EDUCATED GUESS ABOUT WHAT HAPPENED TO DIANTHA.
TIME FOR US TO WIPE OUT THE RIFF-RAFF!
OBLIV-ION AWAITS ...
HOLD IT!
CEASE FIRE!
BOSS'S OR-DERS!

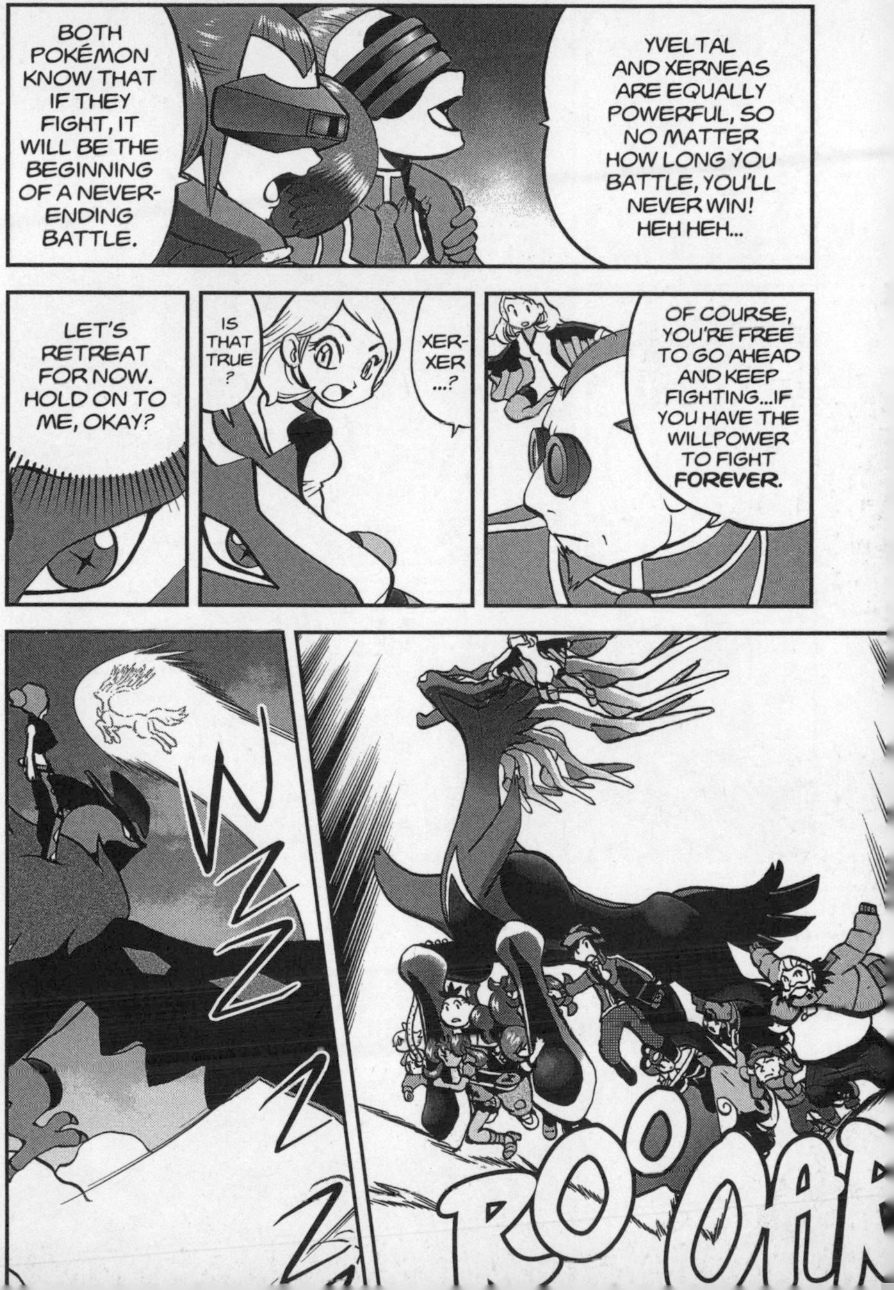
YVELTAL AND XERNEAS ARE EQUALLY POWERFUL, SO NO MATTER HOW LONG YOU BATTLE, YOU'LL NEVER WIN! HEH HEH...
BOTH POKÉMON KNOW THAT IF THEY FIGHT, IT WILL BE THE BEGINNING OF A NEVER-ENDING BATTLE.
OF COURSE, YOU'RE FREE TO GO AHEAD AND KEEP FIGHTING...IF YOU HAVE THE WILLPOWER TO FIGHT **FOREVER.**
XER-XER...?
IS THAT TRUE?
LET'S RETREAT FOR NOW. HOLD ON TO ME, OKAY?
ROOOAR

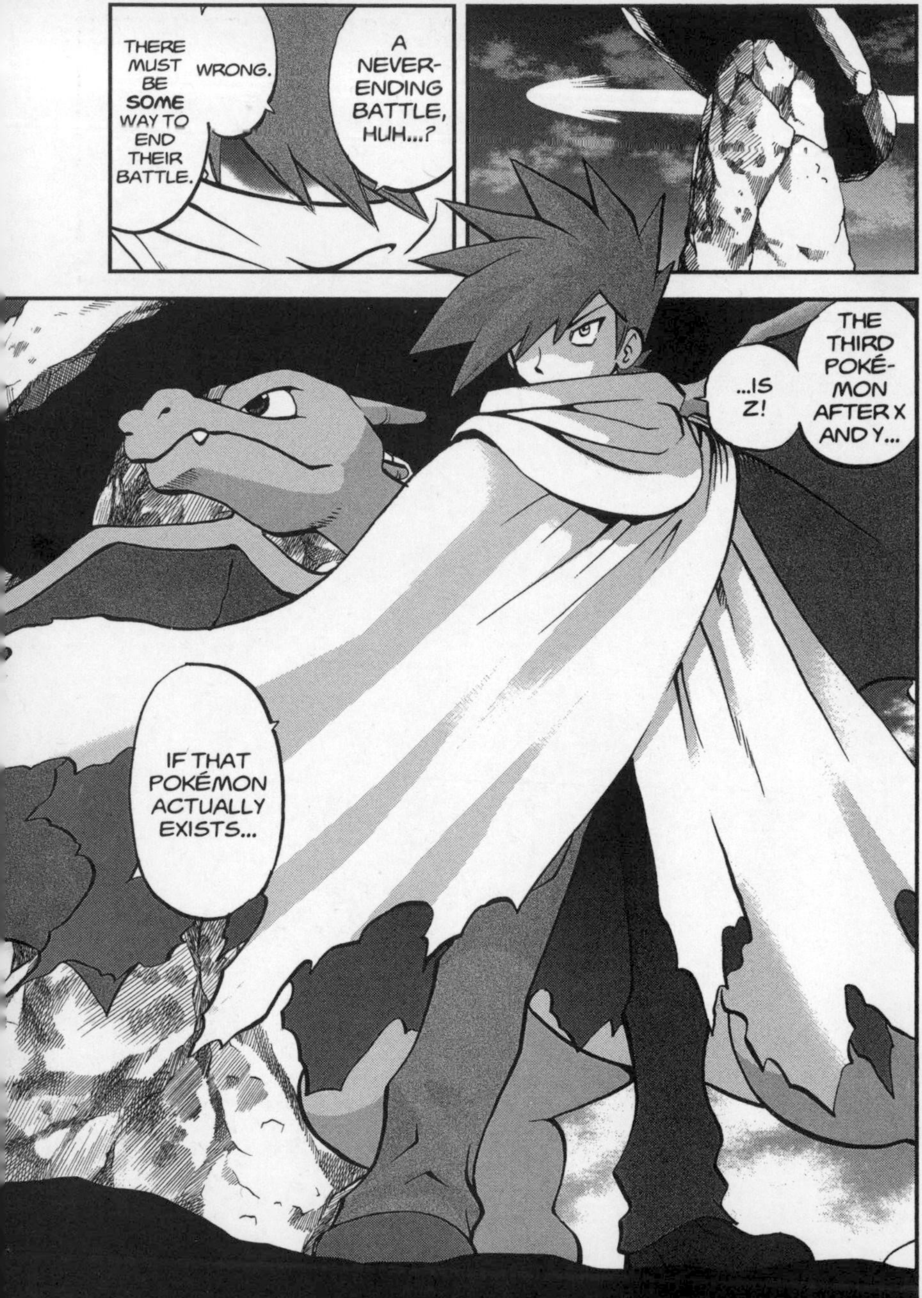
A NEVER-ENDING BATTLE, HUH...?
WRONG.
THERE MUST BE **SOME** WAY TO END THEIR BATTLE.
THE THIRD POKÉMON AFTER X AND Y...
...IS Z!
IF THAT POKÉMON ACTUALLY EXISTS...

Current Location

Geosenge Town

A town lined with mysterious stones and encircled by strange ruins of old.

Adventure 27 Pinsir Glares

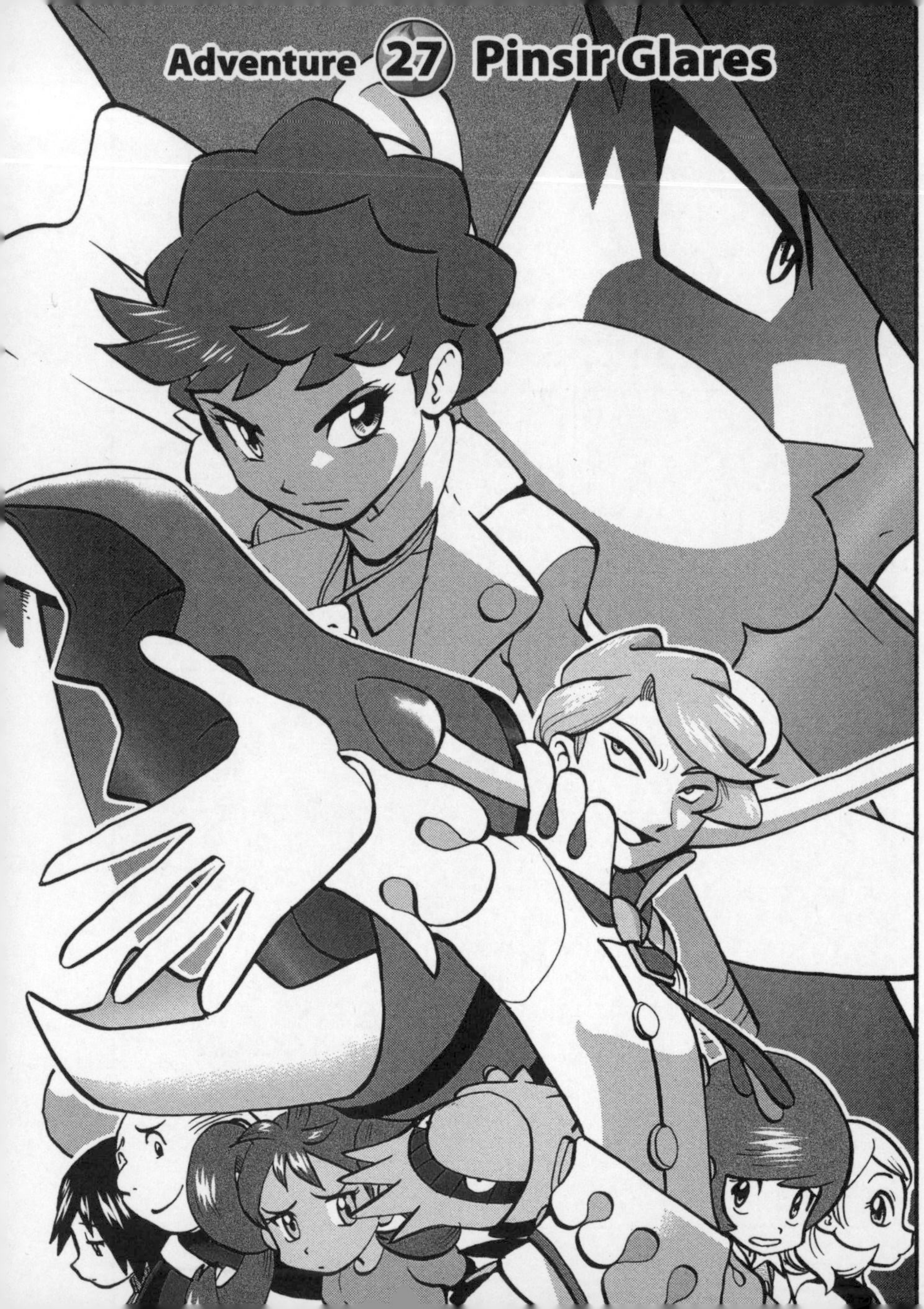

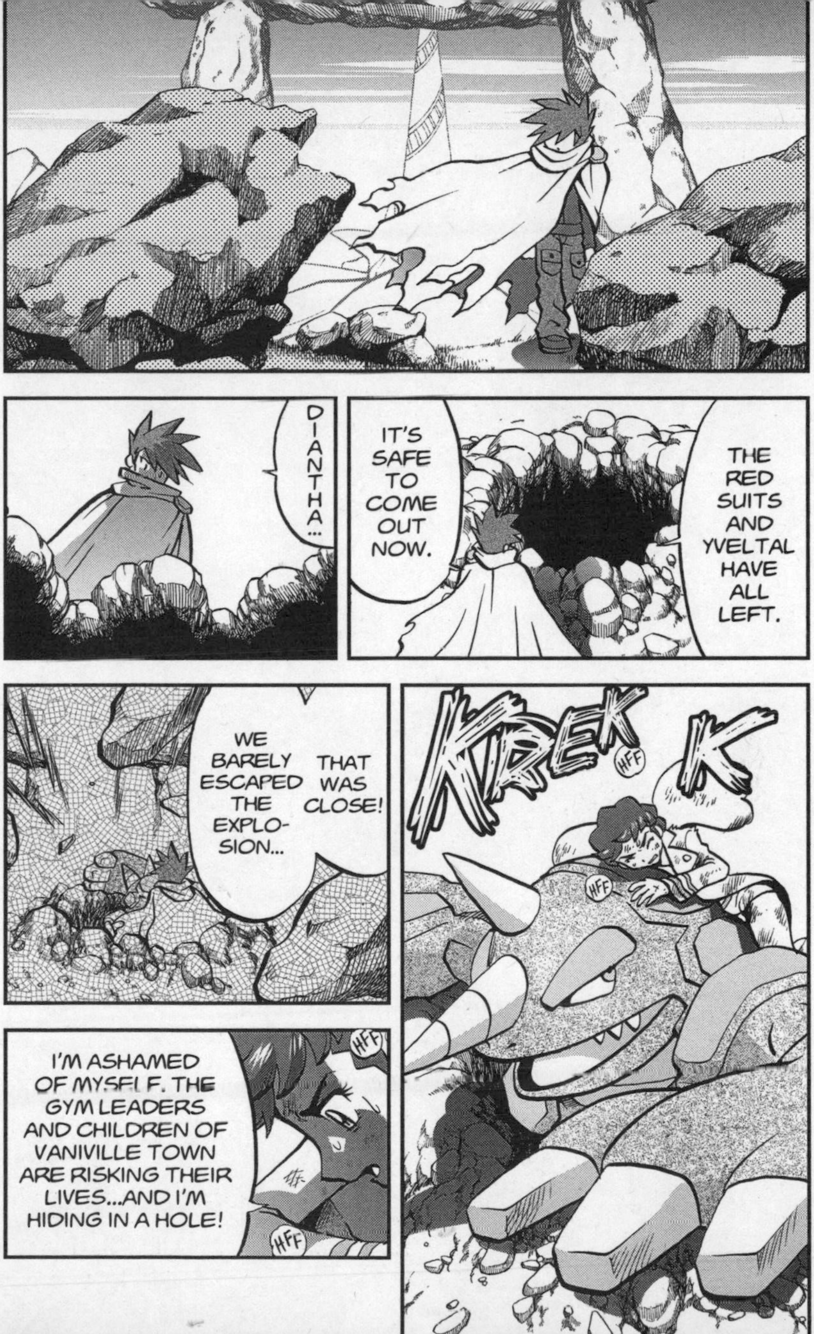
THE RED SUITS AND YVELTAL HAVE ALL LEFT.
IT'S SAFE TO COME OUT NOW.
DIANTHA...
KRBEK K
HFF
HFF
THAT WAS CLOSE!
WE BARELY ESCAPED THE EXPLOSION...
HFF
I'M ASHAMED OF MYSELF. THE GYM LEADERS AND CHILDREN OF VANIVILLE TOWN ARE RISKING THEIR LIVES...AND I'M HIDING IN A HOLE!
HFF

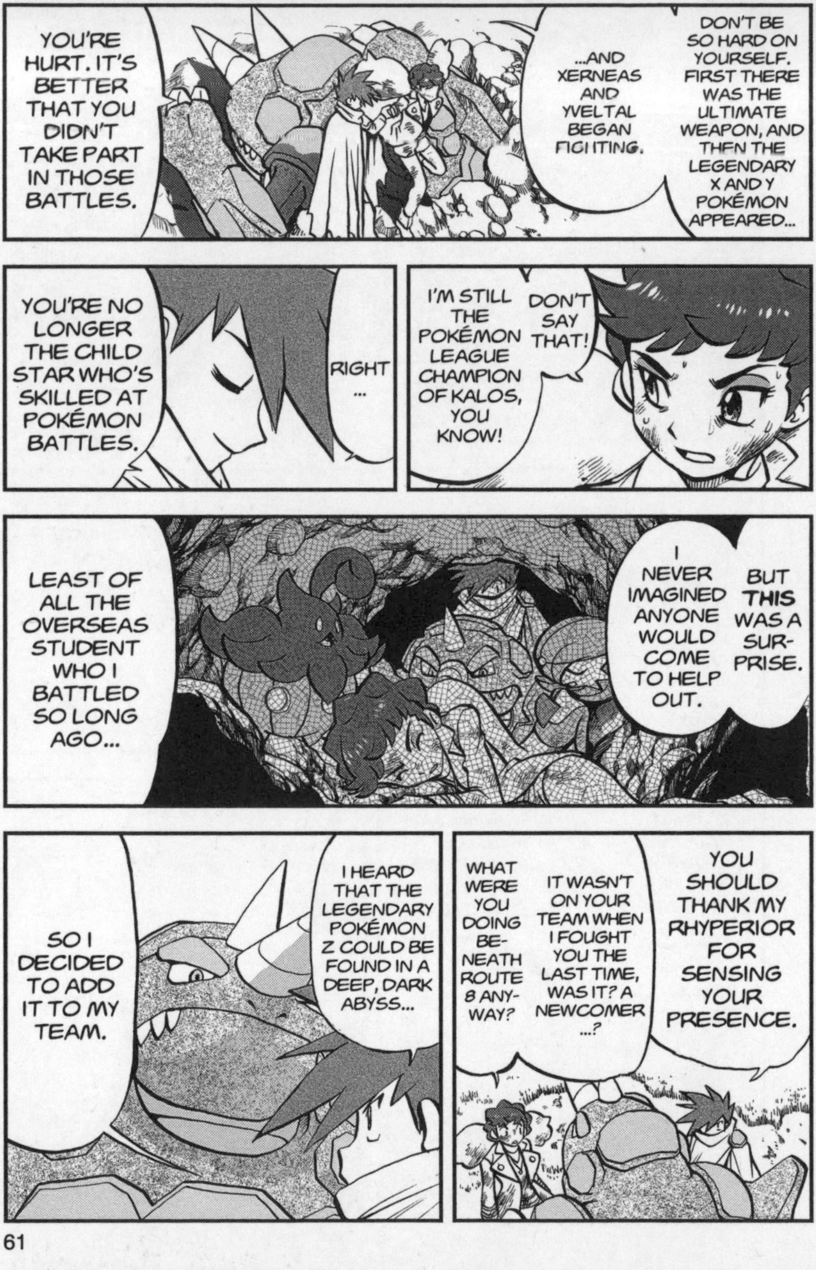
DON'T BE SO HARD ON YOURSELF. FIRST THERE WAS THE ULTIMATE WEAPON, AND THEN THE LEGENDARY X AND Y POKÉMON APPEARED...
...AND XERNEAS AND YVELTAL BEGAN FIGHTING.
YOU'RE HURT. IT'S BETTER THAT YOU DIDN'T TAKE PART IN THOSE BATTLES.
DON'T SAY THAT!
I'M STILL THE POKÉMON LEAGUE CHAMPION OF KALOS, YOU KNOW!
RIGHT...
YOU'RE NO LONGER THE CHILD STAR WHO'S SKILLED AT POKÉMON BATTLES.
BUT **THIS** WAS A SUR-PRISE.
I NEVER IMAGINED ANYONE WOULD COME TO HELP OUT.
LEAST OF ALL THE OVERSEAS STUDENT WHO I BATTLED SO LONG AGO...
YOU SHOULD THANK MY RHYPERIOR FOR SENSING YOUR PRESENCE.
IT WASN'T ON YOUR TEAM WHEN I FOUGHT YOU THE LAST TIME, WAS IT? A NEWCOMER ...?
WHAT WERE YOU DOING BE-NEATH ROUTE 8 ANY-WAY?
I HEARD THAT THE LEGENDARY POKÉMON Z COULD BE FOUND IN A DEEP, DARK ABYSS...
SO I DECIDED TO ADD IT TO MY TEAM.

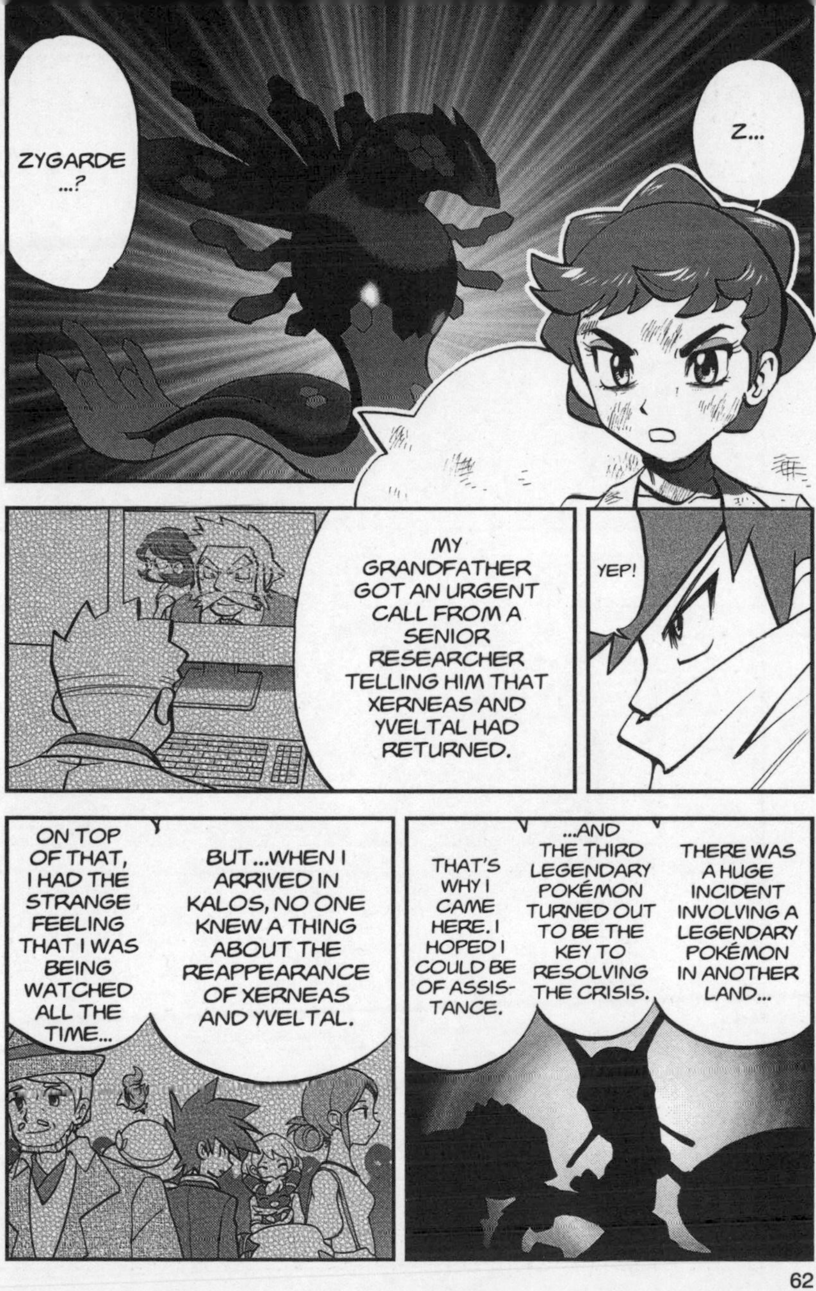
Z...
ZYGARDE ...?
YEP!
MY GRANDFATHER GOT AN URGENT CALL FROM A SENIOR RESEARCHER TELLING HIM THAT XERNEAS AND YVELTAL HAD RETURNED.
THERE WAS A HUGE INCIDENT INVOLVING A LEGENDARY POKÉMON IN ANOTHER LAND...
...AND THE THIRD LEGENDARY POKÉMON TURNED OUT TO BE THE KEY TO RESOLVING THE CRISIS.
THAT'S WHY I CAME HERE. I HOPED I COULD BE OF ASSIS-TANCE.
BUT...WHEN I ARRIVED IN KALOS, NO ONE KNEW A THING ABOUT THE REAPPEARANCE OF XERNEAS AND YVELTAL.
ON TOP OF THAT, I HAD THE STRANGE FEELING THAT I WAS BEING WATCHED ALL THE TIME...

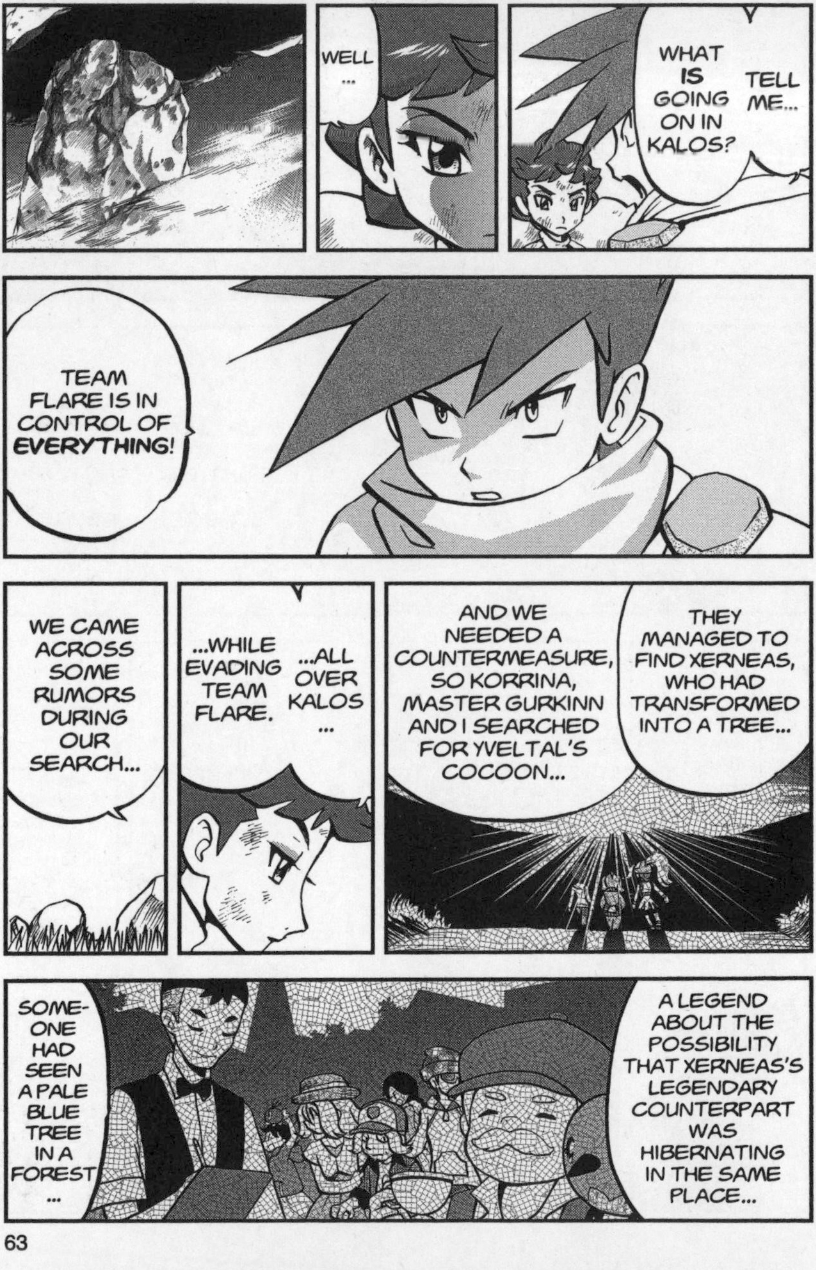
TELL ME...
WHAT IS GOING ON IN KALOS?
WELL...
TEAM FLARE IS IN CONTROL OF EVERYTHING!
THEY MANAGED TO FIND XERNEAS, WHO HAD TRANSFORMED INTO A TREE...
AND WE NEEDED A COUNTERMEASURE, SO KORRINA, MASTER GURKINN AND I SEARCHED FOR YVELTAL'S COCOON...
...ALL OVER KALOS...
...WHILE EVADING TEAM FLARE.
WE CAME ACROSS SOME RUMORS DURING OUR SEARCH...
A LEGEND ABOUT THE POSSIBILITY THAT XERNEAS'S LEGENDARY COUNTERPART WAS HIBERNATING IN THE SAME PLACE...
SOME-ONE HAD SEEN A PALE BLUE TREE IN A FOREST...

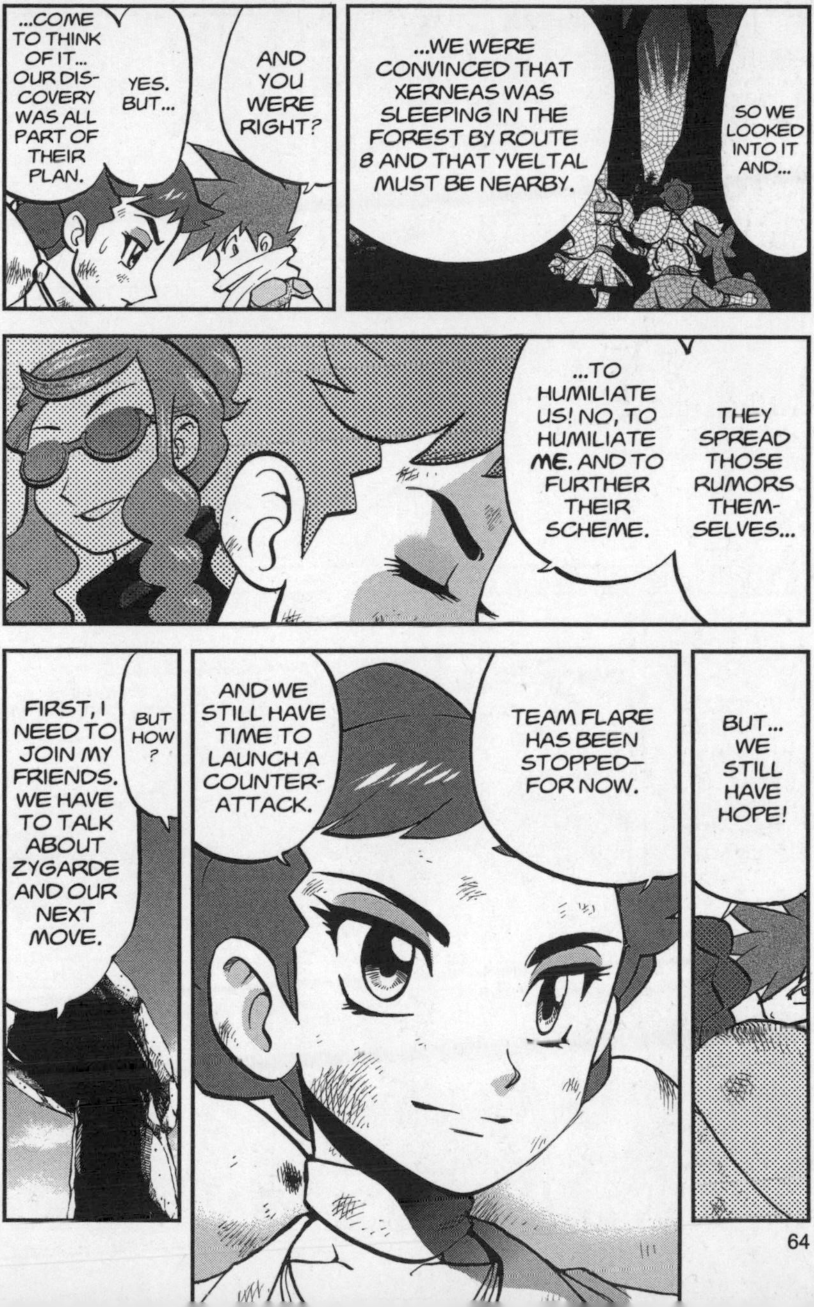
...WE WERE CONVINCED THAT XERNEAS WAS SLEEPING IN THE FOREST BY ROUTE 8 AND THAT YVELTAL MUST BE NEARBY.
SO WE LOOKED INTO IT AND...
AND YOU WERE RIGHT?
YES. BUT...
...COME TO THINK OF IT... OUR DISCOVERY WAS ALL PART OF THEIR PLAN.
THEY SPREAD THOSE RUMORS THEMSELVES...
...TO HUMILIATE US! NO, TO HUMILIATE ME. AND TO FURTHER THEIR SCHEME.
BUT... WE STILL HAVE HOPE!
TEAM FLARE HAS BEEN STOPPED—FOR NOW.
AND WE STILL HAVE TIME TO LAUNCH A COUNTER-ATTACK.
BUT HOW?
FIRST, I NEED TO JOIN MY FRIENDS. WE HAVE TO TALK ABOUT ZYGARDE AND OUR NEXT MOVE.

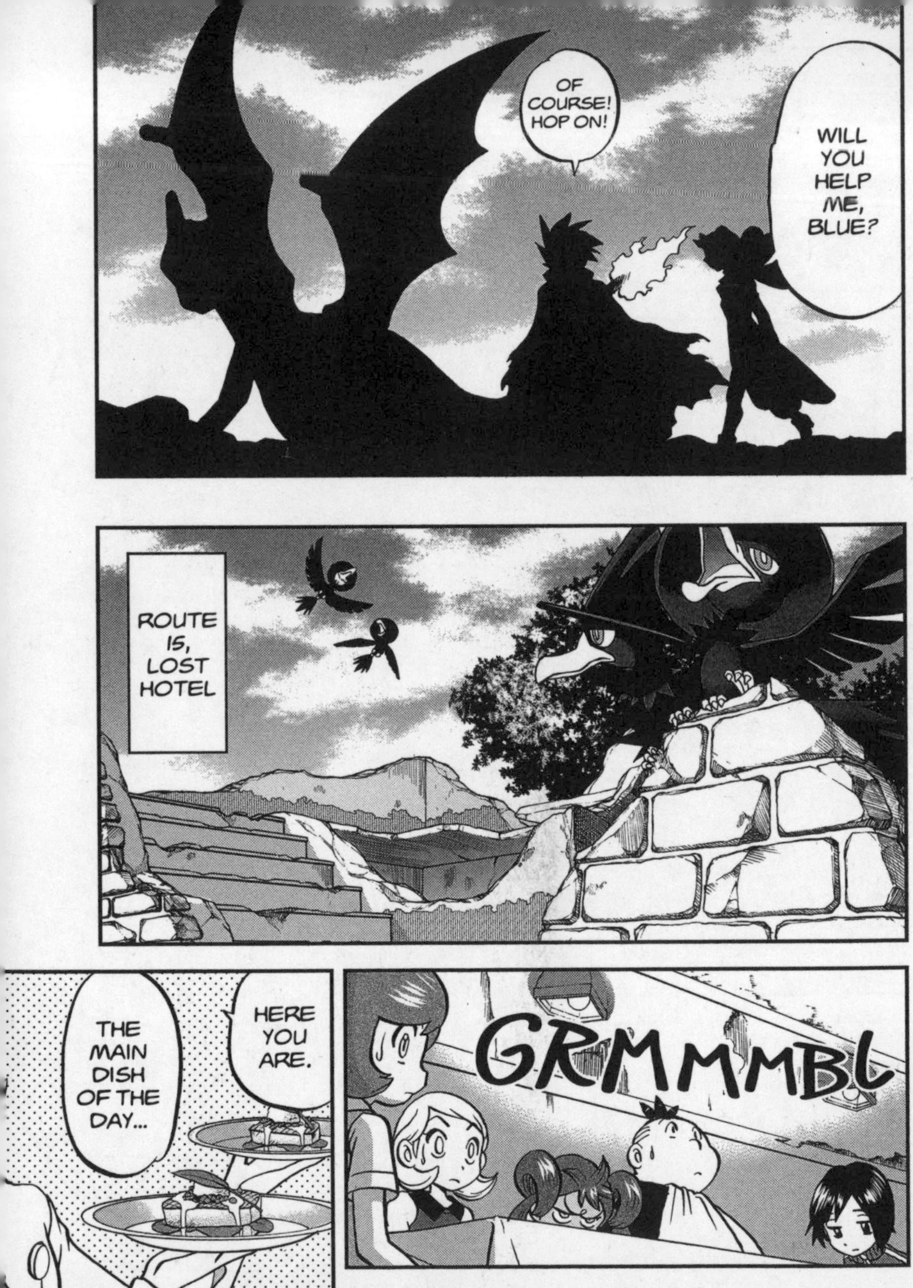
WILL YOU HELP ME, BLUE?
OF COURSE! HOP ON!
ROUTE 15, LOST HOTEL
GRMMMBL
HERE YOU ARE.
THE MAIN DISH OF THE DAY...

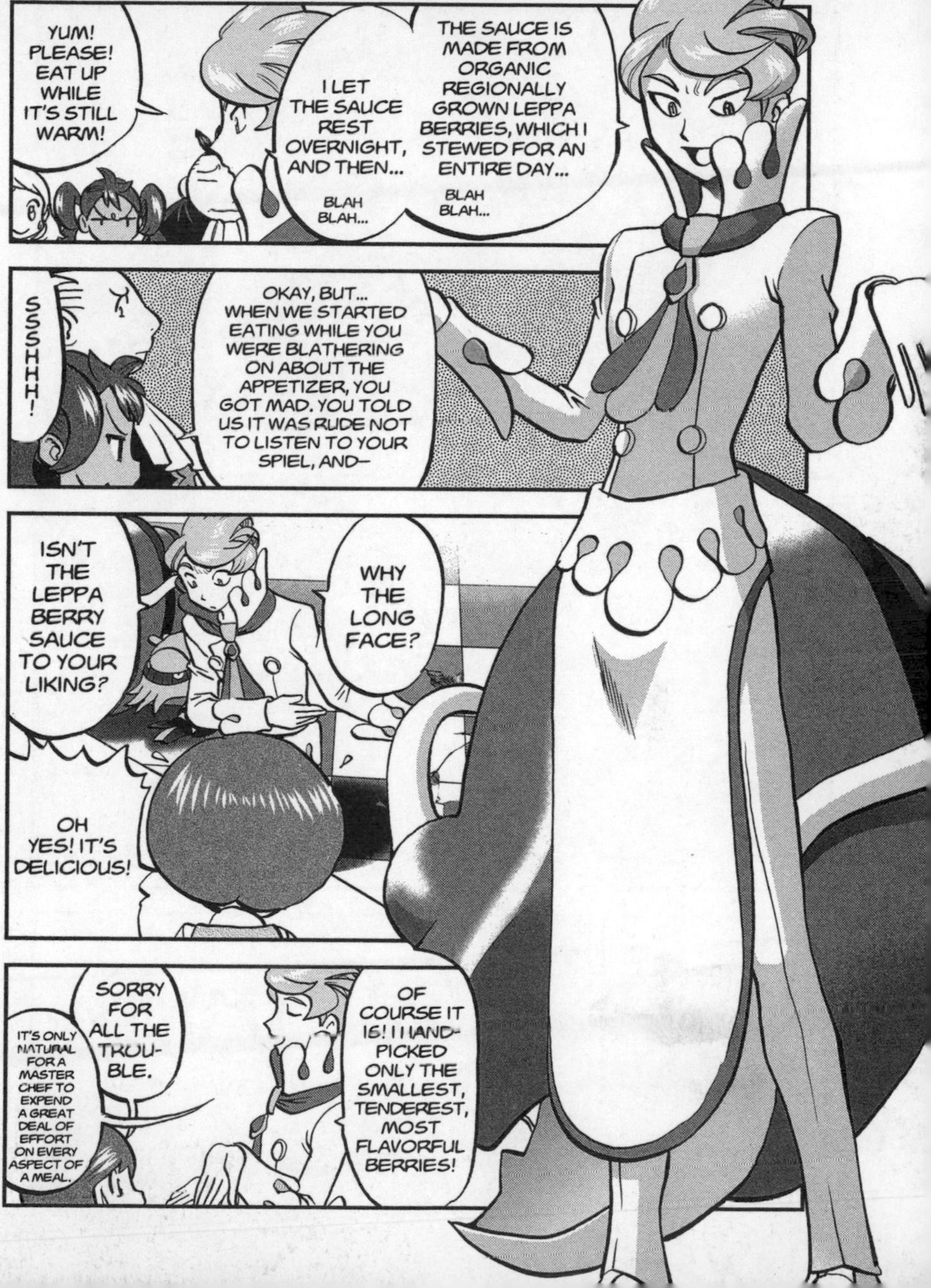
THE SAUCE IS MADE FROM ORGANIC REGIONALLY GROWN LEPPA BERRIES, WHICH I STEWED FOR AN ENTIRE DAY...
BLAH BLAH...
I LET THE SAUCE REST OVERNIGHT, AND THEN...
BLAH BLAH...
YUM! PLEASE! EAT UP WHILE IT'S STILL WARM!
OKAY, BUT... WHEN WE STARTED EATING WHILE YOU WERE BLATHERING ON ABOUT THE APPETIZER, YOU GOT MAD. YOU TOLD US IT WAS RUDE NOT TO LISTEN TO YOUR SPIEL, AND—
SSSHHH!
WHY THE LONG FACE?
ISN'T THE LEPPA BERRY SAUCE TO YOUR LIKING?
OH YES! IT'S DELICIOUS!
OF COURSE IT IS! I HAND-PICKED ONLY THE SMALLEST, TENDEREST, MOST FLAVORFUL BERRIES!
SORRY FOR ALL THE TROUBLE.
IT'S ONLY NATURAL FOR A MASTER CHEF TO EXPEND A GREAT DEAL OF EFFORT ON EVERY ASPECT OF A MEAL.

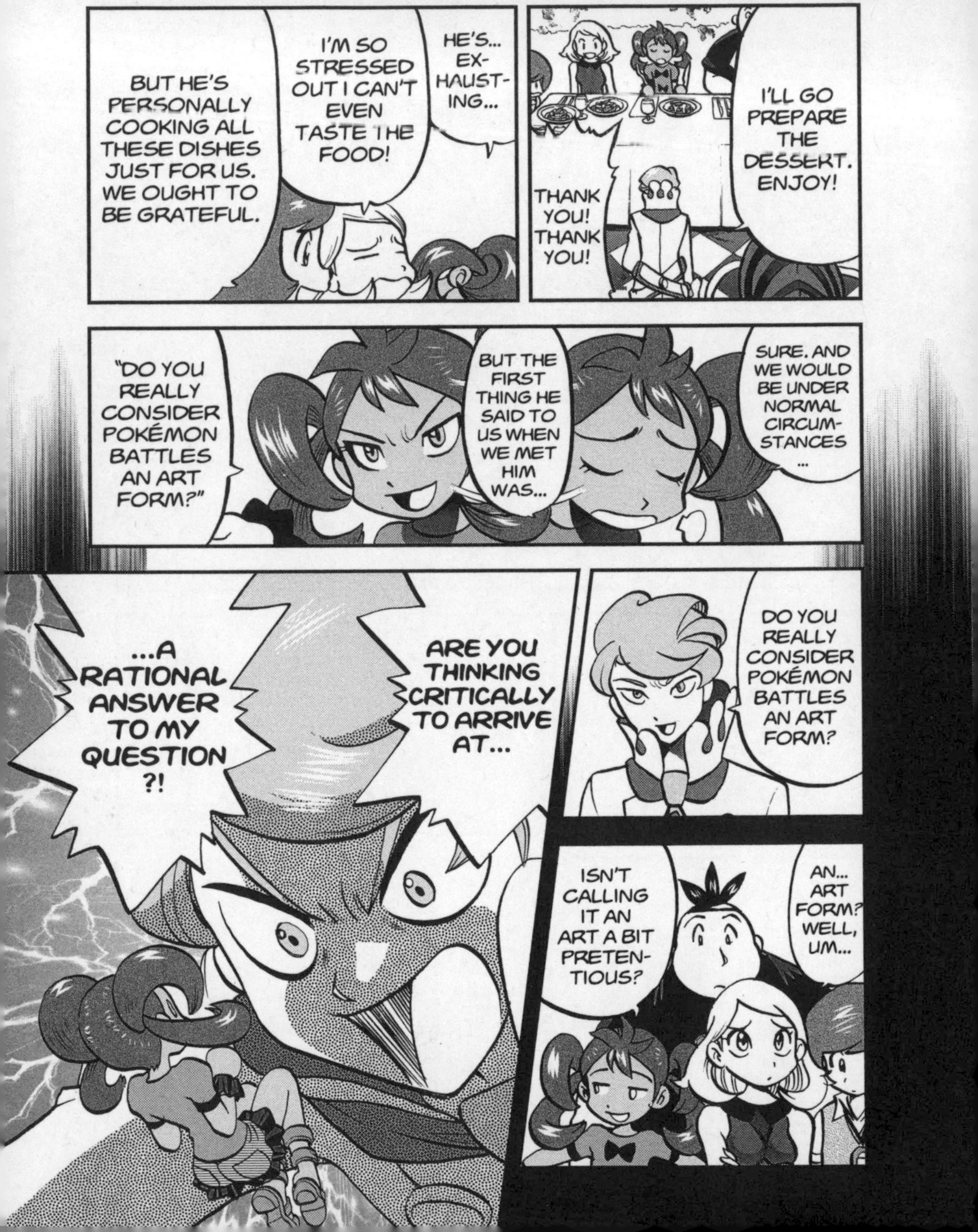
I'LL GO PREPARE THE DESSERT. ENJOY!
THANK YOU! THANK YOU!
HE'S... EX-HAUSTING...
I'M SO STRESSED OUT I CAN'T EVEN TASTE THE FOOD!
BUT HE'S PERSONALLY COOKING ALL THESE DISHES JUST FOR US. WE OUGHT TO BE GRATEFUL.
SURE. AND WE WOULD BE UNDER NORMAL CIRCUM-STANCES...
BUT THE FIRST THING HE SAID TO US WHEN WE MET HIM WAS...
"DO YOU REALLY CONSIDER POKÉMON BATTLES AN ART FORM?"
DO YOU REALLY CONSIDER POKÉMON BATTLES AN ART FORM?
AN... ART FORM? WELL, UM...
ISN'T CALLING IT AN ART A BIT PRETEN-TIOUS?
ARE YOU THINKING CRITICALLY TO ARRIVE AT...
...A RATIONAL ANSWER TO MY QUESTION ?!

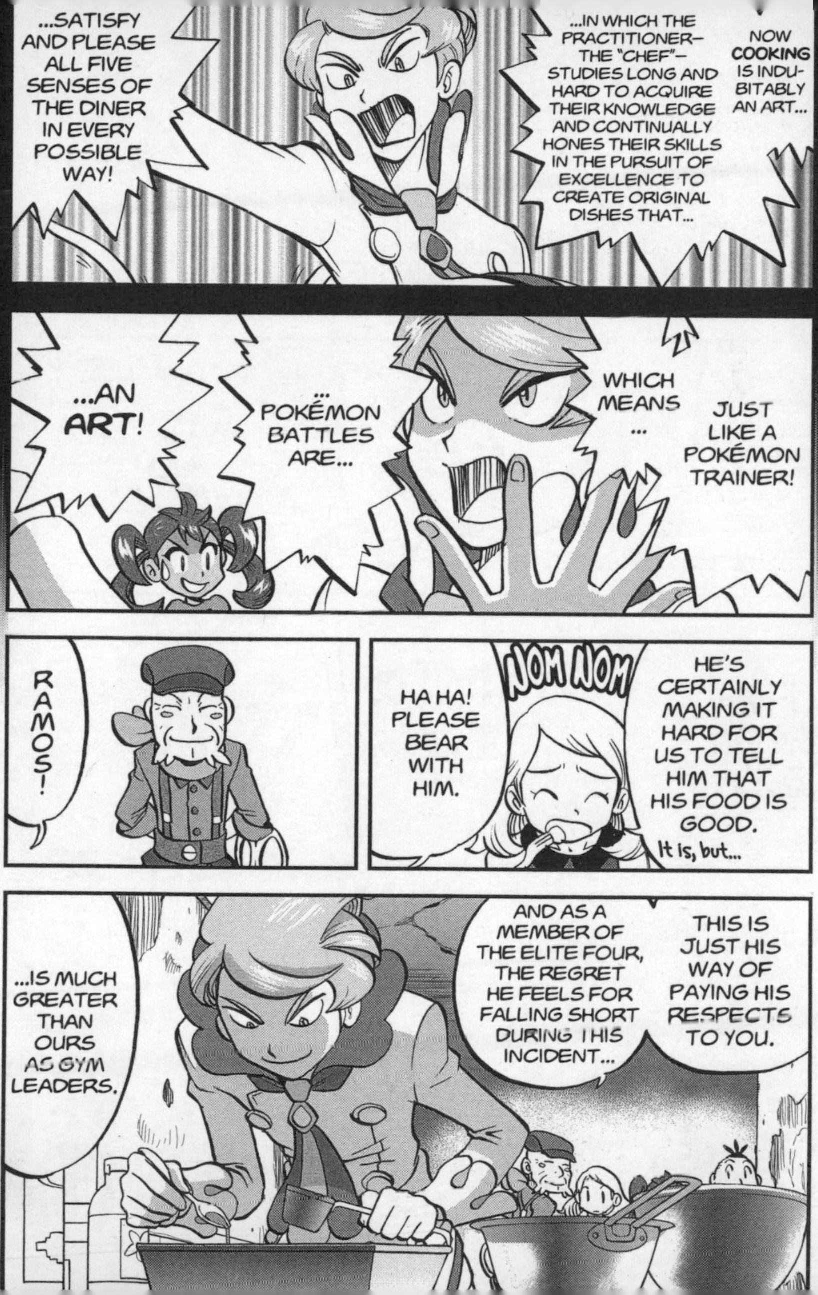
NOW **COOKING** IS INDUBITABLY AN ART...
...IN WHICH THE PRACTITIONER—THE "CHEF"—STUDIES LONG AND HARD TO ACQUIRE THEIR KNOWLEDGE AND CONTINUALLY HONES THEIR SKILLS IN THE PURSUIT OF EXCELLENCE TO CREATE ORIGINAL DISHES THAT...
...SATISFY AND PLEASE ALL FIVE SENSES OF THE DINER IN EVERY POSSIBLE WAY!
JUST LIKE A POKÉMON TRAINER!
WHICH MEANS ...
... POKÉMON BATTLES ARE...
...AN **ART**!
HE'S CERTAINLY MAKING IT HARD FOR US TO TELL HIM THAT HIS FOOD IS GOOD.
It is, but...
NOM NOM
HA HA! PLEASE BEAR WITH HIM.
RAMOS!
THIS IS JUST HIS WAY OF PAYING HIS RESPECTS TO YOU.
AND AS A MEMBER OF THE ELITE FOUR, THE REGRET HE FEELS FOR FALLING SHORT DURING THIS INCIDENT...
...IS MUCH GREATER THAN OURS AS GYM LEADERS.

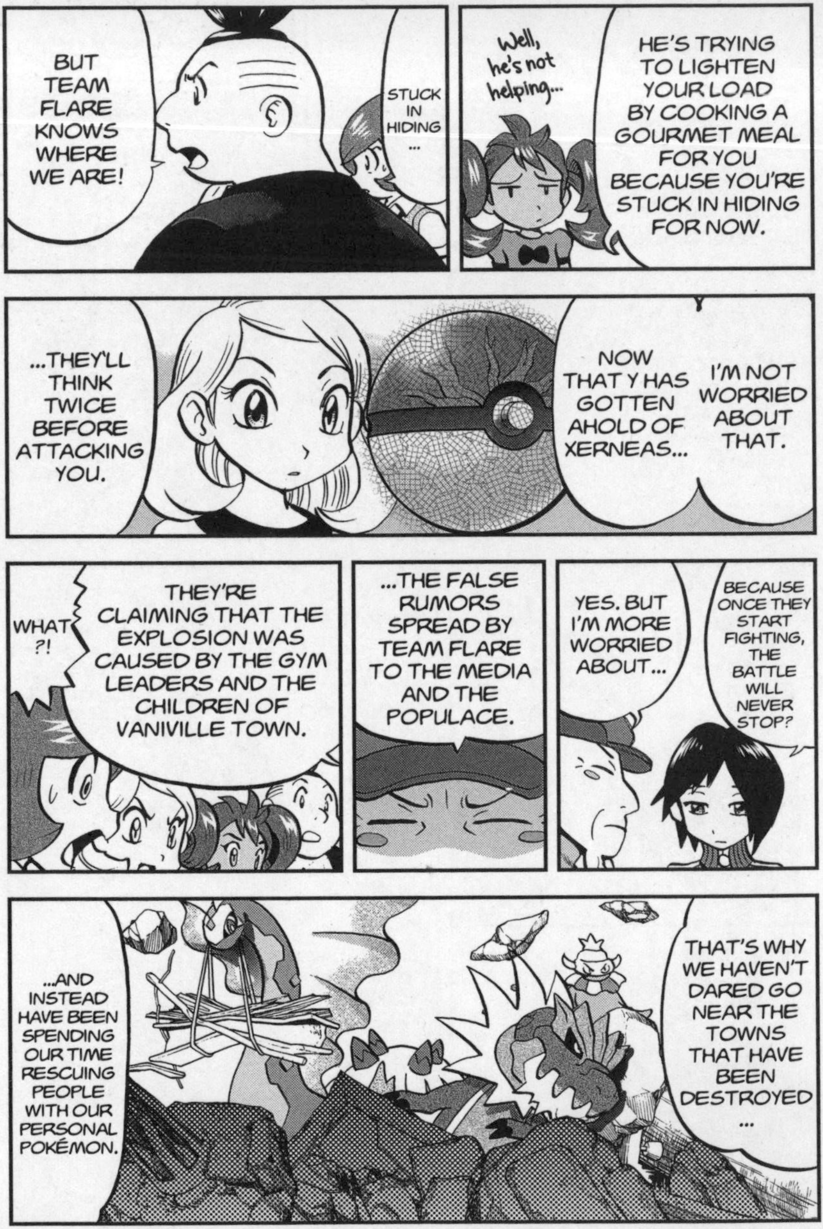
HE'S TRYING TO LIGHTEN YOUR LOAD BY COOKING A GOURMET MEAL FOR YOU BECAUSE YOU'RE STUCK IN HIDING FOR NOW.
Well, he's not helping...
STUCK IN HIDING...
BUT TEAM FLARE KNOWS WHERE WE ARE!
I'M NOT WORRIED ABOUT THAT.
NOW THAT Y HAS GOTTEN AHOLD OF XERNEAS...
...THEY'LL THINK TWICE BEFORE ATTACKING YOU.
BECAUSE ONCE THEY START FIGHTING, THE BATTLE WILL NEVER STOP?
YES. BUT I'M MORE WORRIED ABOUT...
...THE FALSE RUMORS SPREAD BY TEAM FLARE TO THE MEDIA AND THE POPULACE.
THEY'RE CLAIMING THAT THE EXPLOSION WAS CAUSED BY THE GYM LEADERS AND THE CHILDREN OF VANIVILLE TOWN.
WHAT?!
THAT'S WHY WE HAVEN'T DARED GO NEAR THE TOWNS THAT HAVE BEEN DESTROYED...
...AND INSTEAD HAVE BEEN SPENDING OUR TIME RESCUING PEOPLE WITH OUR PERSONAL POKÉMON.

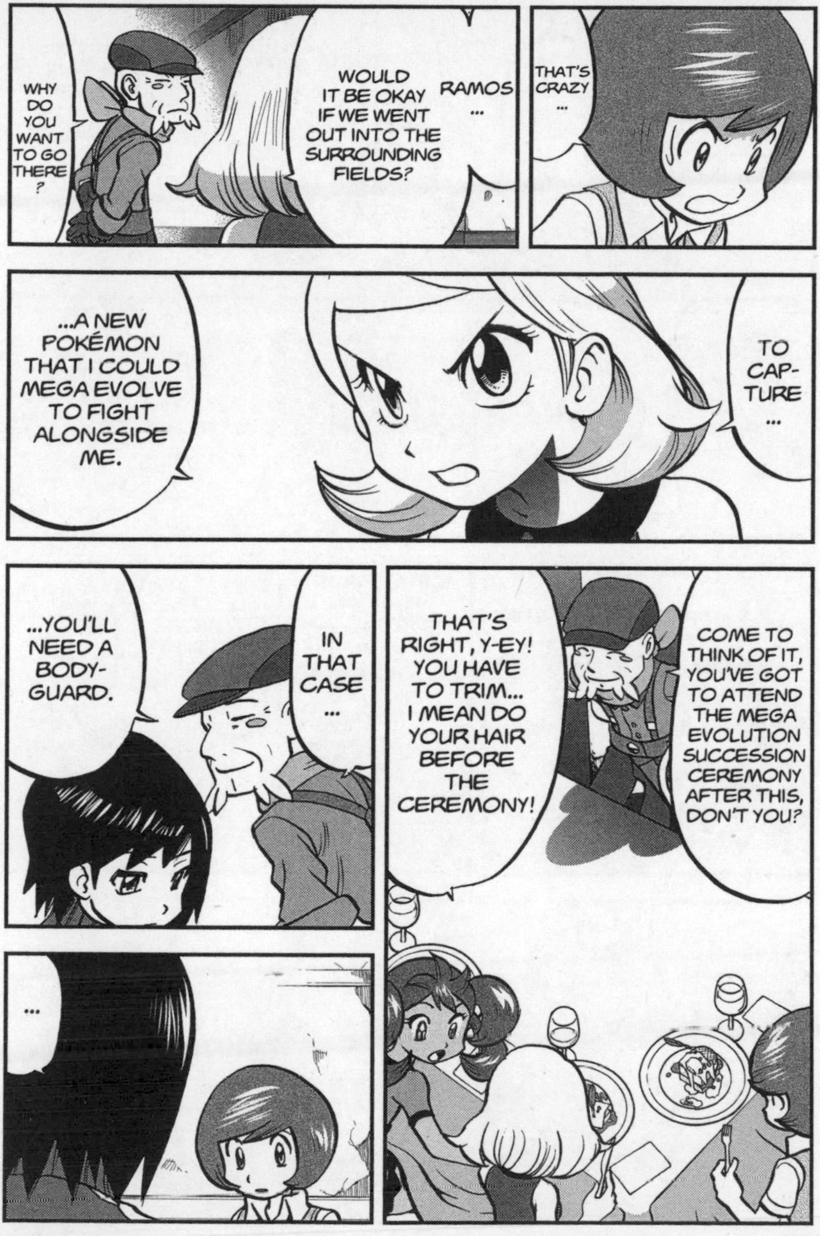
THAT'S CRAZY ...
RAMOS ...
WOULD IT BE OKAY IF WE WENT OUT INTO THE SURROUNDING FIELDS?
WHY DO YOU WANT TO GO THERE ?
TO CAP-TURE ...
...A NEW POKÉMON THAT I COULD MEGA EVOLVE TO FIGHT ALONGSIDE ME.
COME TO THINK OF IT, YOU'VE GOT TO ATTEND THE MEGA EVOLUTION SUCCESSION CEREMONY AFTER THIS, DON'T YOU?
THAT'S RIGHT, Y-EY! YOU HAVE TO TRIM... I MEAN DO YOUR HAIR BEFORE THE CEREMONY!
IN THAT CASE ...
...YOU'LL NEED A BODY-GUARD.
...

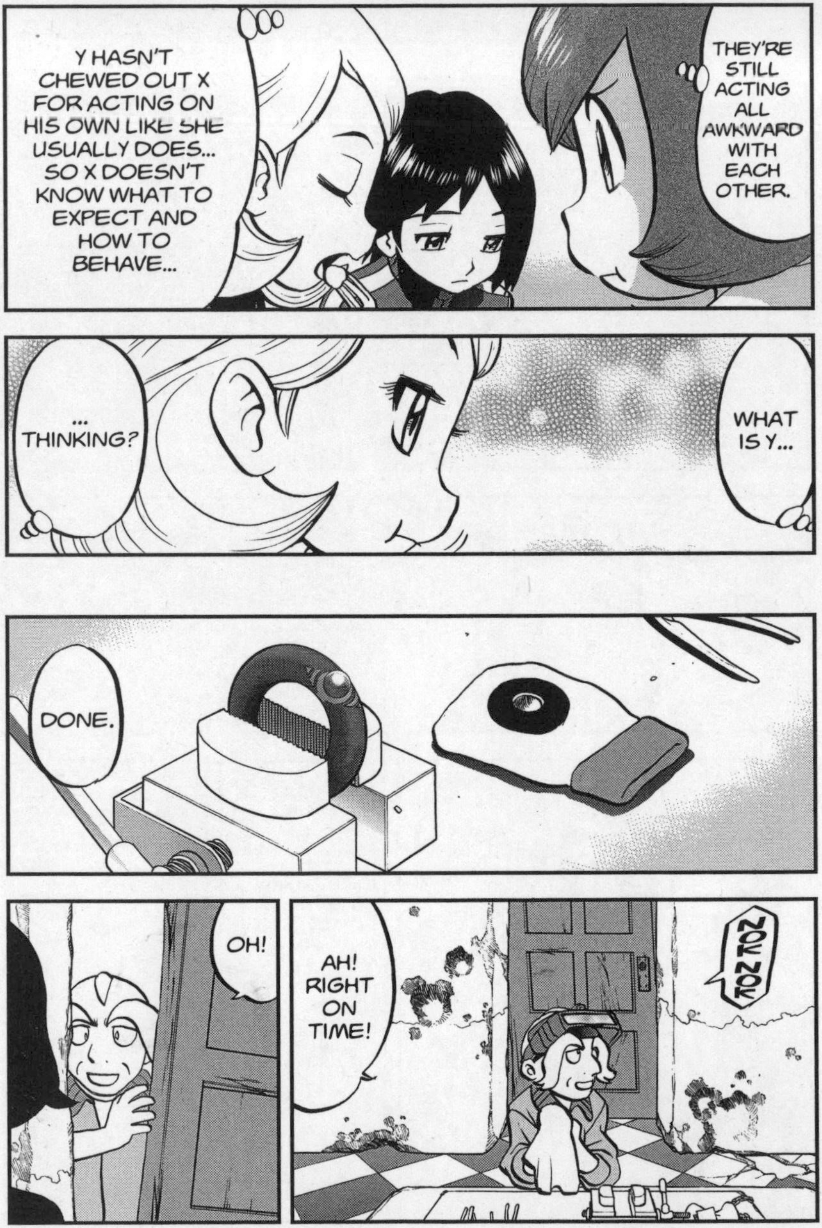
THEY'RE STILL ACTING ALL AWKWARD WITH EACH OTHER.
Y HASN'T CHEWED OUT X FOR ACTING ON HIS OWN LIKE SHE USUALLY DOES... SO X DOESN'T KNOW WHAT TO EXPECT AND HOW TO BEHAVE...
WHAT IS Y...
...THINKING?
DONE.
NOK NOK
AH! RIGHT ON TIME!
OH!

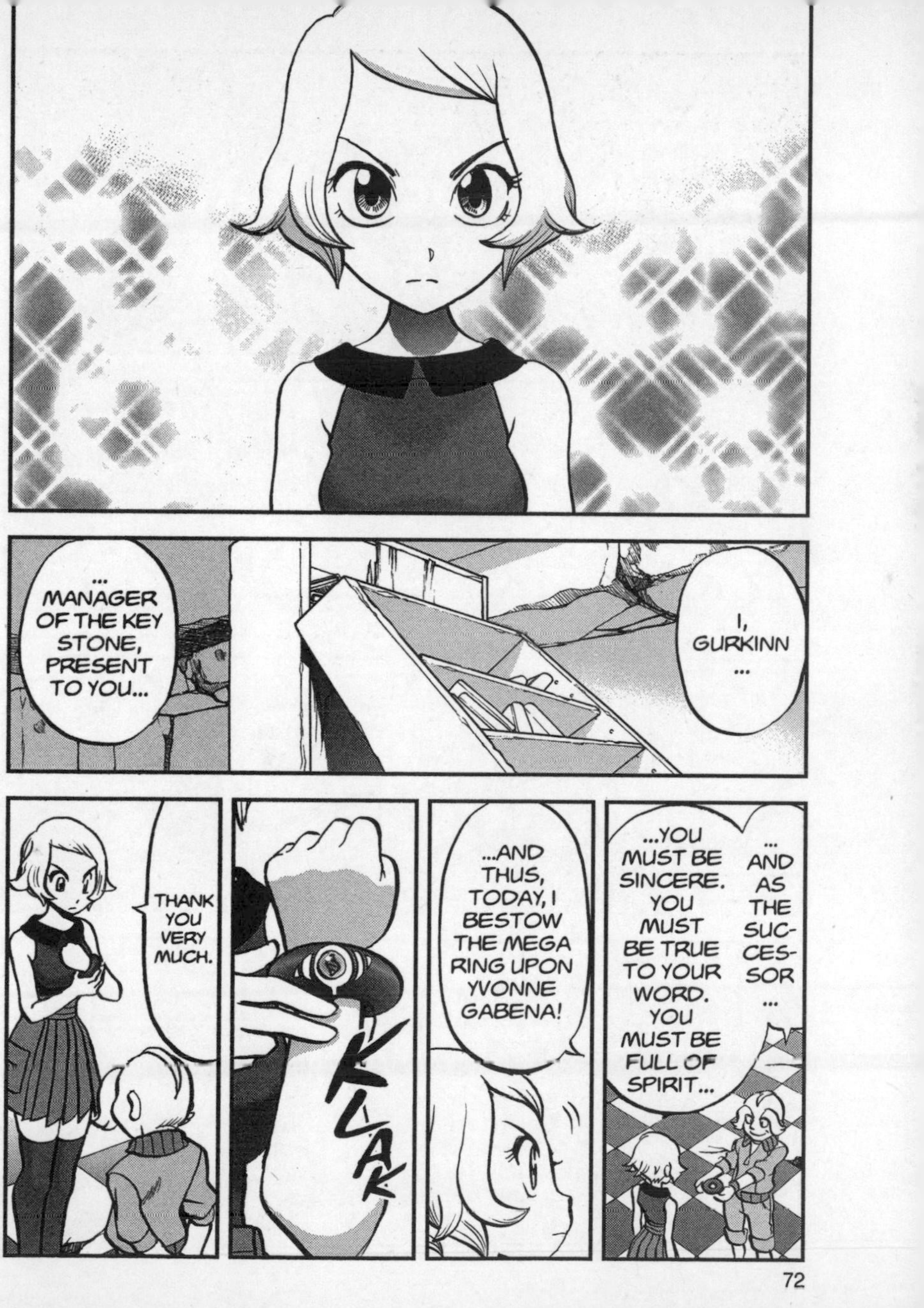
I, GURKINN...
...MANAGER OF THE KEY STONE, PRESENT TO YOU...
...AND AS THE SUC-CES-SOR...
...YOU MUST BE SINCERE. YOU MUST BE TRUE TO YOUR WORD. YOU MUST BE FULL OF SPIRIT...
...AND THUS, TODAY, I BESTOW THE MEGA RING UPON YVONNE GABENA!
KLAK
THANK YOU VERY MUCH.

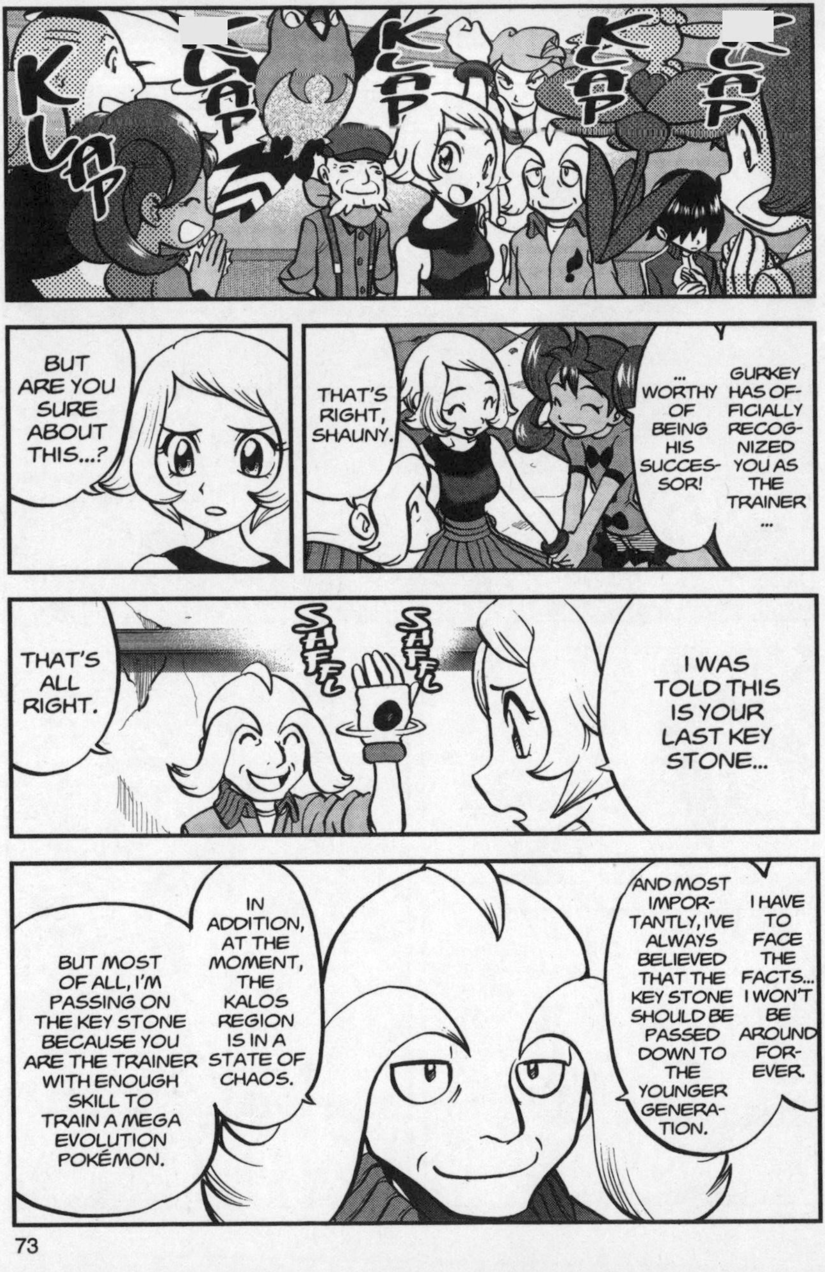
LAP
KLAP
KLAP
LAP
KLAP
GURKEY HAS OFFICIALLY RECOGNIZED YOU AS THE TRAINER...
...WORTHY OF BEING HIS SUCCESSOR!
THAT'S RIGHT, SHAUNY.
BUT ARE YOU SURE ABOUT THIS...?
I WAS TOLD THIS IS YOUR LAST KEY STONE...
SHFFL
SHFFL
THAT'S ALL RIGHT.
I HAVE TO FACE THE FACTS... I WON'T BE AROUND FOREVER.
AND MOST IMPORTANTLY, I'VE ALWAYS BELIEVED THAT THE KEY STONE SHOULD BE PASSED DOWN TO THE YOUNGER GENERATION.
IN ADDITION, AT THE MOMENT, THE KALOS REGION IS IN A STATE OF CHAOS.
BUT MOST OF ALL, I'M PASSING ON THE KEY STONE BECAUSE YOU ARE THE TRAINER WITH ENOUGH SKILL TO TRAIN A MEGA EVOLUTION POKéMON.

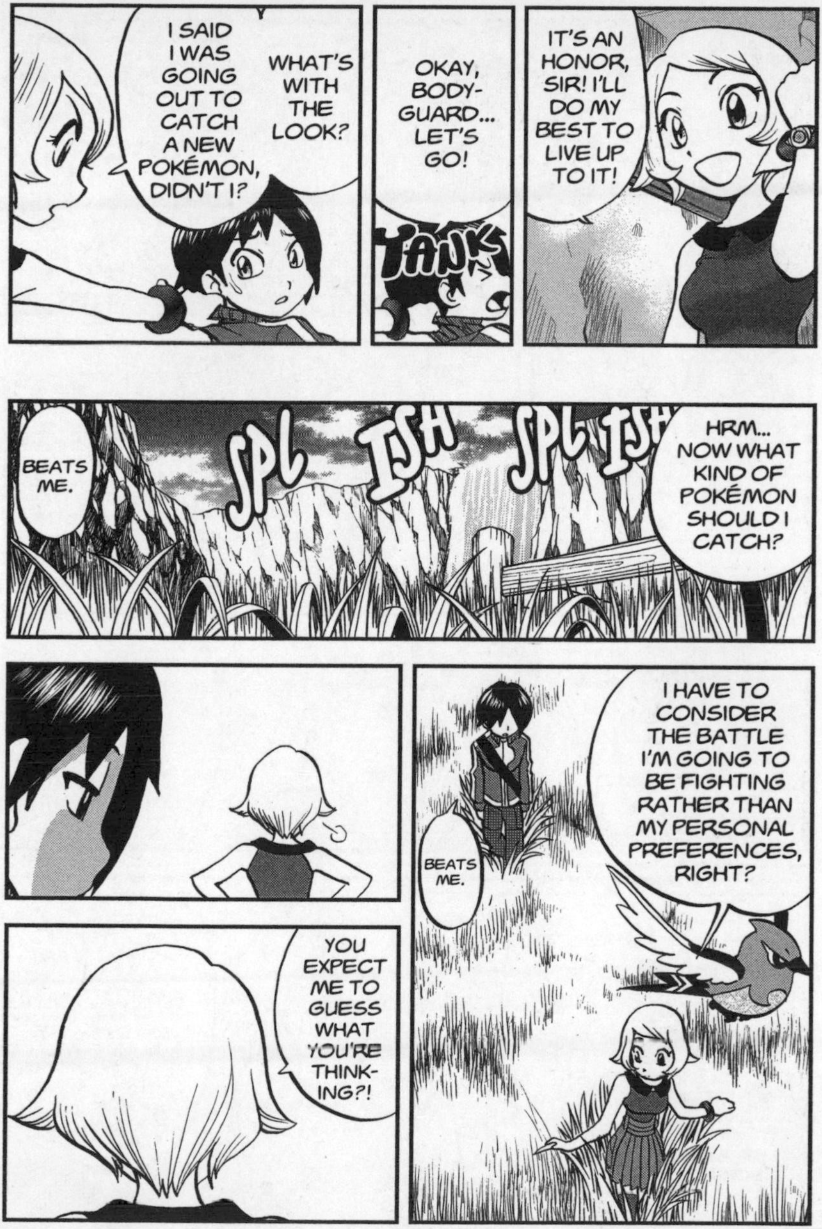
IT'S AN HONOR, SIR! I'LL DO MY BEST TO LIVE UP TO IT!
OKAY, BODY-GUARD... LET'S GO!
YANK
I SAID I WAS GOING OUT TO CATCH A NEW POKéMON, DIDN'T I? WHAT'S WITH THE LOOK?
HRM... NOW WHAT KIND OF POKéMON SHOULD I CATCH?
SPLISH SPLISH
BEATS ME.
I HAVE TO CONSIDER THE BATTLE I'M GOING TO BE FIGHTING RATHER THAN MY PERSONAL PREFERENCES, RIGHT?
BEATS ME.
YOU EXPECT ME TO GUESS WHAT YOU'RE THINKING?!

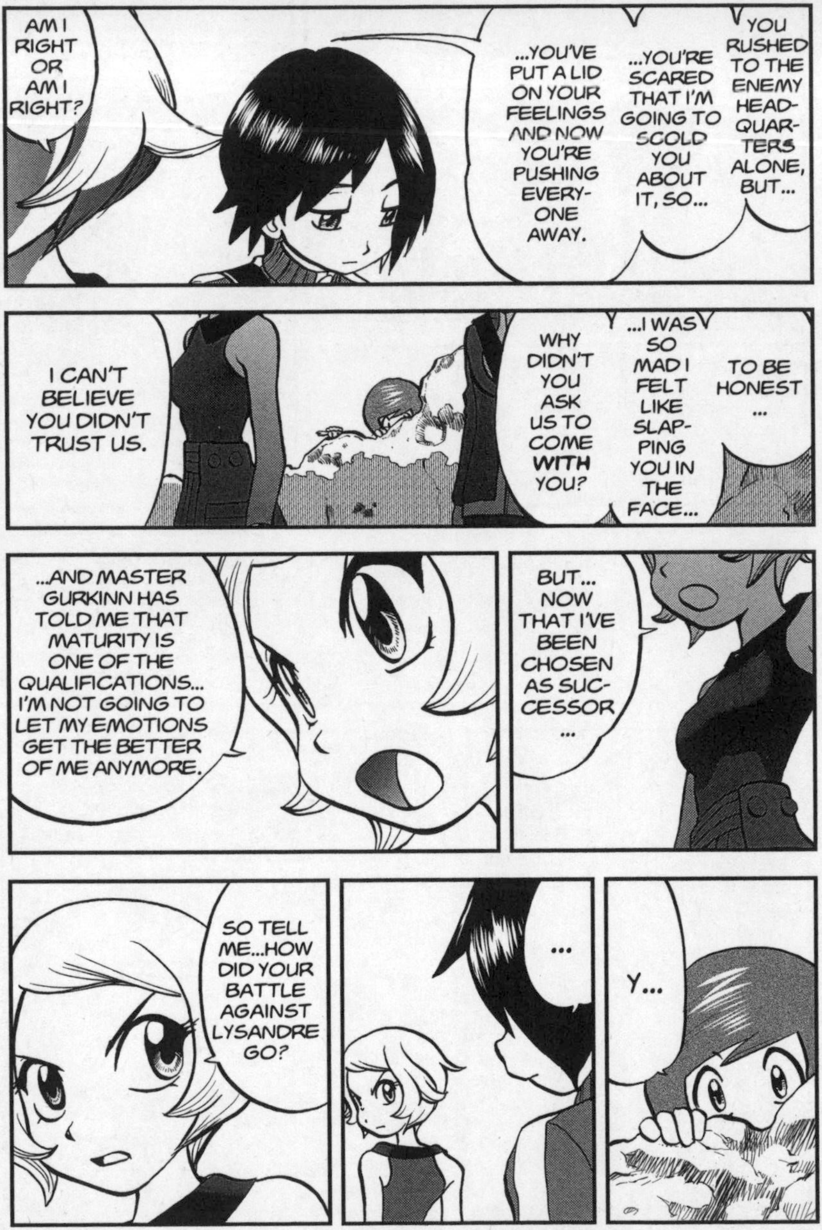
YOU RUSHED TO THE ENEMY HEAD-QUARTERS ALONE, BUT...
...YOU'RE SCARED THAT I'M GOING TO SCOLD YOU ABOUT IT, SO...
...YOU'VE PUT A LID ON YOUR FEELINGS AND NOW YOU'RE PUSHING EVERY-ONE AWAY.
AM I RIGHT OR AM I RIGHT?
TO BE HONEST...
...I WAS SO MAD I FELT LIKE SLAP-PING YOU IN THE FACE...
WHY DIDN'T YOU ASK US TO COME **WITH** YOU?
I CAN'T BELIEVE YOU DIDN'T TRUST US.
BUT... NOW THAT I'VE BEEN CHOSEN AS SUC-CESSOR...
...AND MASTER GURKINN HAS TOLD ME THAT MATURITY IS ONE OF THE QUALIFICATIONS... I'M NOT GOING TO LET MY EMOTIONS GET THE BETTER OF ME ANYMORE.
Y...
...
SO TELL ME...HOW DID YOUR BATTLE AGAINST LYSANDRE GO?

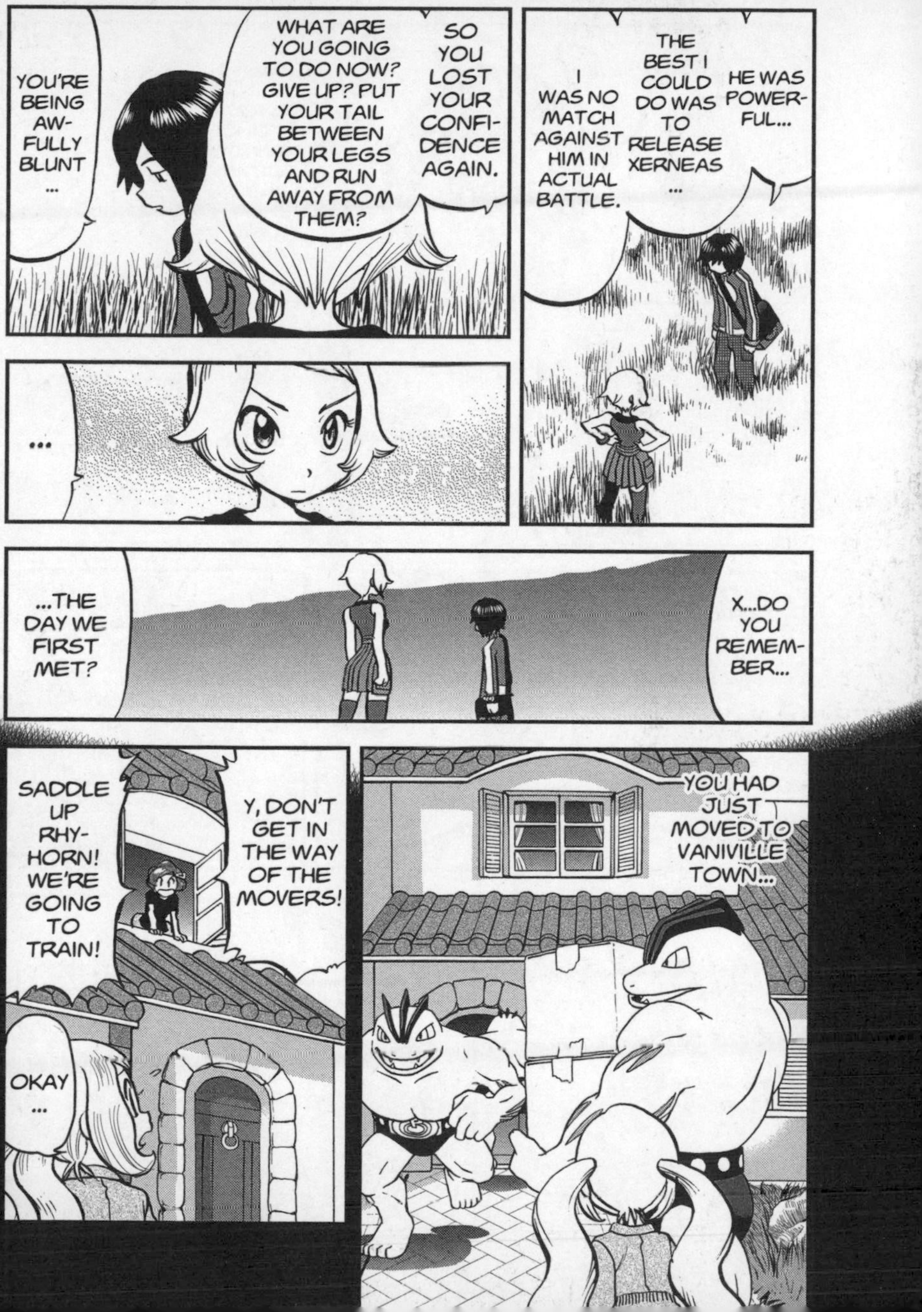
HE WAS POWERFUL...
THE BEST I COULD DO WAS TO RELEASE XERNEAS...
I WAS NO MATCH AGAINST HIM IN ACTUAL BATTLE.
SO YOU LOST YOUR CONFIDENCE AGAIN.
WHAT ARE YOU GOING TO DO NOW? GIVE UP? PUT YOUR TAIL BETWEEN YOUR LEGS AND RUN AWAY FROM THEM?
YOU'RE BEING AWFULLY BLUNT...
...
X...DO YOU REMEMBER...
...THE DAY WE FIRST MET?
YOU HAD JUST MOVED TO VANIVILLE TOWN...
Y, DON'T GET IN THE WAY OF THE MOVERS!
SADDLE UP RHYHORN! WE'RE GOING TO TRAIN!
OKAY...

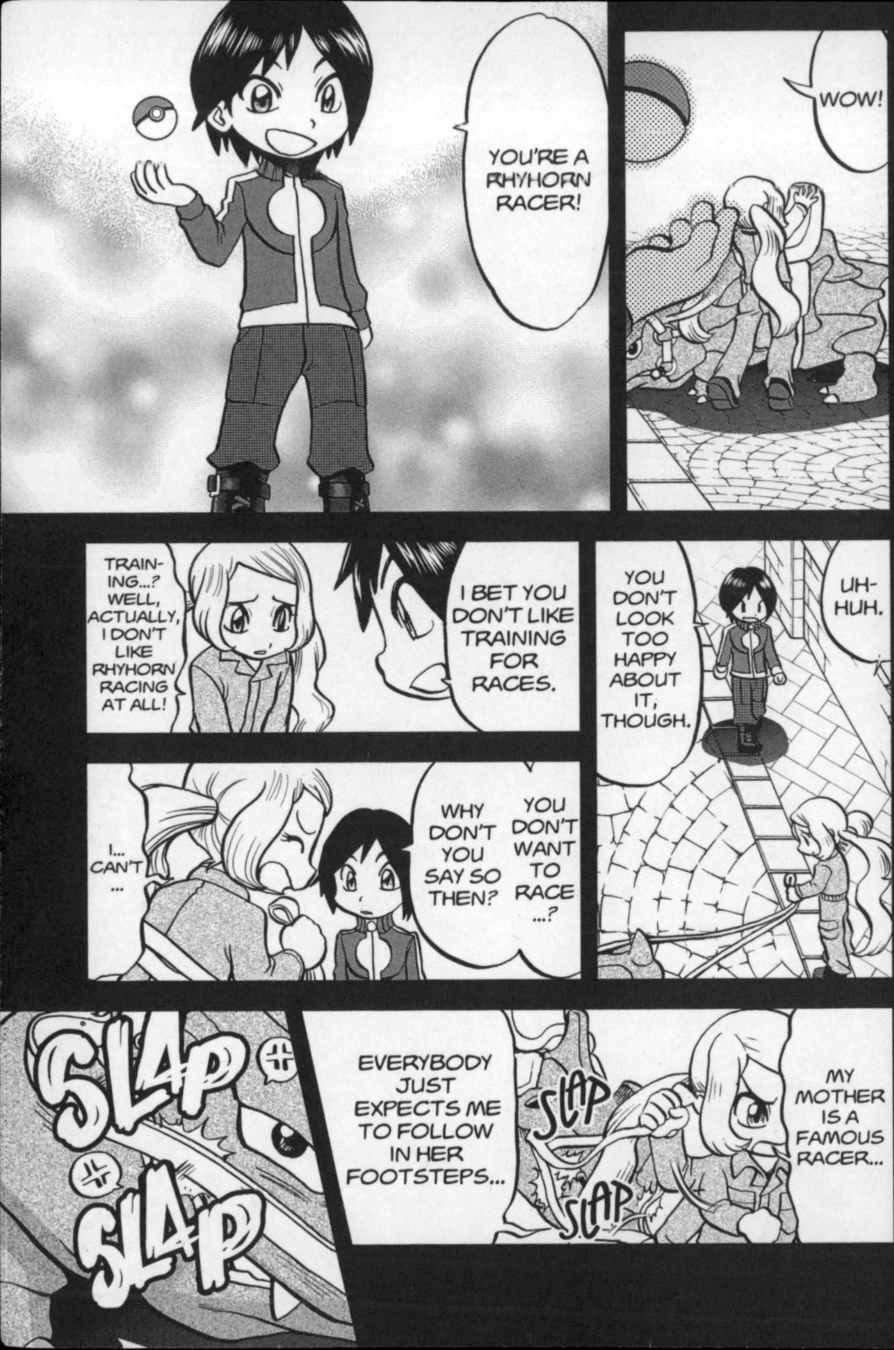
WOW!
YOU'RE A RHYHORN RACER!
UH-HUH.
YOU DON'T LOOK TOO HAPPY ABOUT IT, THOUGH.
I BET YOU DON'T LIKE TRAINING FOR RACES.
TRAINING...? WELL, ACTUALLY, I DON'T LIKE RHYHORN RACING AT ALL!
YOU DON'T WANT TO RACE...?
WHY DON'T YOU SAY SO THEN?
I... CAN'T...
MY MOTHER IS A FAMOUS RACER...
EVERYBODY JUST EXPECTS ME TO FOLLOW IN HER FOOTSTEPS...
SLAP
SLAP
SLAP
SLAP

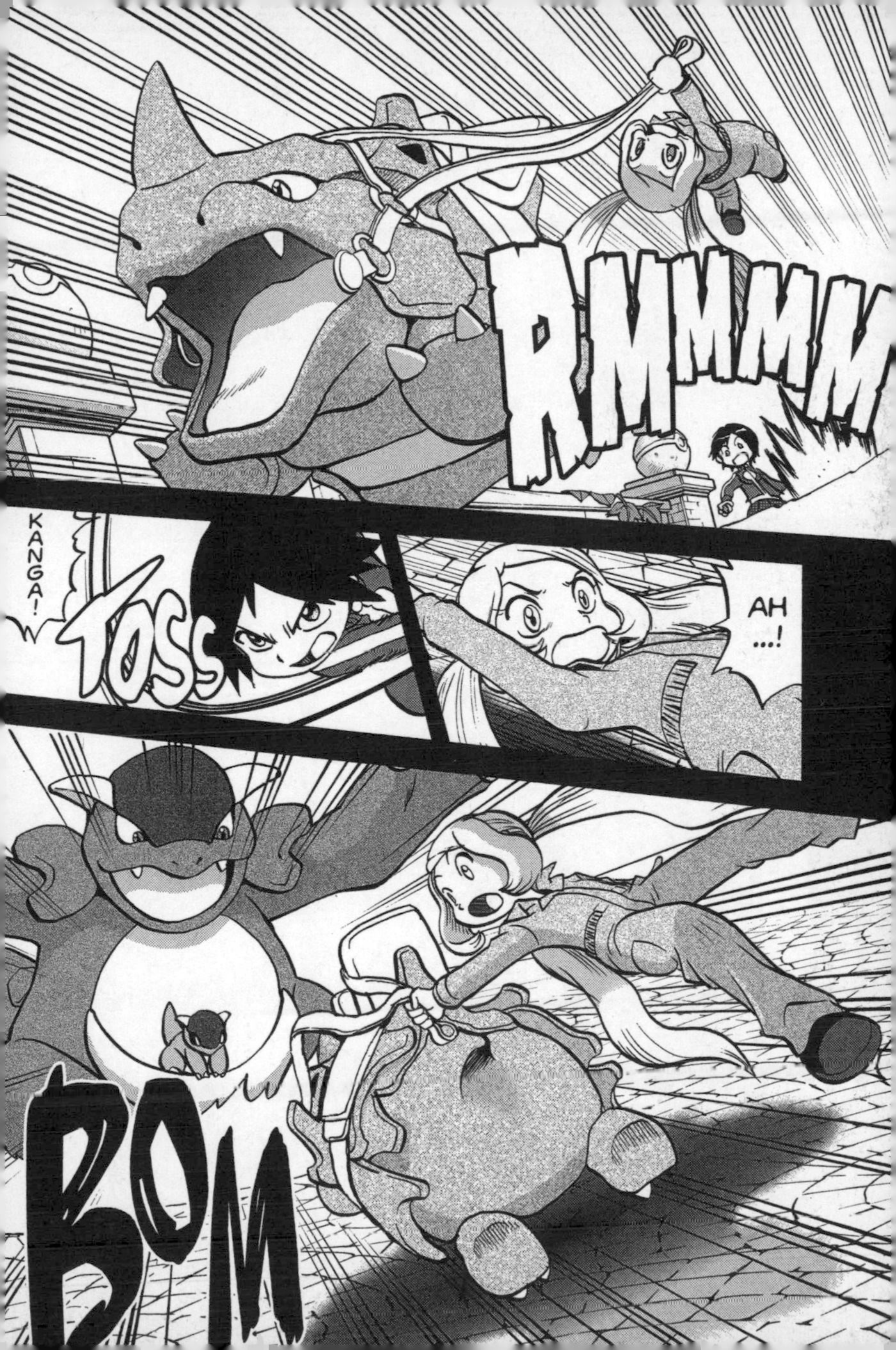
RMMMMM
AH ...!
KANGA!
TOSS
BOM

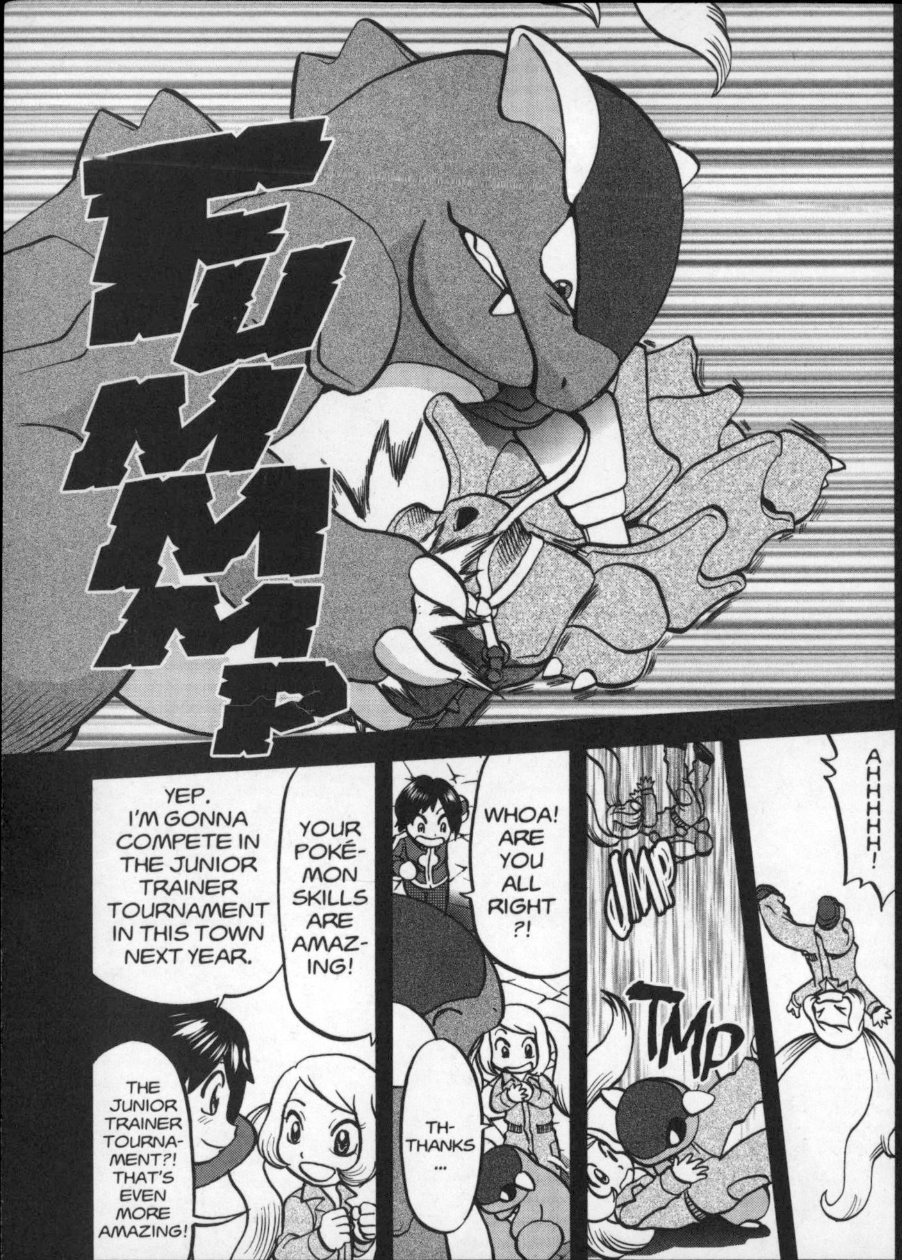
THUMMMP
AHHHHH!
JMP
TMP
WHOA! ARE YOU ALL RIGHT?!
TH-THANKS...
YOUR POKÉ-MON SKILLS ARE AMAZ-ING!
YEP. I'M GONNA COMPETE IN THE JUNIOR TRAINER TOURNAMENT IN THIS TOWN NEXT YEAR.
THE JUNIOR TRAINER TOURNA-MENT?! THAT'S EVEN MORE AMAZING!

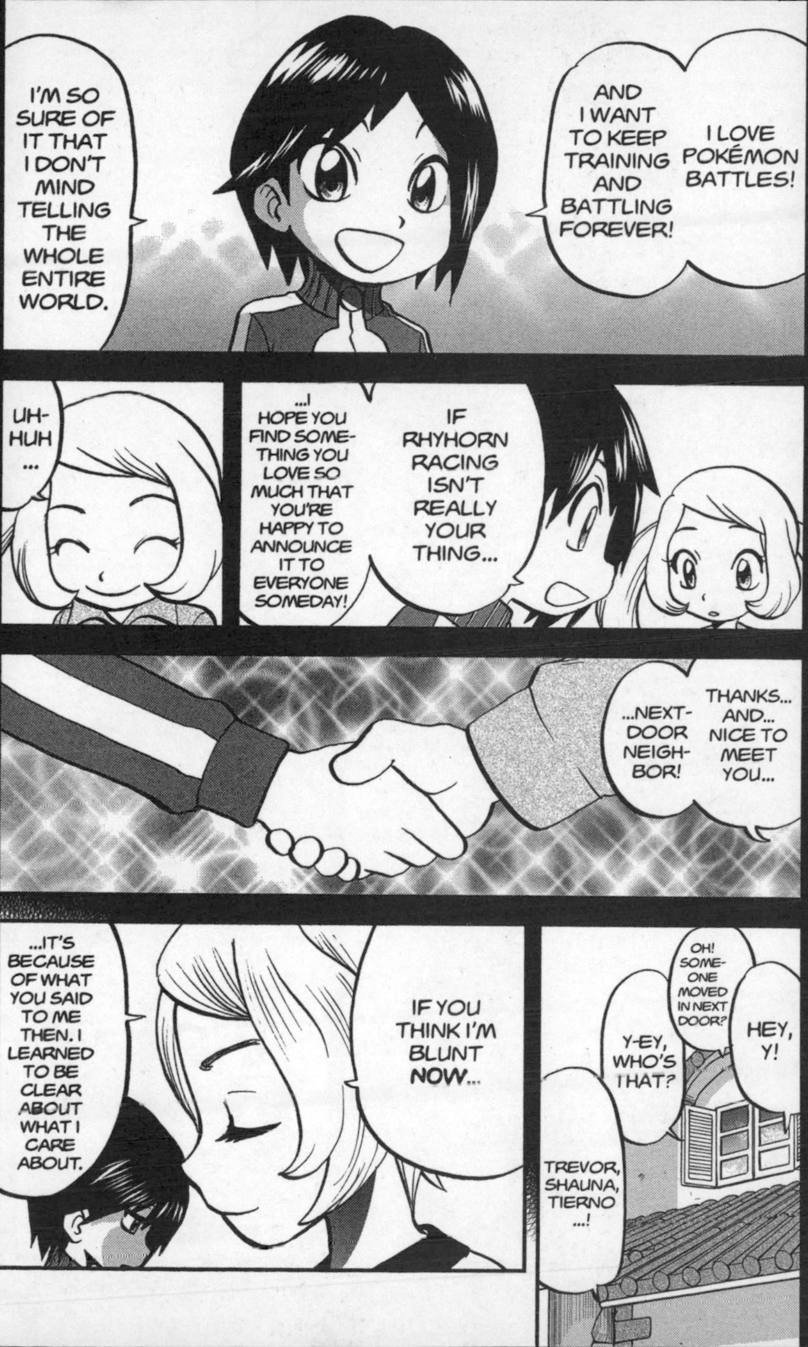
I LOVE POKÉMON BATTLES!
AND I WANT TO KEEP TRAINING AND BATTLING FOREVER!
I'M SO SURE OF IT THAT I DON'T MIND TELLING THE WHOLE ENTIRE WORLD.
IF RHYHORN RACING ISN'T REALLY YOUR THING...
...I HOPE YOU FIND SOME-THING YOU LOVE SO MUCH THAT YOU'RE HAPPY TO ANNOUNCE IT TO EVERYONE SOMEDAY!
UH-HUH ...
THANKS... AND... NICE TO MEET YOU...
...NEXT-DOOR NEIGH-BOR!
HEY, Y!
OH! SOME-ONE MOVED IN NEXT DOOR?
Y-EY, WHO'S THAT?
TREVOR, SHAUNA, TIERNO ...!
IF YOU THINK I'M BLUNT **NOW**...
...IT'S BECAUSE OF WHAT YOU SAID TO ME THEN. I LEARNED TO BE CLEAR ABOUT WHAT I CARE ABOUT.

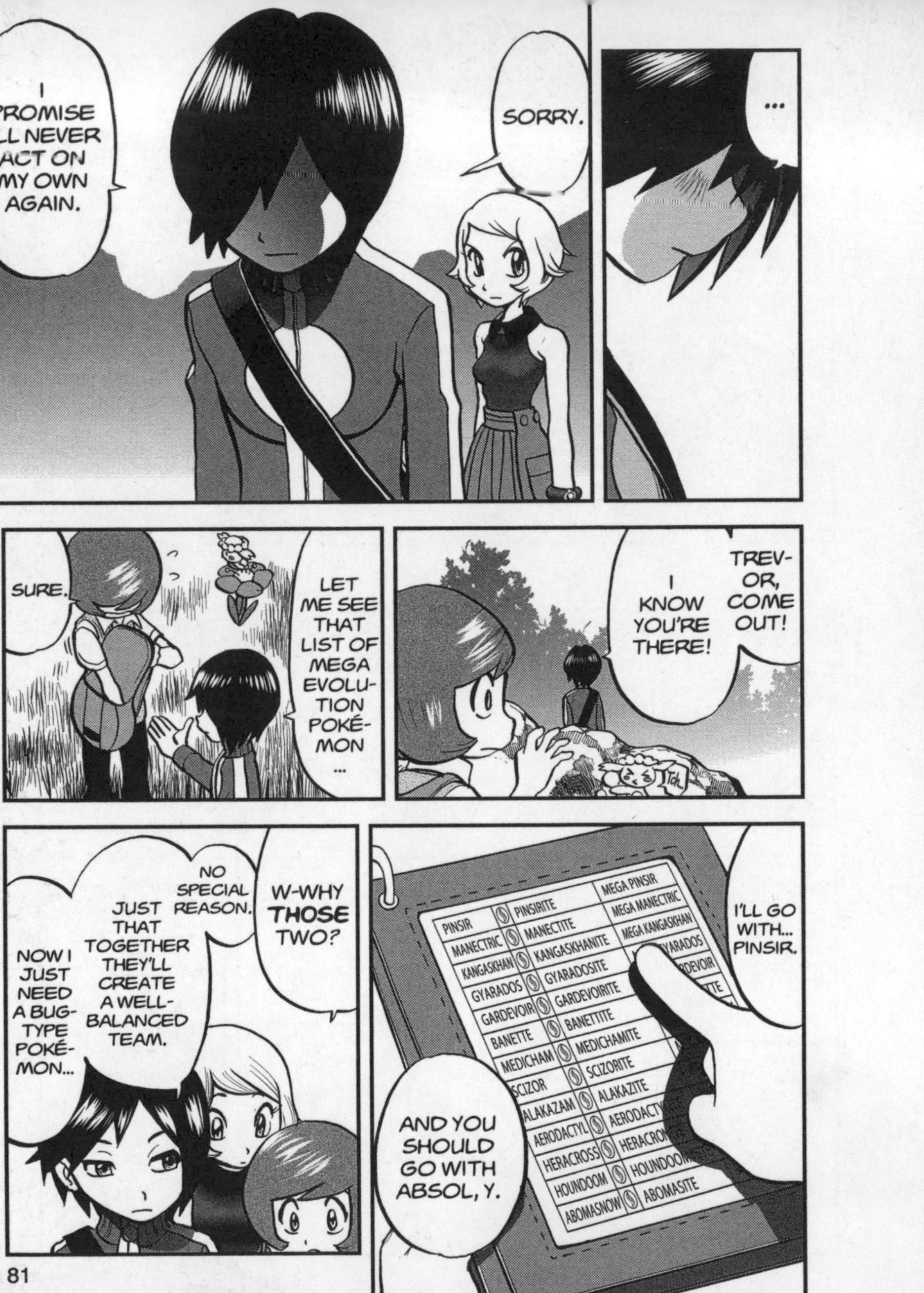
...
SORRY.
I PROMISE I'LL NEVER ACT ON MY OWN AGAIN.
TREV-OR, COME OUT!
I KNOW YOU'RE THERE!
Tch..
LET ME SEE THAT LIST OF MEGA EVOLUTION POKÉMON...
SURE.
I'LL GO WITH... PINSIR.
MEGA PINSIR
PINSIR PINSIRITE
MEGA MANECTRIC
MANECTRIC MANECTITE
MEGA KANGASKHAN
KANGASKHAN KANGASKHANITE
GYARADOS GYARADOSITE
GARDEVOIR GARDEVOIRITE
BANETTE BANETTITE
MEDICHAM MEDICHAMITE
SCIZOR SCIZORITE
ALAKAZAM ALAKAZITE
AERODACTYL
HERACROSS
HOUNDOOM
ABOMASNOW ABOMASITE
AND YOU SHOULD GO WITH ABSOL, Y.
W-WHY THOSE TWO?
NO SPECIAL REASON.
JUST THAT TOGETHER THEY'LL CREATE A WELL-BALANCED TEAM.
NOW I JUST NEED A BUG-TYPE POKÉMON...

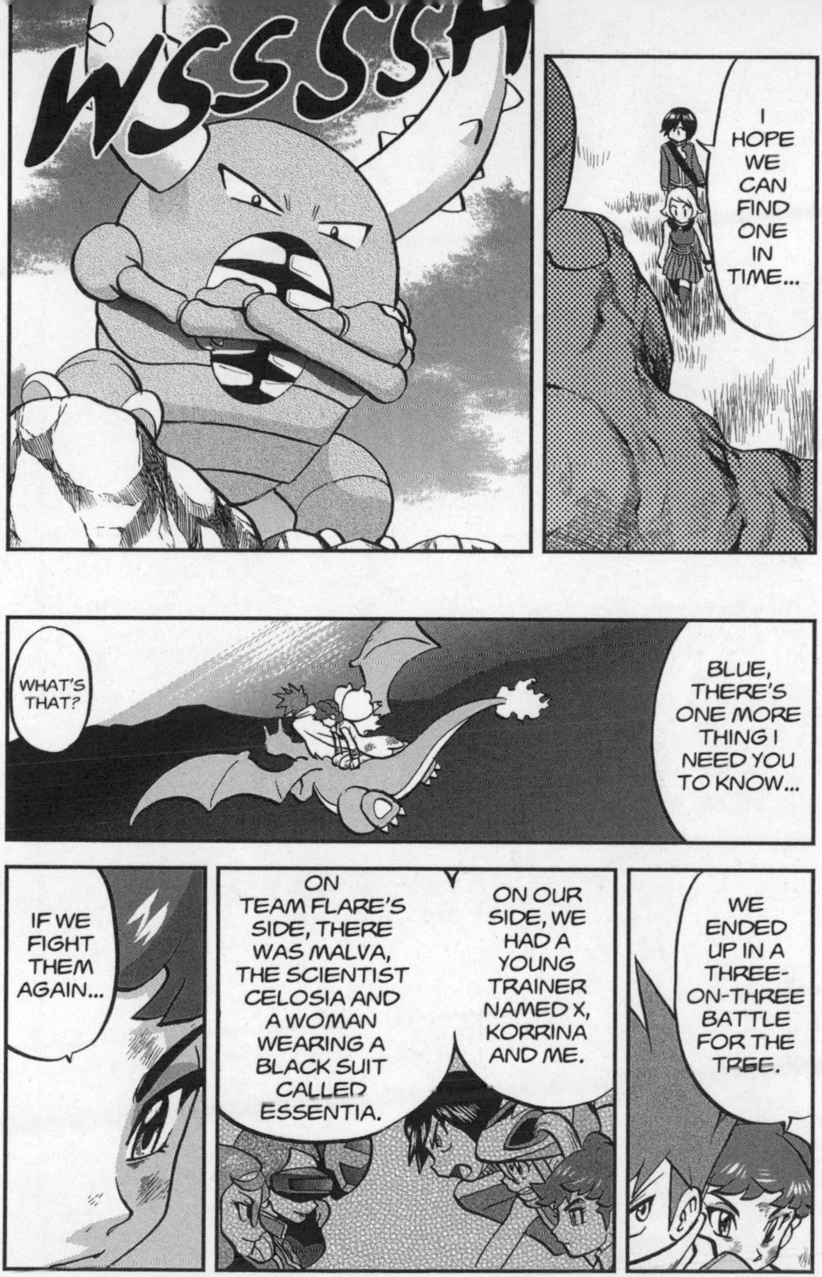
I HOPE WE CAN FIND ONE IN TIME...
WSSSSH
BLUE, THERE'S ONE MORE THING I NEED YOU TO KNOW...
WHAT'S THAT?
WE ENDED UP IN A THREE-ON-THREE BATTLE FOR THE TREE.
ON OUR SIDE, WE HAD A YOUNG TRAINER NAMED X, KORRINA AND ME.
ON TEAM FLARE'S SIDE, THERE WAS MALVA, THE SCIENTIST CELOSIA AND A WOMAN WEARING A BLACK SUIT CALLED ESSENTIA.
IF WE FIGHT THEM AGAIN...

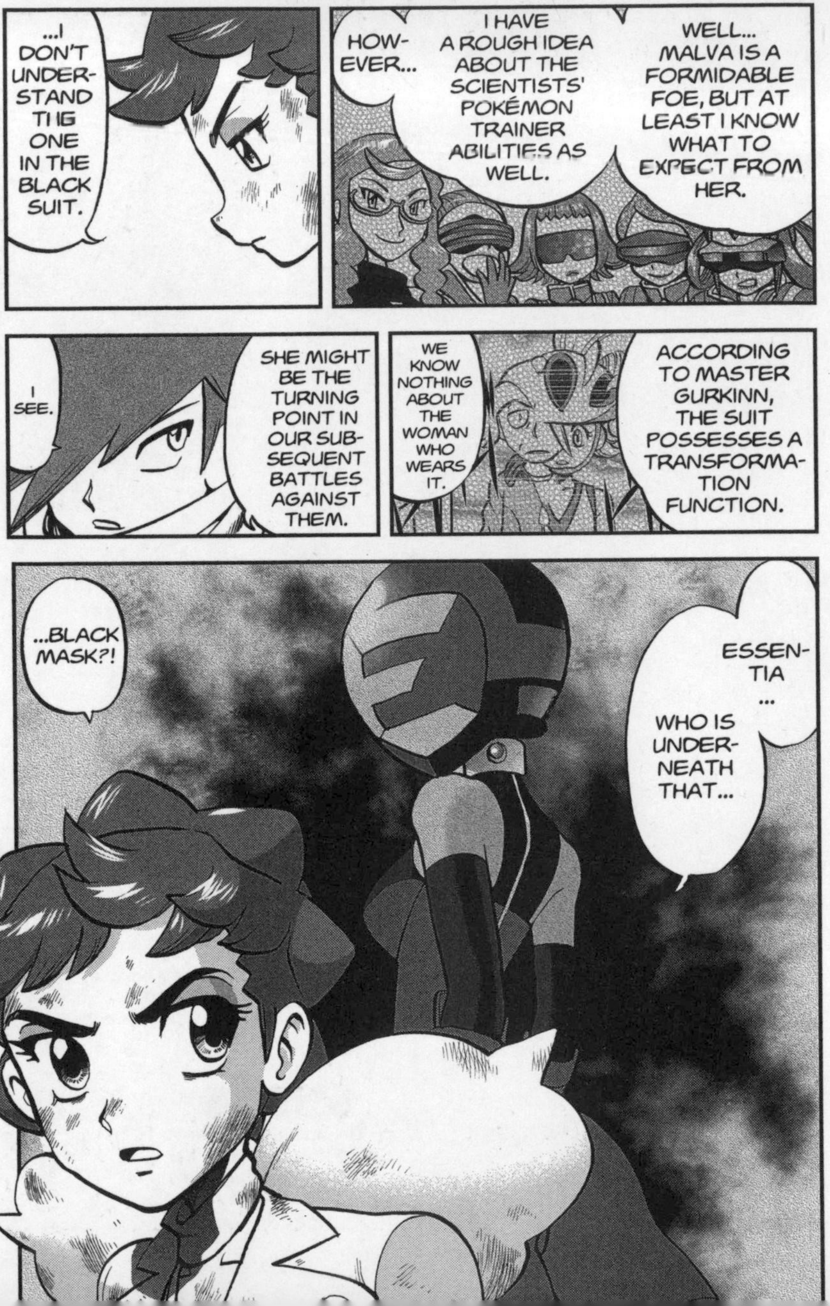
WELL... MALVA IS A FORMIDABLE FOE, BUT AT LEAST I KNOW WHAT TO EXPECT FROM HER.
I HAVE A ROUGH IDEA ABOUT THE SCIENTISTS' POKÉMON TRAINER ABILITIES AS WELL.
HOW-EVER...
...I DON'T UNDER-STAND THE ONE IN THE BLACK SUIT.
ACCORDING TO MASTER GURKINN, THE SUIT POSSESSES A TRANSFORMA-TION FUNCTION.
WE KNOW NOTHING ABOUT THE WOMAN WHO WEARS IT.
SHE MIGHT BE THE TURNING POINT IN OUR SUB-SEQUENT BATTLES AGAINST THEM.
I SEE.
ESSEN-TIA ...
WHO IS UNDER-NEATH THAT...
...BLACK MASK?!

Current Location

Route 15
Brun Way

This path has become a popular hangout for the wild and directionless youths of Lumiose City.

▼

Lost Hotel

The once-famous hotel clings to the shade of its former glory after tragedy left it in ruins.

No.

Date

◆ CURRENT DATA ◆

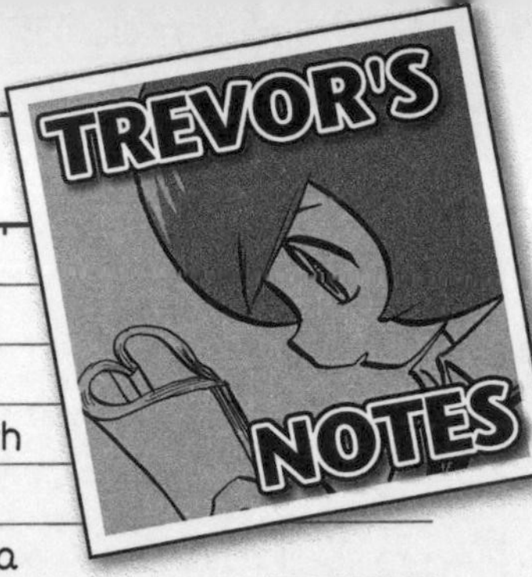
TREVOR'S
NOTES

- Korrina's stolen Key Stone has been made into a ring by Team Flare for Lysandre to wield. When combined with the Mega Stone (Gyaradosite) that Lysandre procured, his Gyarados Mega Evolved into Mega Gyarados and fought with X.

- An area named the "Magic Room" was created during the battle in the forest. This special room has the power to suppress the effects of all the items held by the Pokémon within it. However, it doesn't seem to cancel the effect of the Mega Stone. Therefore, even if a Mega-Evolved Pokémon is dragged into a Magic Room, it won't be turned back into its regular form.

- X currently has three Mega-Evolving Pokémon: Kangaskhan (who uses Kangaskhanite), Manectric (who uses Manectite) and Gengar (who uses Gengarite). Now X has begun to search for a Bug-type Pokémon to add to his team...

- Y has been recognized by Master Gurkinn as the official successor to the Key Stone. She is wearing a Mega Ring like X. The Key Stone was transferred from Master Gurkinn's Mega Glove to Y's Mega Ring.

- Y has begun searching for a new Pokémon, Absol, in hopes of Mega Evolving it. But even if Y and X manage to find and capture Absol and a Bug-type Pokémon, they must search for the Mega Stones (Absolite and the Mega Stone that matches the Bug-type Pokémon) to Mega Evolve them...

TOP SECRET

TEAM FLARE CLASSIFIED FILE

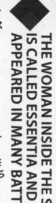

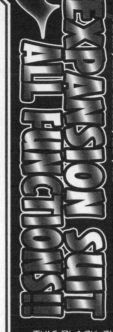

EXPANSION SUIT ALL FUNCTIONS!!

THIS BLACK-CLAD WARRIOR SUDDENLY APPEARED BEFORE OUR FRIENDS. THE SUIT HAS INCREDIBLE PHYSICAL AND POKÉMON-WIELDING ABILITIES. TEAM FLARE'S EXPANSION SUIT IS ONE OF A KIND.

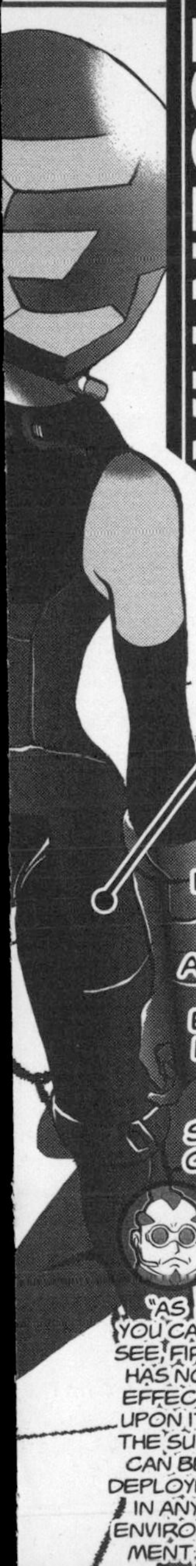

THE WOMAN INSIDE THE SUIT IS CALLED ESSENTIA AND HAS APPEARED IN MANY BATTLES.

ESSENTIA

ESSENTIA IS THE BLACK-SUITED TRAINER X FOUGHT IN THE BATTLE FOR THE GREAT TREE IN THE FOREST. SHE LOOKS VERY DIFFERENT FROM THE OTHER TEAM FLARE MEMBERS AND HER IDENTITY IS UNKNOWN. THE ONLY THING THAT IS CERTAIN IS THAT THIS TRAINER MAKES USE OF THE VARIOUS FUNCTIONS OF THE SUIT TO FIGHT IN UNIQUE WAYS. LET'S TAKE A LOOK AT THE FIVE FUNCTIONS OF THIS SUIT AND LEARN ITS SECRETS...

1 TRAINER ENHANCEMENT FUNCTION

ESSENTIA'S MOVES ARE INCREDIBLY QUICK AND POWERFUL DURING BATTLE. APPARENTLY THESE MOVES ARE ENHANCED BY THE FUNCTION OF THE EXPANSION SUIT. THE EXPANSION SUIT CAN TURN ANY ORDINARY TRAINER INTO A SUPER TRAINER.

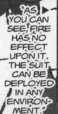

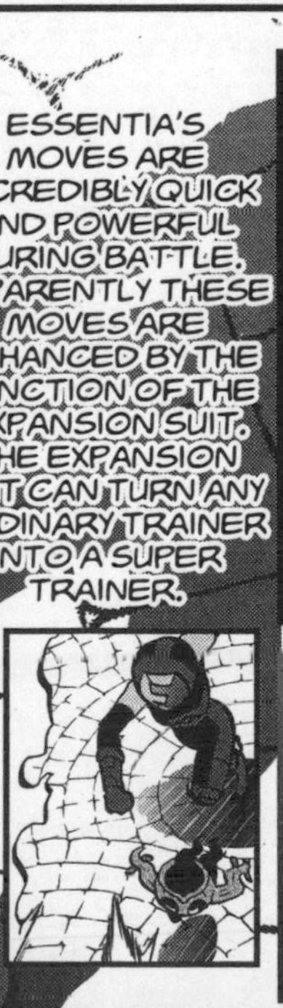

"AS ▶ YOU CAN SEE, FIRE HAS NO EFFECT UPON IT. THE SUIT CAN BE DEPLOYED IN ANY ENVIRONMENT."

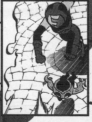

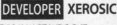

DEVELOPER XEROSIC

THIS MAN STANDS OUT AMONG THE TEAM FLARE SCIENTISTS FOR CONDUCTING THE MOST EXPERIMENTS WITH THE SUIT. DUE TO HIS EXPERTISE ON THE EXPANSION SUIT, HE WILL NOW PROVIDE US WITH SOME INFORMATION...

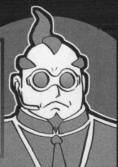

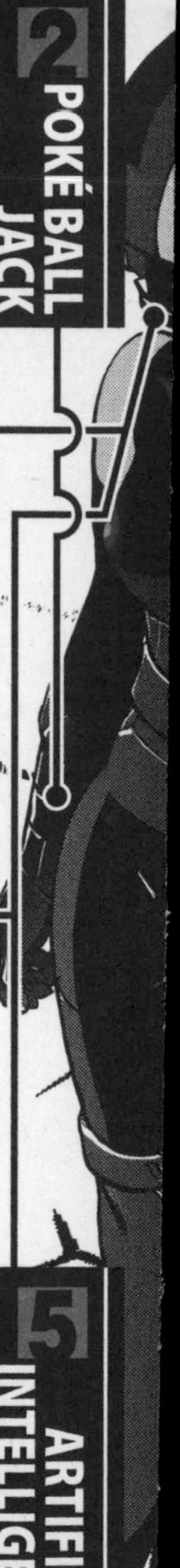

2 POKÉ BALL JACK FUNCTION

THE POKÉ BALL JACK FUNCTION ENABLES THE SUIT TO SEIZE CONTROL OF OTHER PEOPLE'S POKÉ BALLS AND POKÉMON. THE SUIT INFECTS THE POKÉ BALL WITH A VIRUS THAT STRENGTHENS THE POKÉMON.

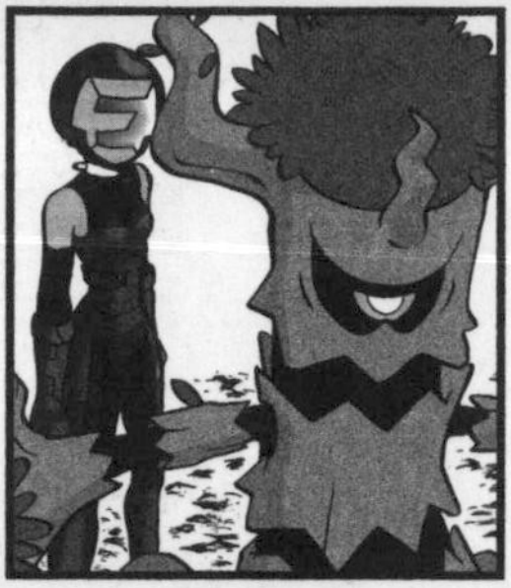

▶ "ESSENTIA'S TREVENANT IS CURRENTLY UNDER THE POKÉ BALL JACK'S INFLUENCE."

3 OPTICAL DISGUISE SNEAKING FUNCTION

SIMPLY PUT, THE SNEAKING FUNCTION ENABLES YOU TO CHANGE INTO SOMEONE ELSE. YOU CAN COMPLETELY TRANSFORM IN A MATTER OF SECONDS, SO IT CAN BE VERY USEFUL WHEN INFILTRATING ENEMY TERRITORY FOR AN OPERATION.

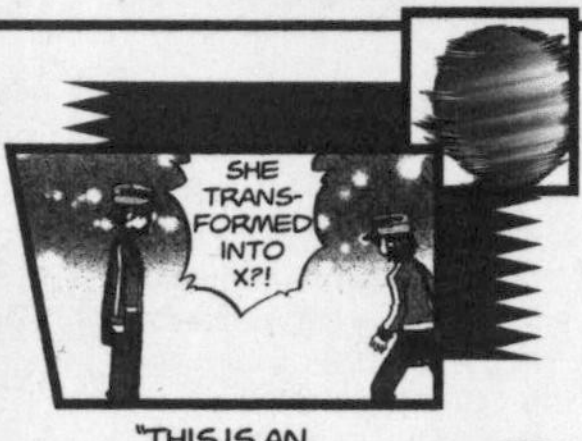
SHE TRANSFORMED INTO X?!

▲ "THIS IS AN INCOMPLETE FUNCTION THAT I NEED TO CONDUCT MORE TESTS ON. I WILL BE MAKING THE FINAL ADJUSTMENTS ON IT SOON."

4 REMOTE CONTROL FUNCTION

THE SUIT CAN BE REMOTE CONTROLLED IN CASE THE SUIT MALFUNCTIONS OR THE WEARER GOES OUT OF CONTROL.

▼ "A PART-TIME WORKER WHO APPLIED TO BECOME THE TEST SUBJECT LOST IT WHILE WEARING THE SUIT, SO I NEEDED TO INSTALL PRECAUTIONARY MEASURES. THIS FUNCTION IS FOR EMERGENCIES."

5 ARTIFICIAL INTELLIGENCE FUNCTION

IF THE WEARER IS KNOCKED OUT OR FALLS ASLEEP, AN ARTIFICIAL INTELLIGENCE WILL AUTOMATICALLY TAKE THEIR PLACE AND CONTINUE THE BATTLE. TRULY AMAZING!

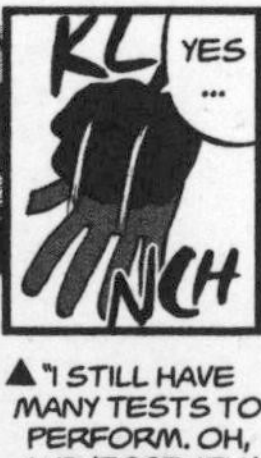
YES ...
KL NCH

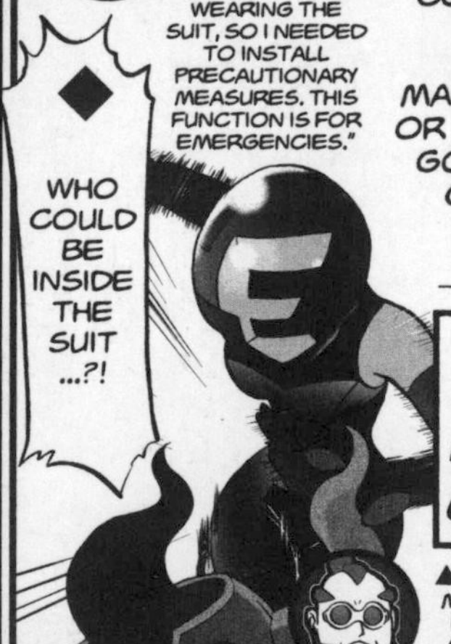
WHO COULD BE INSIDE THE SUIT ...?!

▲ "I STILL HAVE MANY TESTS TO PERFORM. OH, AND 'ESSENTIA' IS JUST THE PROTOTYPE CODE NAME I CAME UP WITH FOR THIS SUIT."

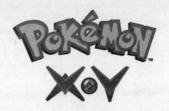

Pokémon X • Y
Volume 8
Perfect Square Edition

Story by HIDENORI KUSAKA
Art by SATOSHI YAMAMOTO

©2016 Pokémon.
©1995-2016 Nintendo/Creatures Inc./GAME FREAK inc.
TM, ®, and character names are trademarks of Nintendo.
POCKET MONSTERS SPECIAL X·Y Vol. 4
by Hidenori KUSAKA, Satoshi YAMAMOTO
© 2014 Hidenori KUSAKA, Satoshi YAMAMOTO
All rights reserved.
Original Japanese edition published by SHOGAKUKAN.
English translation rights in the United States of America, Canada, the United
Kingdom, Ireland, Australia and New Zealand arranged with SHOGAKUKAN.

English Adaptation—Bryant Turnage
Translation—Tetsuichiro Miyaki
Touch-up & Lettering—Annaliese Christman
Design—Shawn Carrico
Editor—Annette Roman

Printed in the U.S.A.

Published by
VIZ Media, LLC
P.O. Box 77010
San Francisco, CA 94107

10 9 8 7 6 5 4 3 2 1
First printing, October 2016

  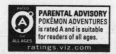

www.viz.com

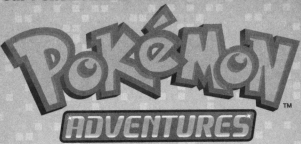
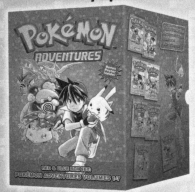

The adventure continues in the Johto region!

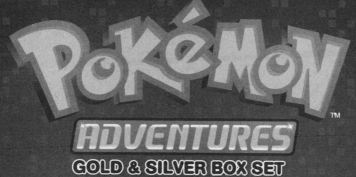

POKÉMON ADVENTURES

GOLD & SILVER BOX SET

Includes **POKÉMON ADVENTURES** Vols. 8-14 and a collectible poster!

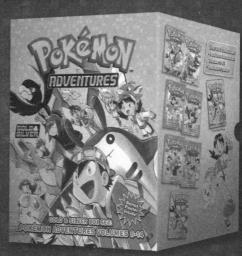

Story by
HIDENORI KUSAKA

Art by
**MATO,
SATOSHI YAMAMOTO**

More exciting Pokémon adventures starring Gold and his rival Silver! First someone steals Gold's backpack full of Poké Balls (and Pokémon!). Then someone steals Prof. Elm's Totodile. Can Gold catch the thief—or thieves?!

Keep an eye on Team Rocket, Gold... Could they be behind this crime wave?

 viz media www.viz.com

 PERFECT SQUARE

 RATED ALL AGES rating.viz.com

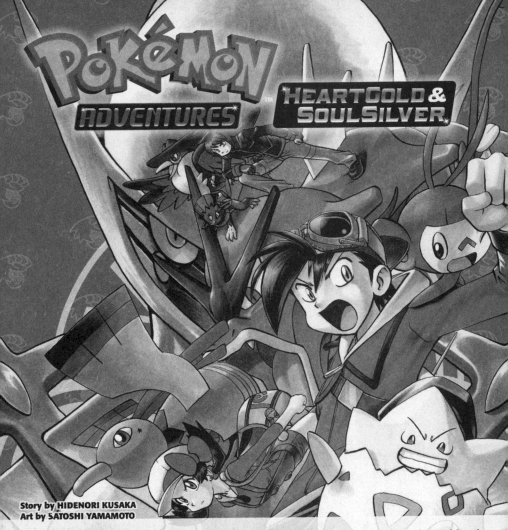

Story by HIDENORI KUSAKA
Art by SATOSHI YAMAMOTO

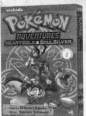
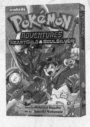

In this **two-volume** thriller, troublemaker Gold and feisty Silver must team up again to find their old enemy Lance and the Legendary Pokémon Arceus!

Available now!

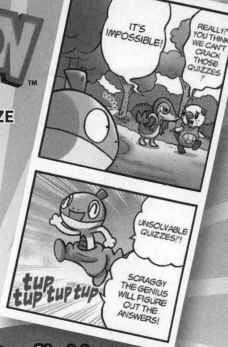
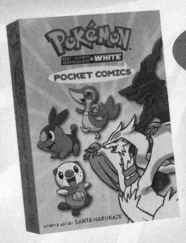

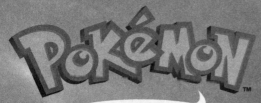

POCKET COMICS
Legendary Pokémon

STORY & ART BY **SANTA HARUKAZE**

FOUR-PANEL GAGS, POKÉMON TRIVIA, AND FUN PUZZLES BASED ON THE CHARACTERS FROM THE BEST-SELLING POKÉMON BLACK AND WHITE VIDEO GAMES!

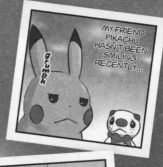

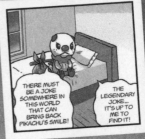

  Available now!

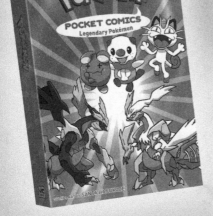

To the forest! To the sea!
To Legendary Island!

Join our Pokémon pals on their quest through Unova—while testing your knowledge and laughing all the way!

Ask for it at your local comic book shop or bookstore!

ISBN: 978-1-4215-8128-6

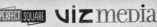

www.PerfectSquare.com   www.viz.com

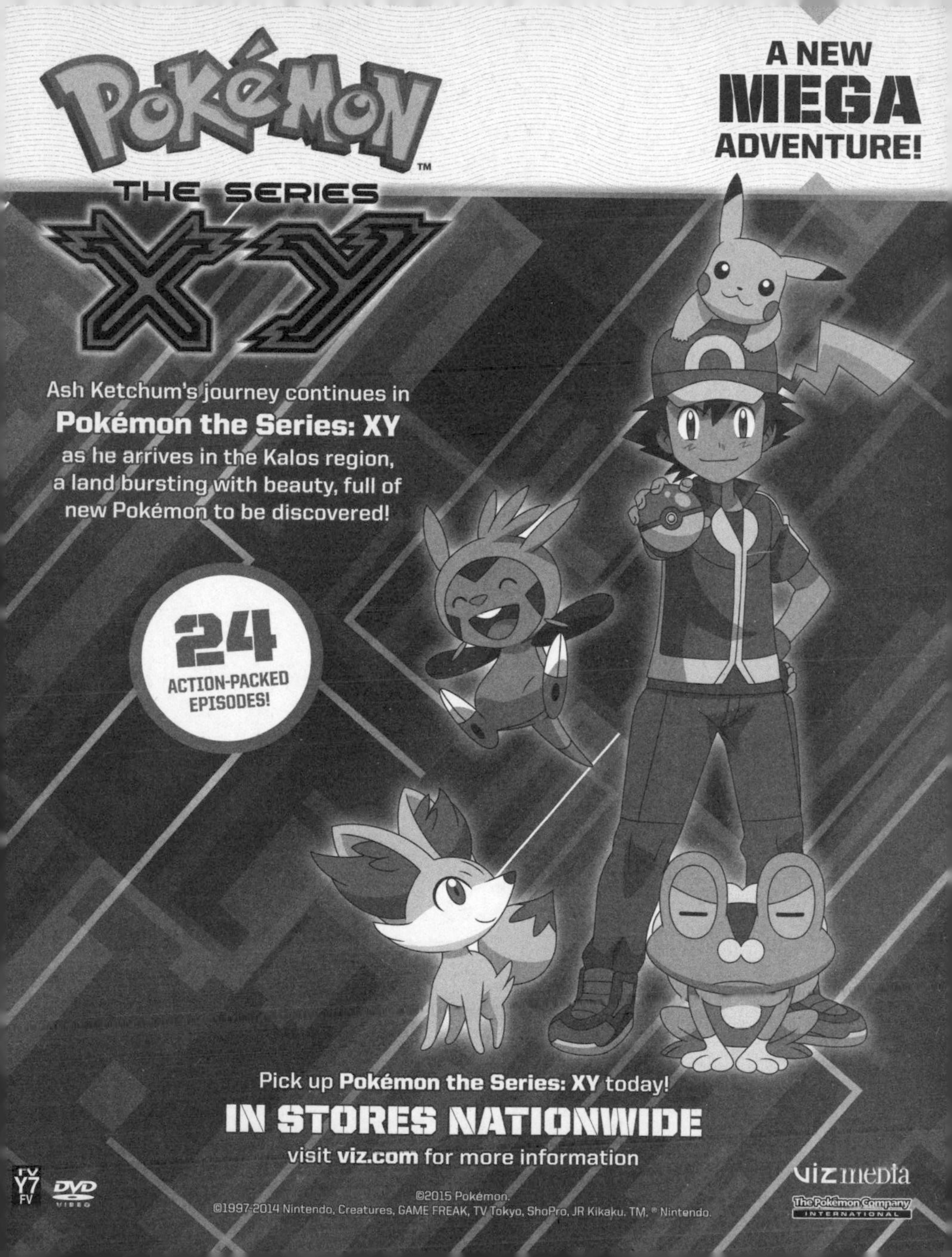
POKÉMON™
THE SERIES
XY
A NEW
MEGA
ADVENTURE!
Ash Ketchum's journey continues in
Pokémon the Series: XY
as he arrives in the Kalos region,
a land bursting with beauty, full of
new Pokémon to be discovered!
24
ACTION-PACKED
EPISODES!
Pick up Pokémon the Series: XY today!
IN STORES NATIONWIDE
visit viz.com for more information
TV Y7 FV
DVD VIDEO
©2015 Pokémon.
©1997-2014 Nintendo, Creatures, GAME FREAK, TV Tokyo, ShoPro, JR Kikaku. TM, ® Nintendo.
viz media
The Pokémon Company INTERNATIONAL

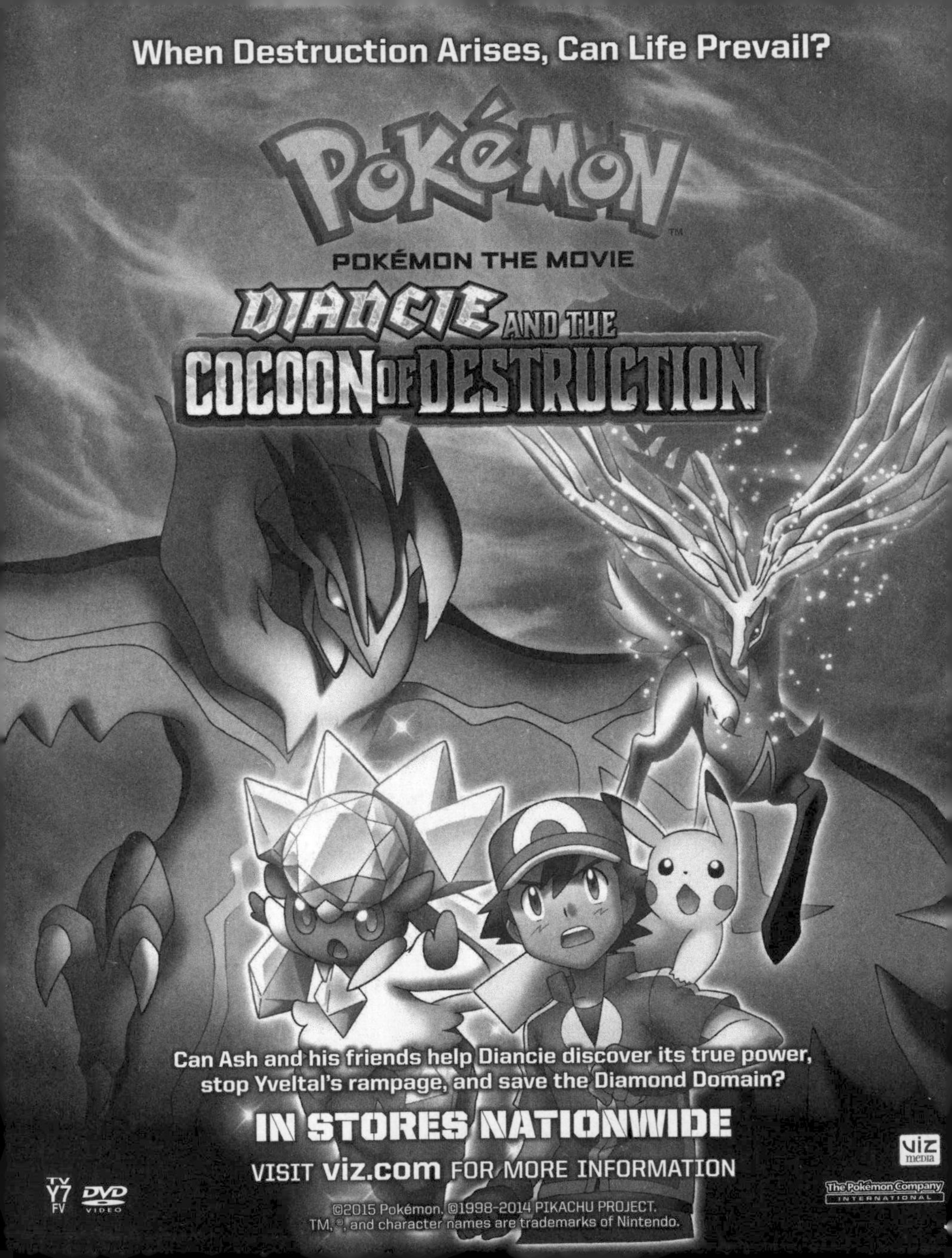

When Destruction Arises, Can Life Prevail?

POKÉMON

POKÉMON THE MOVIE

DIANCIE AND THE COCOON OF DESTRUCTION

Can Ash and his friends help Diancie discover its true power,
stop Yveltal's rampage, and save the Diamond Domain?

IN STORES NATIONWIDE

VISIT **viz.com** FOR MORE INFORMATION

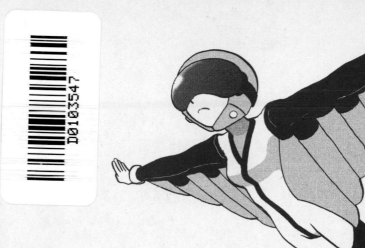

‹‹‹ READ THIS WAY!

THIS IS THE END OF THIS GRAPHIC NOVEL!

To properly enjoy this VIZ Media graphic novel, please turn it around and begin reading from right to left.

This book has been printed in the original Japanese format in order to preserve the orientation of the original artwork. Have fun with it!

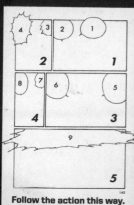

Follow the action this way.